Perfect PRAISE

GRACE PEARCE

Author's Note

This book is intended for people 18+. It is different from my first two books, and the plot relies heavily on spice. It includes, but is not limited to, the following themes: light domination, praise kink, degradation, edging, biting, use of inanimate object during sex, spanking, gagging, minor breath play, use of ropes for restraints, and explicit language (everything listed is consensual). It also includes profanity, a cheating and manipulative ex-boyfriend, references to child neglect and foster care, and references to drug use and drug addiction. Please proceed with this knowledge.

For myself: I don't give a shit.

THE CLOSET
Maren

I'M STILL SCARED OF the dark.

Never mind my age (twenty-nine) or the fact that there's a room full of people packed shoulder to shoulder (press conference) in the next room of this country club.

The hairs on my arm stand in a wave as I grope the wall, searching for the light switch and reminding myself for the thousandth time to never let the door shut before I flip it on.

My fingertips catch warmth. It's round, I think, as I try to wrap a thumb around it. It moves, tenses. And...?

"That's my bicep."

I shriek.

"Those *were* my eardrums."

I flatten my back against the far wall of the closet, which isn't very far at all, at the sound of the deep male voice. I could still kick this guy in the groin—well, where I'd assume his groin is since I'm temporarily blind.

"Maren," he says into the dark.

The light flicks on, flooding my small photography closet with too-bright fluorescent light and filling the space with a low buzz that emits from the long bulbs.

My thudding heart slows at the sight of Locke Hughes.

His deep brown eyes are smirking at me. His lips are even, but I can somehow still see him laughing at me.

Blond hair combined with dark brown eyes is so strange, but it definitely works on Locke in a weirdly sexy and intense way. Maybe it's the lighting—even under the ugly too-white hue of humming fluorescent bulbs, Locke is undeniably gorgeous.

Light: possibly my favorite thing. It's why I became a photographer.

The shadows it casts, the way it lands on things, brightens them. You can completely change the effect of something by simply altering the lighting around it—highlight a smile, darken a look, emphasize an emotion. You can make people see things they couldn't see before.

Except Locke's eyes. They're almost black—and black is the absence of light.

Now, Locke's face, on the other hand, is made to be in front of a camera. It's a travesty he wants nothing to do with one.

"How'd you know it was me?" I accuse him.

His eyes lift over my shoulder, sweeping an arc over my head as he surveys all the camera equipment I use to take pictures of him and every other golfer on the PGA Tour, and land above my other shoulder. "Who else uses this closet?"

"*You*, apparently."

He shrugs. "I'm avoiding the press conference until the very last minute."

"Right," I say, waving a hand toward him. "Cameras. People. Talking."

I think Locke hates the fact that my camera is practically an extension of my arm and that I'm always following on his heels on the golf course, so ipso facto he hates me.

He says nothing, but I didn't expect him to.

I turn and stand on my tiptoes to reach the camera lens sitting on the top shelf. I hear Locke shuffle silently across the two-foot gap between us to reach high above my head and grab it for me.

"Thank you," I gush, maybe too much.

All I get is a head nod.

Locke Hughes doesn't give anyone anything. His time? Fuck you. A hello? You're not worth it. A smile? He'd rather melt his lips off in a fire.

So, I'm still surprised that he stooped so low as to lift his arm and use his neck muscles for me. And I'm still beaming about it back out in the hallway when I leave him to continue his isolated avoidance for another minute.

"Why're you so happy?" a familiar voice says.

I snap my head up, and a groan escapes my mouth before my body can react. I don't stop until I'm close enough for Russell to lay his hand on my shoulder. Delicate, tentative, just like the tone of his lying, traitorous voice.

I skirt out from underneath it and try my best to ignore the blinking red light from the one camera on Earth that I've grown to despise.

As a photographer, I never imagined I would think these thoughts or harbor a hatred for a camera and the person behind it, but here I am—hating that I photograph pro golfers, one of whom is my ex-boyfriend who convinced me to do a reality show with him. Now I'm unfortunately roped into finishing out my contract, even though we've been broken up for months.

"What do you want?" My voice comes out sad rather than angry like I intended.

"I wanted to see if you needed hel—" Russ cuts himself off when his eyes dart over my head.

I can almost feel Locke's intensity moving toward us.

Russell tracks him.

So does the camera.

Locke doesn't even bother to look at any of us as he passes. "Get that fucking camera out of my face, Craig."

Craig, the cameraman, sighs.

We—well, most of us—are supposed to act like it doesn't exist. That's the point of a reality show, obviously, but Locke has the luxury of doing whatever the fuck he wants since he isn't on the show. Or because he's the best golfer in the world?

I thought it would get easier to ignore it, that eventually the camera would become a part of my landscape. And it did for a while—until three months in when Craig caught me catching Russell with a girl wedged against a wall. His tongue down her throat. His hand up her dress. While he was dating me.

Now, it just makes me feel like an anxious ball of sunshine during a solar eclipse. It's smothering and blackens my otherwise bright and happy heart.

When Locke is out of earshot, Russell focuses back on me with a glint of an accusation burning in his eyes. "What were you doing?"

"Nothing," I insist, biting the inside of my cheek. I go against my natural instinct to talk too much. What I do is none of his goddamn business anymore. I am allowed to be in a closet with Locke doing whatever the hell I feel like doing.

But it's two-fold:

One, I don't want the world to see me break down on a future episode of this stupid show because Craig is filming our conversation. They're already going to see me be humiliated on national television in a matter of hours when the next episode airs our dramatic break-up that happened in real life months ago.

Two, I'm too nice. I still care about Russell's feelings and want him to like me, because I want everyone to like me.

I'm light personified.

I care too much about everything, about everyone else, and in the process, I sacrifice myself to make others happy. I'll mold—and then I'll mold again. To brighten others. To try to make them feel good. Let them take what they want from me. One thing I am constantly molded into is a doormat to avoid conflict at all costs.

Russ drills into my brain with a death stare of skepticism mixed with a healthy dose of *I don't want you, but no one else can have you.*

"It's nothing," I say, pushing past him before I can't help but add a sincere, "I promise."

I'm proud that I at least don't look back when I whisk myself through the double doors and into a room full of men.

No one looks at me, and no one continues to look at me as I wind to the other side of the conference room and set up my camera.

That's supposed to be my purpose as a sports photographer though, so I guess I'm the best person for the job. Blend in, catch the moments around me. The blips in time that are otherwise missed. No one ever really notices me or thinks about the person actually taking the picture.

Think about it next time—there's a whole person looking through the viewfinder with wants and dreams and feelings, capturing other people's mid-air moments of greatness. We may hide behind the camera, we may seem invisible, but we're not.

Sports photography isn't really my passion, though. Do I want to be taking mid-swing golf shots of men with five-hundred-dollar clubs? No. I wish I was capturing newborn babies and families and birthdays—lifestyle photography.

Unfortunately, this word snags on my mother's voice in my head every time I think it.

"*Lifestyle* photography?" it rings like a high-pitched squeal. She has this way of saying not-so nice things in a way-too nice tone. Her chuckle always makes me clench my teeth. "That's not a real job, sweetie. There can't possibly be that much money in any photography. When are you getting a real job?"

Anything can be made into a real job so long as people pay you for it, but I got a 'real' job, courtesy of my brother-in-law, the go-to physician for professional golfers. Blame nepotism all you want (I do), but I'm also not bad at it.

Locke is positioned at the long table on the stage with a skinny microphone in front of him. It looks like he's pushed it to the side as much as it will go. I take a few test shots and adjust my camera settings as Russ joins him on stage and sits in front of his own matching microphone.

The number one and the number two pro golfers in the world, and they couldn't be more different.

Number one, Locke Hughes, keeps to himself. He glares at everyone. He doesn't smile. You question if he gets any sleep because he practices every minute of every day, and if he actually does tear himself away from the golf course for longer than a minute, then he's in the gym. Simply put, he doesn't give a fuck about anyone or anything except himself and golf, and he doesn't give a fuck what you think.

Number two, Russell Ashe, likes to be front and center. He wants to make the room laugh. He wants all eyes on him. He thinks he's entitled to the world, and it bugs the shit out of him that there's one person who stands in his way to the top.

Russ doesn't give a fuck about anyone or anything except himself either. But he wants the world to love him, and he cares *a lot* about what other people think.

Locke on the left, Russ on the right. Only a matter of feet separates them. Brown eyes connect with blue eyes when they look at each other. Blond hair gets pushed to the side. Brown hair gets pushed back.

It's like they have the coloring that the other should have. I want to swap their hair or their eyes like one of those magnetic dress-up games I used to play with as a child.

They both sit up straight, and I realize they're the exact same height.

Someone speaks from the crowd. "Gentlemen," his voice says loudly, quieting the murmur. "New year, new you? How are you both feeling going into this tournament?"

Locke sits back and crosses his arms over his chest, like he's bored, at the same time Russ eagerly leans in and clasps his hands in front of him.

Russ smiles and takes the first question. "I've never felt better."

You'd think he'd feel a little less better after betraying his girlfriend of two years.

I focus my lens and snap a few pictures of him as he recites his canned response that he probably practiced in the mirror earlier this morning. "I learned a lot last year, corrected my mistakes, and I'm playing these courses better than I ever have."

"Locke?" the man asks.

Locke keeps his arms crossed and speaks into the microphone. "I feel like the same Locke as last year."

The man chuckles and follows with, "Do you think you'll have a competitive advantage over Russell as you're not a part of the documentary?"

"I haven't thought about it," Locke responds.

The reporter repeats his question, directing it at Russ. "Cameras following you everywhere. Your personal life being shown every week on national television. Does it have an impact on your mindset?"

"Not at all," Russ replies confidently. "This is what we signed up for; to show everyone that golf isn't boring. We're not boring, excluding present company"—Russ follows with a humorous I'm-just-joking laugh, even though he's not—"and we have lives and families outside of the bubble. We aren't serious and focused one hundred percent of the time. The goal is to give everyone a behind-the-scenes look of what we're like as players and people. Besides, we all have our own distractions. People and *personal* things get in the way."

The inflection in Russell's voice wouldn't be missed by the naivest person in the room. It doesn't help that his eyes are dark, eyebrows flattened, and he has his head turned ninety degrees to stare Locke down. Then Russell looks straight at me.

I can't look him in the eye for longer than a second because I feel like he's blaming me for him not being good enough. And why do I even care? He's not my boyfriend anymore, and he's still not good enough.

"Oh," the reporter pipes up. "Locke, care to elaborate?"

"No," he says matter-of-factly.

The reporter laughs. "We don't get to see your relationships play out every week on the screen. Is this new? Will she be joining you at these tournaments? You've never once confirmed any relationship you've had, even when a rare photo emerges."

"On purpose," Locke says.

Craig, standing off to the side of the stage, swivels the blinking light of his camera in my direction, which causes the entire room to follow suit slowly as they collectively notice.

Russell smirks. Locke's face remains unchanged.

All eyes in the room give me an unappreciated once-over, putting together who I am. Whose I *was*.

My heart beats behind my eyes. I know my cheeks and neck are splotched in shades of red.

Russell thinks he can rattle Locke, and he's loving every second of it. To hell if it's at my expense. And Craig just wants to stir drama for the sake of good reality television and make it seem like I was in the closet hooking up with someone; tie it in a nice bow.

My eyes connect with Locke's, but I try my best to ignore the shiver that zigzags down my spine.

Maren and I hardly know each other.

Maren and I work together and nothing more.

Maren and I are like oil and water, the sun and the moon, a mosquito and... everything else.

There are so many options he could choose to tell the reporter if he could mind-read, but of course, he's going to go with whatever he wants to say anyway. He flicks his eyes off me as quickly as humanly possible, like I'm the mosquito in this scenario.

Locke mimics Russell's posture as he speaks into the microphone, and everyone turns back to him. "If I were dating someone, I wouldn't confirm it. If I weren't dating someone, I wouldn't confirm it."

The smile Locke gives Russ makes him seethe behind his fake look of camaraderie.

My mouth drops open behind my camera. It takes everything in me to remain professional and not cry out of mortification. But my face doesn't emerge from behind my viewfinder until every mundane question has been asked, until they've both explained their outlook on this week's upcoming tournament in San Diego, until almost everyone is out of the room.

I leave every piece of equipment I have behind as I rush out the back door, praying no one steals my stuff.

I spot Locke through the enormous glass doors of the country club first, talking to his caddie. Behind him, Russ climbs into a golf cart and drives away before I practically smash through the door into the bright Florida sun.

"What the hell was that?" I huff before I second-guess my anger. I hardly know the guy, and it already annoys me that no matter how many times I smile at him, he blankly stares and looks away. "I mean, what was that?"

I register the tiniest bit of shock in Locke's eyes before they calm. "What was what?"

His caddie shrinks off inside, like he wants no part in this conversation, leaving the two of us alone.

"*That*! Everyone was staring at me, waiting for you to acknowledge our *relationship*. Then you got all mysterious and let everyone just believe we're together."

He shakes his head before his hand comes up to smooth the back of his hair. "I did no such thing."

"Yes. You. Did."

"I didn't confirm it or deny it," he insists.

"They're going to air that, Locke. The entire world will think I'm your girlfriend."

"I think you've misplaced your anger. Blame Russell for the shit he pulled."

I swallow down my feelings. "I can't."

"You can't?" he says. "Whatever, never mind. You're in the clear anyway. Your dumb show can't air me."

"Trust me. They'll edit it and get across exactly what they want, despite the truth—and that press conference will be on TV."

He shrugs. "So? Don't watch it."

I fist the sides of my golf dress. I have a right to be mad, right? I have a right to express it, right?

"Right. So easy for you to say. I've had to follow you around and take your picture for years. You don't care about anything or anyone. As long as it doesn't mess with your golf game or your workout schedule or your domination of all things male."

"How would you know what I care about?" he asks flatly.

"This is the longest conversation I've ever had with you, and you're literally telling me not to watch my life fall apart."

"You don't know anything about me."

"Well, you know about me," I say, a pathetic twinge hollowing out my voice. "All you do is glare at me when I try to take your picture and do my job. The helpless sports photographer who dated Russell Ashe and was the only one who didn't know he was a lying, cheating asshole."

Locke opens his mouth and quickly closes it. Lines etch near the corners of his mouth in a frown.

"Locke?"

This girl appears out of nowhere. Not nowhere exactly. She's sitting in a car with the window rolled down. Beautiful—no, gorgeous—blonde, and just as mysterious looking as he is. Someone who would never take anyone's shit.

"You couldn't have just said you were dating *her*?" I sigh.

"She isn't my girlfriend." His chuckle catches me off guard, and he doesn't even glance her way. "She doesn't give a shit about me."

As if on cue, she curses under her breath, rolls the window up, and looks at her phone.

"Why don't you give a shit about anything?" I question him.

His dark brown eyes twinkle in amusement and pity. "You should try it."

"But how do you do it?"

The idea blooms from the dreading jealous pit in my stomach, and I will literally die if I don't speak the words that are now clogged in my throat. I want to be as nonchalant as he is. I want the I-don't-give-a-fuck attitude.

"Teach me." My words are barely audible.

"What?"

"Teach me," I whisper slightly louder.

Locke looks startled. "Teach you *what*?"

"How to not give a shit."

He looks at me like I've completely lost it.

It's definitely up for debate.

I resort to pleading. "Please."

THE PROPOSITION
Locke

I scowl. "No."

Maren swallows, like she's second-guessing whether she should have spoken.

"Fuck no," I add for emphasis before she can say please again like that. I thought she was going to ask me to teach her how to play golf—which might be an even less ridiculous idea than that, and that's saying something.

She taps her tiny foot an inch off the ground. "Why not?"

"That's... mildly cute," I say, eyeing her long legs. "Answer's still no."

She scrunches her face in offense. Her button nose is sexily speckled with freckles, but I doubt she'd be thrilled if I said that either.

"Please don't call me mildly cute."

I'm not unaware of the effect it has on people, so flashing her a rare smile is all it takes to make her soften. "What do you want to be called?"

Nope, back to mad.

Her body stiffens. "I'm not doing that so you can get inside Russ' head," Maren says.

"Do what?"

"Whatever you're trying to do; psychological warfare so you can win. Pissing contest. Arm wrestle. One-upmanship. Dick measuring.

Whatever. I really don't want to be a part of whatever was going on between you two. I'm not going to play your weird alpha-male game."

"Weird alpha-male game," I repeat slowly. "Has anyone ever told you that you talk a lot? What are you even saying?"

She waves her hand at my face like I should know exactly whatever the hell she's talking about. "Like hook up with you or be your fake girlfriend or something to give a giant middle finger to Russ."

"Fake girlfriend?" I laugh. That sounds like a lot of fucking work with zero reward. "Pass. You went there rather fast. And that is the furthest thing from what I was trying to do."

A blush creeps over her cheeks. Her patience is growing thin, even though she's trying to hide it, and she asks me rather nicely, "Then what were you doing up there?"

"Like you said, I wasn't giving a shit. You should try it some time," I say, lifting an eyebrow.

She sighs and tucks a strand of her long brown waves behind her ear. "You're... infuriating."

I laugh internally. Even insulting me, she sounds like she's elated. Poor girl has zero chance.

"You don't need someone to teach you. It's easy. I don't tell people my business, Maren. Let them think whatever they want to think. I'm not going to change anyone's mind."

"Do you watch *Triple Bogey*?" she asks.

I roll my eyes. The name alone is enough to make my brain shrivel from severe stupidity. "What do you think?"

"Do you know what it's like for people to think they know you when they don't at all? Like half of America hates me and half loves me. And all they really know is what the show chooses to show them. They don't really know me at all."

"Nope," I deadpan. "No idea what that could possibly be like. Besides, all of America is not watching your little show." My own annoyance is bubbling to the surface, so I slip a hand in my pocket and thumb the tee I have in there at all times. "Is this conversation over?"

I expect her to fight me harder, longer, but she just sighs and accepts defeat. The competitive asshole in me almost feels disappointed.

"Sure," she concedes.

I glance over my shoulder and motion for Casie to roll down the window. "I don't feel like hanging out anymore," I tell her. "Going to go practice."

Casie whines out a "Loccckkkeee," that sounds nothing close to nice, rolls her eyes, and practically peels out of the parking lot.

"I'm sorry," Maren mutters apologetically to my back as I walk off, "for ruining your mood and messing up your plans."

I stop short and turn slowly. Her face starts to lift, grow brighter, thinking I've somehow changed my mind. I slip my hat from my back pocket and put it back on my head. My voice comes out harsh. "Here's one for free—don't say sorry."

I just catch her start to smile as I backpedal around the corner. That's the only piece of life advice she'll get from me, so she should wipe that look off her face quickly.

The driving range is surprisingly quiet this morning. Conrad, all alone, has parked himself at the very far left bay.

I saunter up quietly, eyeing his nearly perfect backswing, and joke loudly, "Why did I hire you to be my caddie again?" He flinches, and the ball shanks hard right. "God, you suck."

"Asshole," he laughs. "Speaking of..." He takes his time putting another golf ball on the tee. "What was that up there?"

"It was nothing," I say. "Just Russ being Russ."

Conrad holds his eye contact like he knows I'm lying. Which he does.

Sometimes I wish he didn't know me so well, but he's the only real person in my life—technically my brother and definitely my cousin.

We have the same dirty blond hair, but Conrad got the blue approachable eyes to go along with it.

"I'm not in the mood to talk," I add.

He nods. "Got your ass chewed out by that girl you love to hate?"

"No," I counter. "She wouldn't be capable of chewing out anyone. And I don't hate her. I hate how her camera is always pointed at me."

"That's literally her *job*."

I shrug. That has zero relevance to the fact that I hear the click of her camera shutter all day on seventy-five percent of the days in a year, and the sound grates me down my spine.

"You're impossible," Conrad says.

"Let's not talk about me. What's new with my favorite girl?"

He pauses then happily relents because like every new parent, he'll take any excuse to talk about his daughter, Emmie. "As of this week, she's holding her head up now. You should see how cute she looks in her little seat, looking around at the world all happy that she can see it. And then, of course, she's a terror at night because she's hit a four-month sleep regression."

I nod in understanding. Four months ago, I had no fucking clue that a one-day-old baby couldn't hold their head up or what a sleep regression was or that babies can't drink water. Now, I babysit.

Conrad is in the middle of a story about how she shat in various shades of green and yellow all over his lap after a bath when my phone starts ringing.

I slide it out of my pocket and step away to let him go back to his practice swings.

"Word travels that fast?" I say.

"Pleasure, as always," Graham replies, "and as your agent, I'm expected to know these things before they happen."

"Nothing is happening."

He ignores me. "Rooting around in rivals' ex-girlfriends? Bold move. One that I can't control the narrative of when you don't talk to me."

"There is nothing to control," I try again. "That fucking reality show was trying to make good TV. I hardly know the girl."

"Well, shit," he sighs. "I thought I stumbled on something. Would it kill you to date someone? Show the world you can be a cute boyfriend in a serious relationship?"

"You think I'm cute?" I joke.

Again, Graham ignores me. "You know what would be a PR dream? Showing the world how much of a better boyfriend you are than Russell Ashe. Doesn't even need to be real. Do you think this Maren woman would agree to that? It might make you appear more... human."

"As opposed to?" I question.

"Robotic?" he says with a question mark.

"My AI is showing?"

He scoffs. "Actually, this may be my best idea yet. What about Casie?"

"Over," I say, playing with a tuft of grass under the toe of my shoe and deciding in the moment.

"Locke."

I shrug like he can see me. "I'm bored."

Which I know is a byproduct of not letting someone in, but I don't care. It's not worth it, and I have no interest in it. Surface level is all I want, until, well, until I get tired of it and move on to the next temporary surface level thing that satisfies me for a couple of months. Nothing about me screams that I'd want to enter into a fake relationship to better my image, especially when I don't care about that image.

"Think about it," Graham insists.

"Thought about it—no."

"How's Florida?" he asks, changing the subject.

"Sunny."

"So is San Diego. I've got a few commitments lined up. And before you complain, you *have* to do at least some of this. It's required, per your contract, and it won't kill you. This is part of your job. Press conferences, interviews, dinner and drinks with sponsors, among other things. I'll email you the schedule tonight. Look it over."

Among other things sounds suspicious.

"I told you this year was the year of less," I say. "Less tournaments, less obligations. I want more time with my family, especially my niece, and Conrad deserves it. He's been traveling with me for a decade. If you're not going to do what I want, what do I pay you twenty percent of my marketing dollars for?"

Graham doesn't miss a beat. "To show people you are actually a human with a soul, no matter how much you hide it. And trust me, Locke, it's not an easy job."

"I'd tell you to fuck off, but I know you won't."

"Get back to doing what you do best; playing golf," he laughs.

After he hangs up, I settle in the bay next to Conrad. With him, I never have to pretend. He just lets me be.

I pull my driver out of my golf bag that Conrad hauled over here. That feeling when the golf ball hits the sweet spot is the closest thing I have to pure love.

THE SHOW
Maren

CAMILLE WADDLES ACROSS THE living room, balancing a plate of nachos on her stomach as we get ready to watch the episode of *Triple Bogey* we recorded.

"Don't use my nephew as a shelf," I say.

She rolls her eyes and places the heaping pile of cheese on the coffee table in front of me. "It's the least he could do. My sciatic nerve will never recover from the damage he's doing in there."

"I want some tortilla chips with that cheese," I tease, eyeing the overflowing plate.

"They're under there," she says and plops down next to me on the couch. "If you're not going to be nice to me, be nice to baby boy. *He's* the one who wants all this food. And yeah, be nice to me. I'm almost seven months pregnant."

I tsk. "You have to love me anyway."

The cardinal sibling rule. And Camille and I are about as close as you can get without being actual twins. Eleven months apart, we have been together every step of the way—you know, except for those eleven months I lived without her. Maybe you could even say it was only the two months before she was conceived.

We also coincidentally look almost identical—except for that year she had purple hair. Somehow, our mother was never able to talk her out of it. It was Camille's choice *alone* when she decided to pivot to the balayage craze. If it was our mom's choice, Camille would have caramel-highlighted brown waves—like me.

Even though we were close growing up, I constantly lived in my little sister's shadow. Camille was scoring the soccer goals and back handspringing over me in gymnastics. She was kissing boys first and sneaking out, all while making better grades.

But you'd think she was living in mine the way my mom showered her with attention like she was compensating for something. Maybe that's why Camille's the confident one—she had some deep-seeded childhood experience that allowed her to spread her self-assured wings. The one I didn't get, the one that left me aiming to please everyone.

"How's Mom?" I sing. "In grandmother shopping heaven?"

"She hates the crib I picked out."

"Shocking," I deadpan, munching on a nacho that I had to dig out from the shredded three-cheese mound.

"I don't care. The one I want is gorgeous. Besides, that's all we bought today because she insisted that I keep looking at ugly cribs, so I humored her, then rejected every one that she liked more."

I snort. "Living vicariously through you since the early 2000s."

"Maren, I swear. When you have a baby, you better not buy the crib *she* wants—"

"I need a boyfriend first," I stop her. "When's it getting delivered?"

"He's backordered," she quips. "But I got you the extra-large. I hope it fits."

A groan slips out of my mouth. "Jesus, Camille. That is not a visual I want in your head."

She waves her hand in my face and smirks. "Russell wasn't cutting it—obviously."

Since she's indifferent to all sports in general, I doubt she saw the press conference today, but that doesn't stop my mind from drifting to Locke.

"What do you mean *obviously*?" I shoot back before I quickly follow with, "No, don't answer that. When is your *crib* getting delivered?"

"While you're in San Diego. It's going to look perfect in front of the window in your room."

I sigh. "It's not *my* room. It's the nursery, and I promise I will help you set it up as soon as I get back. Then the very next thing I'll do is look for a new place. It's time, and you and Parker need alone time before the baby comes anyway. I've already been here too long invading your space."

"Please," she says. "Parker and I don't care. Between the hospital and his personal patients, I'm surprised he even found the time to knock me up."

She gets a heavy eye roll from me because my room isn't *that* freaking far down the hallway, and I have above-average hearing.

"Where is he anyway?" I ask, looking at my watch.

"He couldn't take this show anymore," she laughs, "so he's braving the gym."

"After tonight, when we watch Russell humiliate me in front of half of America, maybe let's not do this anymore?"

Camille's eyebrows fly up in surprise. "Seriously?" Her face softens before she smiles wide. "I like it. But also, it isn't half of America."

Here comes Locke again through my thoughts, eyeing my legs like he'd eat them and telling me all of America doesn't watch my little show.

It's not *my* show.

She leans over as much as she can to pick up the remote off the coffee table, scrunching my nephew in the process, and hands it to me.

"Ready?" Camille asks.

I nod and press play. A half second of the theme song blares through the room before I quickly hit pause.

"Did you know Locke Hughes has dimples?"

I think cheese comes up through Camille's nose when she laughs. "What?"

And he asked me what I want to be called, I don't add.

Strangely, I think I'd like it if he called me something. Despite thinking about it all day, I'm just not sure what. Though I *am* fairly sure that he's calling lots of women lots of things. But that smile. I can't erase it from my mind.

"He has dimples," I repeat.

Her grin starts slowly and widens so far she might split her face. "And...? How do you know that?"

"He smiled at me for the first time today."

"Huh," Camille remarks. "I've never seen him smile. Or look happy. Or register an emotion." She wiggles her eyebrows. "Did you give him something to be happy about?"

"No," I insist. "I wasn't even that nice to him."

She laughs. "So, you were absolutely delightful? Got it."

Then I humiliatingly remember that I implied he wanted to use me as a fake girlfriend. I still can't keep the blush from returning, so I cover my face with my hands. "I accused him of trying to sleep with me to mess with Russ."

Camille gasps into a fit of giggles and kicks me in the side. "What! You did not. Why?"

"Just this stupid press conference thing. It doesn't matter. I don't even know what I was thinking," I admit. "He was looking at me with those eyes. They're way too dark, by the way. And they were up and down my legs, my body. I swear he was looking at my freckles, and I just went blank."

What do you want to be called? makes a husky reappearance in my brain for the thousandth time.

I shake it out of my head. "Let's just get this over with. Please."

She nods, but I can tell she wants to push me, wants to tell me to have some fun. Even though Locke is not anything close to the word fun.

The theme song of *Triple Bogey* stops her before she can open her mouth.

I curl up under a blanket and prepare my heart to watch my already unfolded life through the eyes of everyone else. I can't stop myself from seeing how the show portrays me. Because the way I remember it and the way they edit it usually come out as two different versions, and I want to see what everyone else sees.

I've psyched myself up all day to relive it—not that I don't find myself reliving it often.

Russ had just moved up to number two in the World Rankings. He'd been ecstatic all week, wanting to celebrate when we got back to Palm Beach after a tournament. We were hosting a dinner party when I excused myself, with Craig at my heels, to grab my camera from our room to document the moment, and there was Russ against the wall with some woman I barely knew.

It was a quiet fight, because Craig was filming it, and I moved out the next day.

I think about it daily, wonder what I could have done differently to make him happy, keep him faithful. But this time I don't have to relive it through reality television because after every commercial, I think it will be next, and it just isn't. They never air it, and when the credits start rolling, my mind is in complete disarray.

If Russell had anything to do with it, maybe he has a sliver of a heart left. Maybe he still cares.

It's depressing thinking that this little closet is the only thing I have in my life that is *mine*. And even other people borrow it sometimes.

No house—I moved out of Russell's and into Parker and Camille's the day after he cheated.

No furniture—I sold it all when I broke my lease to move *in* with Russell.

No boyfriend. No pets.

Now that I think about it, not even this closet is really mine. I have the key, but it belongs to the golf club.

I suppose I have my car—which is on its last leg and makes a weird sound that I ignore when I accelerate.

As I've been packing up my camera equipment for the tournament in San Diego this week, all I've been able to think about is Russ.

I thought I had been exactly what he wanted—always by his side, smiling and supportive. I gave him space when he asked for space. I held his hand through every loss.

So now, I'm wandering out into the sun with a smile on my face and my camera slung over my shoulder in search of him—to what, I'm not sure. Make up? At the very least, I need to know if he had anything to do with last night's television omission.

I find him on the practice green, deep in concentration.

When he feels my presence, he looks up and slightly startles at the sight of me. "I didn't know you were here today," he says, a little wisp of softness in his voice that reminds me of the man I thought he was.

Back then, Russ caught my eye because he seemed larger than life, but I also wasn't sure I wanted to date a professional golfer. It seemed daunting, almost exhausting. He persisted though, made me feel wanted, special. He was always the first one to text or call. Always asking me on another date, even when I hadn't kissed him. I was blinded by the over-the-top dedication and the excitement of being in a new city every week. I'd always end up caving to him, anything he wanted I'd eventually give him. Maybe that was what he saw in me—a weakness, a person who was easy to manipulate. And once he had me, it was like a knife cutting into soft butter. Zero resistance.

And even when it came down to infidelity, I'd still considered taking him back. He promised he'd only let the fame go to his head, how all these girls threw themselves at him. The evening that it happened, when I spent the first night at Camille's, she'd begged me to be done with him forever. She didn't think he would ever change. But can't everyone change, or at least have the ability to?

"I'm just packing up equipment for tomorrow. Lots of lenses and boxes and equipment." I hesitate while I muster the courage. "Did you watch last night's episode?"

He shakes his head. "No, I didn't. I was at dinner."

The sting radiates outward from my chest. We used to watch it together—he always insisted. Now, I'm sitting here every week on my little sister's couch, spiraling into dark black holes, while he's out here living his best life, moving on.

He opens his mouth to speak again but decides against it, almost like he wants to wait to see what I have to say.

"Oh, okay," I say, trying to keep my voice level. "I thought—"

"I tried, Maren," he says quickly, glancing around. "But you know how these things go. Producers and editors and scheduling. I promise I tried so hard to convince them not to show it."

The cadence of my voice quickens, brightens. "So, you did have something to do with it?"

"What?" His brow knits together when his eyes spring back to my face. "They didn't air... it?"

It.

He doesn't know what else to call *it*.

This is what our relationship has been reduced to. Two little letters. The moment everything shattered.

But maybe he still cares? Maybe he still feels some protectiveness over my feelings. Enough to ask them not to put our deep personal issues on the show. And should I let one mistake define him? Especially if he's trying?

"Russ?"

It wasn't my normally sing-song voice saying his name.

I whip around to see *her*.

Her.

Three little letters that ruined everything.

She's standing there with a pink golf bag, her set of pink golf clubs poking out the top with tie-dye club head covers and her long blonde hair blowing in the wind.

"Hi," she says hesitantly, looking between us.

"Hi," I reply. She shifts from one leg to the other, and I wish I knew where she got her outfit. "Your golf dress is really cute."

Then I laugh. Sure, there are tears behind them. What do you expect? I'm not that strong, and I haven't seen her since that night. And I definitely had no inkling that they were still seeing each other.

Humiliation washes over me. Again. I've become accustomed to it at this point. Here I was thinking Russ cared just a little. When am I going to learn that everything out of his mouth is a lie?

Just another day in the life of—

"Maren."

Russ' lips aren't moving. I squint at him, convinced I'm hallucinating, but now he's looking at me like *I'm* the bad guy for some reason.

"You're an ass—" I start, my voice wavering.

"Maren," the voice says again, stronger this time, and I realize it's behind me.

I turn to see Locke sitting in a golf cart. Like he knew where I was and that I needed saving, but obviously he didn't. His eyes are steady on me, summoning me without another word, so I float like he's enveloped me with the darkness lurking in them.

As soon as my butt hits the seat, he takes off.

Don't look back, I tell myself, even though I know every single person on the practice green is staring. Me getting into a golf cart with Locke Hughes is an everyday occurrence. *Don't let on that he makes you nervous.*

Whatever he wants, he doesn't like it himself. In fact, I think he hates it. But right now, I just want to get away, no matter how much whatever lies at the end of this little ride terrifies me.

Away, away, away is my mantra.

I can finally breathe when the clubhouse comes into view.

"Thanks," I mutter when he slows. Before the cart can come to a full stop, I'm practically trying to sprint off of it.

"Wait." Locke reaches out and holds my wrist softly, tugging me back to the seat. The smirk radiating off his face without a trace of a smile unnerves me.

"He's teaching Lydia how to play golf. He never taught me how to play golf," I blurt.

His face wipes clean somehow. "What?"

"Lydia. That's her name. Such a refined name, I guess. Better than Maren. And I don't even like golf, but I wanted to learn for him."

Locke blinks. "You don't like golf?"

My laugh comes out forceful and abrupt before I compose myself to a semblance of a normal human and remember he stopped me from leaving. "What do you want?"

"I'll teach you," he says.

I stare in confusion. "Golf?"

"No," Locke sighs. "How to not give a shit."

It takes a minute for the hamster wheel in my brain to stop spinning.

"That would require you to actually talk to me," I laugh.

He stays silent.

"So, we'll hang out more? Spend time together?"

"Do you have a point?"

"Everyone will think we're together."

"I don't care," he says. "Let them."

Attempting to redeem myself from my earlier nonsensical accusation, I joke, "Ohhh, so exactly like fake dating?"

THE OXYMORON
Locke

"Fake friendship," I scowl. This might be my worst idea ever. "If anything."

Maren crosses her arms. "What do I have to do?"

She's quick.

"Simple. We can both get what we want. Come with me to obligations I have during tournaments and whatever else, and talk. I'm sick of it, and you say a lot of words."

She raises her eyebrows and laughs. "So, like a fake girlfriend?"

"There is zero dating in this scenario," I say with a deeper voice. No part of me is going to act like I'm in a relationship when I'm not. "Fake friends."

"And when people question why we're hanging out so much?"

I refrain from rolling my eyes. "Again, I do not care. Let them think whatever they want to think. I won't be making any statement about what we are or aren't doing. It's no one else's business."

Maren surveys me with a look of curiosity, like she doesn't believe it's that easy. But it is.

"You're okay with that? Everyone discussing you behind your back?" she asks. "Even when they're wrong?"

"I have to be."

She folds her lips together and thinks on that without offering her thoughts.

"So, that's it?" she asks skeptically. "All I have to do is go to some stuff that I was already going to be attending as part of my job anyway but talk to the people you're supposed to talk to for you?"

"Oh no, one more thing." I pause to let my dimples sway her by themselves. "And stop taking pictures of me."

"That's my *job*," she huffs after pulling her eyes off of my smile.

"Is there some type of quota you need to fill of me?" I question.

"Well, no, but I can't just not take pictures of you. You win almost everything. You're at every press event. That's impossible, and I'll get fired. If you didn't want your photo taken, ever, then you shouldn't have become a professional athlete."

"The old 'I owe everyone my life because I get paid to play a sport,'" I say. "Do you believe that?"

Maren shakes her head. "You know what I mean. And I'm not a crazy fan running up to you on the street with a cell phone shoved in your face. My photos go to websites and social media and newspapers and commercials. They're for the PGA—you know them, my employer."

"Take less," I counter. "The bare minimum. One per press conference. I'll allow you to make your own judgment call when I play—as long as you stand farther away from me while I swing so I can't hear the shutter."

She scoffs and narrows her eyes at me. "You cannot *hear* me taking pictures of you."

"I can," I insist, "and my life would be a lot more pleasant if I couldn't."

Her mouth snaps shut. She sits back and crosses her legs as she considers my offer.

Quiet, less, is just within reach, but I give her a few seconds while I let my eyes drift.

I wish her legs weren't so long. I bet they're even softer than her wrist. And why does she always wear short, tight golf dresses if she doesn't play golf, let alone *like* it? Yesterday was pink. Today is light purple.

"Well?" I challenge her, trying to distract myself from checking out the neckline of today's purple. She brings her wide, green, still-teary eyes to mine. "Offer expires in three… two—"

"I'm in."

"Good." I go to reach for her thigh without thinking and divert my hand at the last second. "Phone," I demand with my palm out. "First lesson."

She ogles my arm for a second too long, unlocks her iPhone with her face, and places it gently into my hand. "You're like this hot icicle, and I think you know it. Throwing your smile around whenever you feel like it's convenient to melt people."

"That's an oxymoron," I say.

"You know what I mean," she replies slowly, then at the same time seems to realize what exactly she said. The blush starts in her ears and makes its way down her neck and over her chest.

Confidence will have to be a lesson for another day, but I still can't help myself. "Own it, Maren."

"What?" she whispers.

I refuse to break eye contact. "What you said. You think I'm hot."

"I said *you* think you're hot," she argues, looking down at her feet. The red pushes up against her skin stronger and brighter. "There's a difference."

"Uh huh," I chuckle before I decide to let her off the hook.

Her phone looks like an OCD person's nightmare. The social media apps on her phone are exactly what I imagined—red bubbles with numbers reaching the hundreds. "You read all these comments?"

She blanches instantly and lunges across the foot-wide gap between us for her phone, but she's not that type of quick. I hold it out of her reach until she slinks back into her seat.

"No," she lies.

"None of these people would say this shit to your face. You have to stop reading them."

"I don't read them."

Every line in her face gives her away.

"What do they say?" I press.

Maren looks away with a shrug and sighs out, "Everything. Read them for yourself."

I tap on the one with the most notifications. Under the latest picture of Maren with a woman who could be her twin—I tell myself not to ask because I'm not trying to get to know her—there are hundreds of comments.

I skim to get the general idea:

Maren is gorgeous.

Maren is hideous.

She's just keeping her engagement private since there haven't been any photos of her with Russell lately, and they can't spoil Triple Bogey.

No, Russell's dumped her because he deserves better than a groupie.

There's two of them, and thank god her sister isn't on the show, too, to make it double annoying.

Oh my god, there's two of them, and her twin needs to be on the show as soon as possible because they're adorable together.

I can't read any more.

I switch to her contacts and save my number before I text myself without her noticing. Then I let my irrational instinct to protect this woman overpower my brain for a split second. "From where I'm sitting, you're incredibly beautiful, and Russell doesn't deserve you." When she looks back at me with narrowed eyes, unsure what my motivation is, I hold out her phone to her. "Delete them."

"The apps?"

"Yes, the apps."

She pauses, unsure of what to do, and then lets out a sigh. "How am I supposed to know what people think?"

"Why do you care?" I scoff. "You think you can please everyone?"

"I try," she says with a shrug.

"That is literally impossible. Delete them."

Her eyes drop to her phone and back up to mine, debating with herself, before she nods.

I watch one by one as she holds down and presses delete three times for each app. "They really want you to be sure," I joke.

"I feel lighter already," she laughs under her breath, but I don't think she believes it. "And thanks for saving me earlier."

"Don't get the wrong idea. That was unintentional," I clarify.

She laughs again, louder this time. "Right, Locke. I know. Still, thanks."

I cock my head to the side to study her. "And did you watch your little show last night?"

"Ugh," she says. "It's not *my* show. Stop saying that."

"Did you watch it?" I repeat, full well knowing the answer is yes. "Don't lie this time. You're not very good at it."

She tips her chin up. "I promise I won't anymore. I already decided last night."

"Good," I say.

"They didn't even show it, you know. The cheating," she says. "I stupidly thought Russ had something to do with it. Which is why I went out searching for him. To say thank you. Can you believe that? Why did I believe that in the first place? Something is wrong with me."

My eyes bounce around her face trying to decipher her emotions as she blinks back happy or sad tears—I can't really tell. I don't have the heart to tell her he would never do something that wasn't for his own benefit. Suddenly, a smile so wide blooms across her face that I instantly relax.

"But," she drawls, "now that I'm going to always be hanging out with you, *friend*, hopefully they'll have less footage of me to use."

I frown. "Always is a huge exaggeration. See you in San Diego. I hear it's sunny."

But when she turns to hop off my golf cart, I can't help myself. Just a second longer won't hurt. "Hey, Maren," I say, wrapping my hand around the back of her arm. Her skin is like silk, and I'm already missing the feel of it in the future version of me who will eventually have to let go.

She looks back over her shoulder. "Hm?"

"Being happy is the best revenge."

THE BEACH
Maren

LOCKE WASN'T LYING—SAN DIEGO is sunny.

As soon as I check in to the hotel, I putz anxiously around doing nothing, waiting for nothing. So, I find myself wandering down to Torrey Pines State Beach with my personal Nikon, that I splurged on with part of my I-signed-my-life-away-to-a-reality-show check, in my tote bag. At least one good thing came from it.

Sure, I see the beach and the Atlantic Ocean almost daily in Florida, touch the sand almost weekly, but something about the entirety of the Pacific feels different.

The air smells fresher and less salty. The shore is jutted with rocky cliffs. And it's freaking bright.

I fluff out a blue striped towel I borrowed from the hotel pool (which I promise myself to remember to return or I'll think about it for a week) and sit down in the center.

A hang glider launches off a cliff to my left, the purple and white triangle soaring expertly in front of the clouds. I watch in amazement until a group of children's laughs brings my attention to their sand-castle.

A cloud moves to cover the sunlight, casting everything in a slightly dull shadow, and I suddenly remember what I came out here to do.

Lifestyle photography is my happy place, no matter how few people will pay me for it.

I take in the shadows: the kids stomping their sandcastle into nothing, a surfer wiping out, the clouds moving across the sky over the ocean. These are the perfect moments of people just being.

I don't even realize how long I've been immersed behind my camera until my phone rings.

My heart flutters stupidly before I remember Locke doesn't even have my phone number. I've been on edge all day, waiting for him to contact me. He didn't ask for it, and I also realize I have no idea what his schedule is—if he's here yet, what events he expects me to go to. Which isn't that surprising. The man expects you to be on the same page as him without communication. I'm sure there's something in San Diego he wants me to be the face and voice of for him. Russell always had functions or press events or obligations outside of golf.

I assume Locke will just show up randomly at my hotel room door whenever he's ready like I should've been on the same wavelength as him.

"Mom," I say cheerily when I answer, trying to curb her inevitably hurt feelings before she makes everything about her. "I'm so sorry I didn't call you when I landed. I've been going, going, going since my feet touched the ground."

"Aw, sweetie," she says, "I know you're busy. I just wanted to check that you made it safely. What did they have you doing as soon as you got there?"

Which is code for *you didn't have five minutes to call when you landed? During your Uber to the hotel? After you checked in?*

It's not that I don't want to talk to her—okay, it's a little that—it's just that every time I do, somehow I end up feeling bad about myself, even when I was happy with myself, and wanting to change to appease her. I recognize I've been on a guilt trip my entire life, but I don't know how to jump off.

She doesn't give me time to reply. "What are you doing now? It sounds windy."

"Just at the beach," I say with a smile before my hair whips into my mouth. "Got a moment away to myself, so I'm taking some photos."

"That's wonderful. At least you don't have to spend every second with Russell. Which reminds me, your dad and I were watching your show the other night, and your hair is getting so long."

Which is code for *you need a haircut.*

"I kind of like it long," I tell her, softening how much I actually like it. "But I'll make an appointment to get it cut in a couple weeks."

I run my fingers through it before twirling it at the end. Why isn't me liking it long good enough for her? Instead, I care more about what she thinks, even when she should be happy that I'm happy.

"Oh, that's good. You know how much I like your hair shoulder length," she says. "Camille's is too long too. Did she show you a picture of the perfect crib she picked out? I would have loved for you to join us."

Of course, now it's perfect since Camille didn't go with the one my mom wanted.

"She did, and I had work, Mom."

"Golf. So many hours and tournaments and traveling. Watching it is like watching a sloth move." My mother chuckles, and my teeth involuntarily grind. "Camille also mentioned you took some maternity photos of her. Please text them to me. I'd love to see them."

"Well, they *are* lifestyle," I say like I'm the only one in on the inside joke, "but they still came out great. I've got to get back now. I love you."

My stomach instantly untangles. Of course, there's guilt there for lying, but being out from underneath her criticism makes me feel lighter.

"I love you too!" she sings. "Oh—"

But I'm already in the motion of pressing 'end,' and I'm not quick enough to stop.

After I hang up, I text her as many photos as my iPhone will allow in one text and watch the blue bar load.

A second later, I get her read receipt and wait.

I wait for her to finish flipping through. I wait for a response that I don't get. I wait until I give up. I wonder if she knows her read receipts are on.

Then I'm looking at the pictures I've already spent a crazy number of hours editing and muttering to myself like a lunatic, "So beautiful. You're such a talented photographer, sweetie. Camille looks so happy, and you captured the natural light perfectly, Maren. Wow, I think you *could* be a professional *non*-sports photographer."

I jolt when my phone buzzes in my hand, thinking I'm getting what I was hoping for, only to see a text message from someone else.

My stomach swirls then pinches tight, and tangled doesn't even begin to cover whatever is happening inside my body. I squint at my phone to make sure I read the name right.

Hottie Icicle? Why am I smiling?

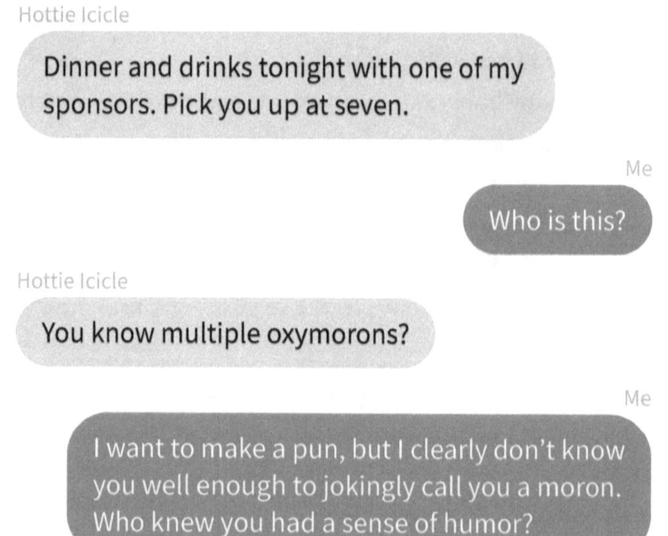

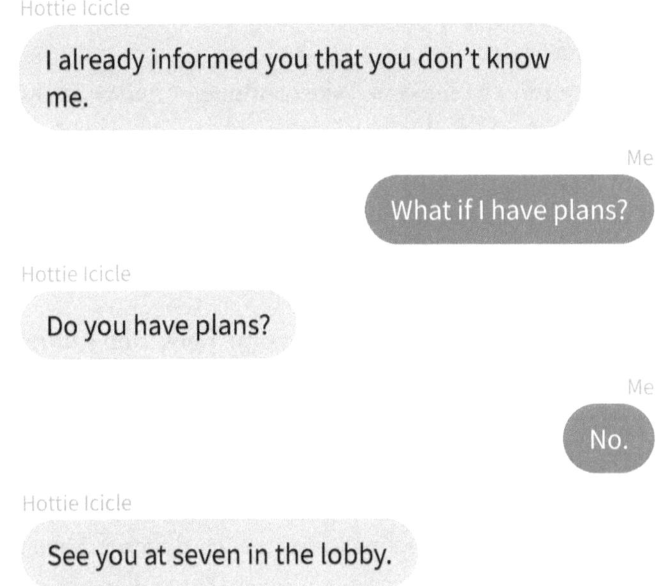

I don't even bother asking how he knows what hotel I'm staying at.

THIS IS NOT A date, but it feels a little bit like a date.

For some reason, my nerves are going kind of haywire, and my heart keeps expanding involuntarily. I think it's in response to the fact that I will be spending time with *Locke Hughes* of all people, the man who hates everyone.

"It's not a date," I repeat for the twentieth time while I'm currently obsessing about the way I look and trying to convince more than just my sister.

Camille leans in closer to her camera and giggles behind her palm. "Do you have a golf fetish?"

"No more golfers," I insist, backing up and twirling to show her my butt and back. I shimmer from shoulders to knees. "What about this one?"

"Too fancy," she says. "Next."

I groan and unzip.

"All golfers can't be the same," she continues. "You could also just have some fun. Locke is obviously not the relationship type."

"They might be all the same, and all of them are probably selfish. They don't even play a team sport," I point out. "I want someone who focuses on me, not their handicap or what number they're ranked. I want an all-consuming love, you know."

Camille scrunches her nose. "Handicap? Look who's using golf terms now."

I laugh and pull another dress over my head. This one is more complicated, and I can't find the armholes in the stretchy, tight fabric. "I don't even know what it is really, and I don't think professional golfers actually keep track of theirs... whatever the word means. Something about comparing them maybe. I don't know. My handicap is probably a thousand. Or wait? Is higher better? Golf is backwards, obviously. Why is it backwards?"

"Don't hold back. Talk birdie to me. Locke could give you a hole in one. It'd be so intense that after eighteen holes with him you wouldn't be able to walk the next day," Camille says before we both burst out laughing. "Yeah, not my best work."

Though I don't tell her, I imagine it would be extremely intense. The way his eyes latch onto me like hooks. I bet he'd have the stamina of a racehorse.

"What about this one?" I ask with my arms finally out to my side, eking out the image of what Locke must look like naked from my brain. While he doesn't smile, he's still very nice to look at, and I'd bet those hours in the gym don't hurt.

"Nope, you look like a middle-schooler who's trying too hard."

"Ouch," I tease her before I rummage around and find an ivory shift dress with brown buttons down the side.

She shakes her head after I put it on. "You look frumpy, Grandma. Like Nana when she wore that nightdress in public. You need something that hugs your hips. What do you have that's in between that?"

"God," I huff. "Good thing I packed half my closet."

I root around in my overflowing suitcase for yet another dress until I find the one I think Camille will like the best. I really did pack eight of them just in case.

"Where is he taking you?"

"I was too scared to ask him."

"That's practical," she teases. "What if you're going ax throwing or rock climbing and you show up in a dress?"

"'Dinner and drinks' is enough to assume a dress."

"'Dinner and drinks' is enough to assume a date."

"It's *not* a date."

She nods like I'm full of shit. "Riiiiight. The fake-girlfriend debacle of the twenty-first century. Explain this arrangement to me again. I'm not quite sure I get it."

"Locke says he's tired of talking. I think he thinks it will take some of the pressure off him if I'm there because I 'talk too much.' And I know he hates me taking his picture because I've been subjected to his glares now for years. He swears he can hear me taking his picture."

Camille munches on a pickle from a jar that appeared from thin air. "No way."

"I don't believe him either. But now, he'll get his wish. Like I told you, selfish."

"Well, he's helping you too," Camille points out. "You haven't sent me a single bitchy social media comment in days."

I don't want to admit how much quieter my brain has been. It's nice not trying to change myself so I come across differently the next time I'm filmed. Camille has been telling me for months to stop reading them, but she never went as far as to stare me down with blackened eyes and demand I delete the apps.

"Yeah, I feel happier," I say lightly and prepare myself for the *I told you so* that doesn't come.

"He's good for you then," she says instead. "Those strangers were hurting you, and they made you compare yourself to every other woman on that show." Her eyes fly down to my dress. "Let me see."

I stand back for the full effect and twirl in place.

"Perfect," she gushes.

"Hair up or down?" I ask, gathering my long hair into my palms.

"Down. It looks so pretty long. Don't cut it. More to grab onto." She winks. "And maybe someone can pull it harder at that length tonight."

I drop my hair. "Worry about your own relationship," I joke. "This one is a non-relationship. I think he called it 'fake friends, if anything.' So eloquent." Sliding on my heels, I glance at the clock. "I've got to go. It's 6:58."

"Okay, but Maren, let a teeny bit of his asshole rub off on you. You could use it." Her eyebrows shoot up at her unintentional words, and she cackles. "Ew. Let's never mention that I just said that ever again—unless you're into that kind of thing."

"You're disgusting," I laugh. "I'm hanging up."

"Wait!" she shrieks before her face turns deadly serious. "Enjoy your date."

"Goodbye," I huff before the screen goes black.

I give myself another four minutes to collect my scattered thoughts. For some reason, I know Locke would never be late and that he's sitting four stories below me at this exact moment, but I don't want to walk down there at exactly seven to find myself having to wait awkwardly alone... just in case.

At 7:03, I grab my clutch and head down to the lobby. As soon as the elevator doors open, I find Locke sitting on the couch directly in front of the desk, eyes trained on me like he knew this was the elevator that I was in.

He stands immediately, and I may not be able to walk just from his eye contact alone.

THE NON-DATE
Locke

I NEVER SHOULD'VE TOUCHED her.

For some reason, I can't get the feel of her skin off my hands. It just lingers there, and adrenaline is coursing through my veins now at the slight thought that she's within reach.

As she walks toward me, Maren tucks her little purse that's only big enough to hold a phone under her arm and drops her eyes to the floor like she's terrified to keep looking at me.

Her black dress has two lines of tiny crocheted holes around her waist, and it's hugging her hips just enough to draw my gaze to them, which immediately goes down slowly to her gold heels.

"I didn't know what to wear," she says quickly when she reaches me. "Is this too much?"

"Is that what you think?" I ask. "That you're too much?"

Her wide eyes meet mine like I've stolen all the oxygen from the room. "Sometimes."

"Take it from someone who actually is, you are not too much."

"Well, all the other times I feel like I'm not enough," she jokes with truth laced into the words. "So... there's that."

I feel it rise in my chest—the urge to prove her wrong, to stamp out whoever made her doubt herself. Russell, I'm sure.

"You look perfect," I say genuinely, ignoring that I'm half-hard. I'd tell her she looks fucking sexy, but I don't think she'd appreciate it, and I'm trying to remind myself every other second that I don't want to have sex with someone who's always around.

Her lips part, but she doesn't respond.

Do not touch her, I tell myself. Instead, I turn and assume she'll follow. When I hear the click-clack of her heels trying to keep up with my long strides, I slow to walk beside her.

"Are you staying in this hotel?" she asks.

"No," I chuckle. "I'm renting a house. I don't like people."

She smiles like I'm joking. "How'd you know where I was?"

"Conrad, my caddie, knew where the PGA staff is staying," I say, holding the door open for her.

"Things come easily to you, don't they?" she muses.

"That takes work," I say, shrugging.

I lead her to my rental car sitting at the curb. She stays silent as I hold open the door for her, and she continues to stay silent when I get in and pull out into traffic.

Every time she crosses her legs in the opposite direction, I find myself wishing I knew what she was thinking, if she is nervous, until out of nowhere she says, "So, you like Conrad?"

I definitely don't appreciate the thought that this whole time she was thinking about my fucking caddie.

"I have to," I joke. "He's my cousin. And my brother."

Maren's mouth forms an *oh*. "I'm sorry. Unless that's an incest joke I'm not picking up on."

"Incest jokes are never funny," I say while I stifle a laugh. "And there's nothing to be sorry for because it's not sad. If my aunt and uncle hadn't raised me then I'd have gone into foster care."

She shifts toward me and lays a hand over mine before I can register what she's doing. It's like a long drag of nicotine that goes straight to my head before I quickly yank my hand back.

Her face drops. "I'm sorry," she says again, flustered.

"Stop apologizing. There's nothing to be sorry for," I tell her probably too harshly, but she doesn't seem to mind.

"I know, I know. But it's sad and beautiful."

"It was a long time ago," I say.

She smiles to herself. "I think I would've liked to see you as a child."

"I'm sure I have a picture."

"I meant *know* you. What you were like," she clarifies. "Wh—"

Before she can ask a follow-up question about me, I'm already cutting her off. "What about your sister?"

"How'd you know I have a sister?"

"You posted a photo of yourself with a girl who looks just like you. I mean it's a given, right?"

"She's my doppelgänger," she says, straight-faced. "I randomly met her at the grocery store."

"So, your twin?"

"Actually, no," she laughs. "Camille is eleven months younger than me. Also, she's married with a baby on the way."

The way she adds the last part makes me think she has to tell men that a lot. "My next question wasn't going to be if she was single."

Maren gives me an appreciative look and tries not to smile. "It's okay if it was. I assure you we've been asked if we're into threesomes more than once. As much as we look alike, she has always been the funnier, prettier, more confident, slightly better version of me. I came to terms with it a long time ago. I just want everyone to like me, so I try to blend in. Give everyone what they want from me."

"You think it's easier to sacrifice yourself?" I ask.

"Sometimes, yeah. Don't you?"

"Not anymore. Someone will always hate you. It doesn't matter what you do or say. One person will think something amazing about you and another person will think the complete opposite. You tell the entire truth to someone's face and you will never be able to change their mind, so I don't try anymore."

"Anymore?" Maren questions me.

I start slowly, unsure how much of myself I want to give to her, but a chuckle slips out first before I can stop it. This is why I'm trying to help her, so I may as well.

"I'm not immune to the internet. Always having it at your fingertips is a curse. Half of us admit it, but don't do anything about it. Every article that was written about me, every video taken, even if I didn't find it myself—and trust me, I found enough myself through Google or social media to last me a lifetime—someone texted one to me. I'd spend hours reading comments or watching a video of me where I was supposedly rude or tired. Every single person would analyze my body language or try to read my lips.

"And then I'd obsess—what could I have done differently, how could I make people happy. Then I'd try to change, be overly nice, but then I would still get misinterpreted as fake or rude, and no matter how hard I tried to change, someone always had something negative to say about me. The best thing I ever did for my mental health was put my phone down. Because I can't control other people's feelings. I know myself and am happy with myself. I'm not living for others. That's all that matters. And for someone like me, it's easier to keep people at arm's length anyway."

"For someone like you?" she repeats.

"Someone who's..."

I try to choose my next words carefully, and I'm about to say *a professional athlete* until Maren turns toward me.

Her eye contact is surprisingly steady before she finishes my sentence like she read my thoughts. "Too much?"

Then Maren goes back to looking out the window.

WHEN WE WALK INTO the restaurant, Graham's eyeline bounces between me and Maren before he stands to greet us.

He buttons his jacket and swipes a hand through his brown curls with his face full of hesitancy.

"He didn't know I was coming?" Maren whispers, confused.

I shrug as we approach. "He assumed when I said I was bringing someone that it was Conrad. He should learn to ask better questions."

"Maren!" Graham smiles brightly and holds his hand out for her. "It's so nice to officially meet you."

"I'm so sorry," she replies, shaking his hand. Her eyes flutter to mine, wondering how he knows her name. "Locke didn't tell me your name."

"Graham, his agent." He sits after I pull Maren's chair out for her and settle into the chair beside her. "He didn't tell me his…"

"Co-worker," I offer before I shoot him a stern look warning him not to mention any fake PR bullshit.

"—co-worker was joining us." Graham's eyebrows fall in disappointment before he places a hand on Josh's shoulder to his left. "This is Josh, VP of marketing at Rival, and his wife, Shelley."

They both smile a little too much, like they're trying to impress Maren. Josh's dark beard surrounds his bright white teeth, making them look impossibly whiter, and Shelley's deep red lips curl up like she's hoping to become her best friend. But Maren doesn't seem to notice.

Instead, she nods and tries to pull a face like she knows exactly what Rival is, though it's clear she has no clue. "Nice to meet both of you. Maren Murray."

For some reason, hearing her say her last name startles me. I'd never thought about it before, but now I'm wondering what her middle name is, how old she is, when her birthday is, what her favorite color is.

After Josh and Shelley greet us, I find myself leaning into the side of her face.

"You're an alliteration," I chuckle for her ears only and watch her shiver. "Rival is a sports drink, by the way." I straighten. "Josh and Graham have been with me since the beginning."

Maren's eyes light up as she looks between them both. "When was the beginning?"

"God," Josh says, thinking. "Almost a decade ago."

"How old are you?" she asks, craning her neck toward me.

"Thirty."

Her smile starts in her eyes first like she likes my answer, then she sticks her tongue between her front teeth and playfully bites it.

My eyes have a hard time pulling themselves from her mouth until she eventually turns back.

"So, what did you do? Force him to give up college?" Maren questions Graham.

"Trust me, I tried," he laughs. "Many times. I backed off. I'm a patient man. And then one day, suddenly, he was ready."

Another turn of her body into mine. "Where'd you go to college?"

I'm equal parts impressed and disappointed she didn't google me because I can tell she truly doesn't know the answer. Of course, the asshole never mentioned it to her. Which then leaves me dreading the moment she learns, "The University of Florida."

Her brows knit, and she chews on her lip as she no doubt does the math in her head.

"Oh," she says, wide-eyed, when she's figured out the answer. Her pupils look like pinpricks against the green shades of her irises. "So, you and Russell were teammates?"

"We were," I confirm, "for a year."

Maren blinks at me then erases all traces of confusion with a soft smile, almost as if she's apologizing. "I'm—he never mentioned that."

I scowl. "You're saying you're sorry in your head, aren't you?"

"No," she says, tipping her chin up in defiance, and changing the subject, thank god. "When did you start playing golf?"

"Don't remember," I say.

Graham knocks a knuckle on the table. "Twelve."

"I thought you had to pick up golf at the age of two to have any hope of turning pro," Maren jokes.

Shelley laughs with her and teases her husband, "Right, Josh? Isn't that why you weren't able to play professionally?"

"Josh isn't half bad," I defend him. I've had to play with him enough times in my life to appease people. "Trust me, if he wasn't, I would have never played with him again. Take Graham, for example, one and done."

"Oh?" Graham laughs in his good-natured tone. "Maren, I just happen to have a picture in my phone of twelve-year-old Locke at his first tournament."

I groan. Maren grins happily.

I know exactly which photo it is: the one Graham had my aunt dig up when he needed it for a commercial. I'm practically scowling into the camera with my first ever medal because I placed second.

"Baby Locke?" Maren breathes delightfully, extending her arm out and curling her manicured fingers toward his phone. "Let me see." Her eyes flash, her smile all teeth, when Graham hands over his phone. I wonder what she looks like when she actually does get mad and is comfortable enough to show someone. "Look at you! You're like the exact same, just a foot shorter. Same frown. Same haircut."

"I don't like change," I mutter. "And I was pissed off I lost."

"You got a medal though." Her foot grazes mine on accident when she crosses her legs underneath the table. I angle my legs farther away from her. "When did you know you were good? Better than normal?"

"I don't know," I say noncommittally before I pick up my beer and try to take a long enough sip that will force Maren to focus back on the group.

This isn't a get-to-know-you game. She's supposed to be talking to them so I can sit here in peace.

Thankfully, she seems to realize this. Her smile loosens a millimeter when she looks up at me and a silent conversation passes through us unintentionally.

She turns away quickly and hands the phone back to Graham. "I was just telling Locke on the way here that I would've liked to see him as a child. That didn't disappoint."

"Everyone knew he was special by at least fifteen," Graham fills in for me. "It's a good thing his aunt suggested golf to channel his emotions into."

"Emotions?" Maren's laugh channels *how can Locke Hughes possibly have emotions* energy. Then her laugh abruptly subsides as she misinterprets his words. She flicks her eyes to mine sadly and silently apologizes.

"Intensity?" Graham humorously corrects himself. "When Locke wants something, he will not stop until he's achieved it. Every piece of himself is focused on it. Similar to a lot of great athletes."

I'm chugging my beer at this point, even though I typically don't drink. I wish everyone would shut up. I don't want to sit here and discuss my personality traits or my life or my habits.

Somehow, Maren picks up on this.

"Shelley," she says, shifting the topic for me on purpose, "what's the world of sports drinks like?"

Josh and Graham fall into their own conversation. Maren and Shelley gush like they've become two best friends.

I'll sit here, thankful for Maren's talkative personality, and drink my beer in silence. This is what I was supposed to get out of this arrangement anyway.

I'm not doing it out of the goodness of my heart.

THE PRAISE
Maren

I spent the entire dinner—and car ride here—ruminating on what it would feel like to be liked by Locke.

He keeps such a small circle that I assume it would be extremely hard to become a part of it, to be allowed in. But if you were, just how special that would make you feel. How much it would mean that he trusted you, that he wanted you. If he gave you his attention and you became his focus, just how intentional he would be. It's hard to even picture the intensity of his eyes falling on you with a look of love, like you're *his*. Because he chose you.

I imagine just the pure weight of *him* would steady you in the strongest earthquake.

Or someone similar to Locke because, of course, actual Locke hates when I touch him.

Our fingers brushed once when I reached for my glass and he reached for his fork at the same time. Another time my foot accidentally grazed his leg when I crossed mine. He jolted each time like I'd shocked him and then proceeded to make a conscious and obvious effort to avoid all my rogue body parts.

After the third time he leans away from me when I go to pick up my wine, I excuse myself to go to the restroom.

What am I even doing? Why am I wishing Locke would touch me in the most innocuous ways when he clearly can't stand me?

His relief when I steered the conversation away from him was palpable.

I talk too much, I smile too much—way, way too much for him. This is why I'm here. I am definitely not emotionless enough for him to even just sleep with for fun. Not that that's what I want. But also, not that I haven't thought about it.

And *I'm* here to be more like Locke. So, I need to pull myself together.

Of course, that plan goes to shit when I step back into the restaurant and weave my way through the bar only to have Russ swivel on his barstool from out of nowhere and trap me with his arm.

"Maren," he greets me, placing a kiss on my cheek so quickly that it shocks me into a coma. Technically, not a hello. "You're the last person I thought I'd see here tonight."

He smells like whiskey, and I instinctively look around—either for Craig or Lydia, I'm not really sure.

The bar area is small, with the typical liquor bottles lining the back wall on glass shelves and a sleek wooden counter. The murmur is dull around us, but enough to make me feel unseen.

"Craig will be here in a minute," he says.

"Oh, okay," I finally say. "I should get back then. It was good seeing you."

His grip tightens on my waist. "So, you're... with him now?"

I don't miss the inflection in his voice. He was about to accuse me of sleeping with him before he attempted to reel back his jealous tone. I made Russell work for it, so I think he knows I wouldn't be having sex with Locke already. Unless maybe it makes him madder that maybe this is something I'm doing just for fun.

My eyes spring to our table, which is in perfect view from here, where I find Locke already staring at us with no emotion. He looks away to say something to Graham like he couldn't care less.

No one cares, and I hate myself that I just want Russ to care about me. It can't be that much to ask someone who you spent years of your life with, even if you're no longer together, to care about your feelings. That's not a wild request.

"It's not like that," I say in a lame attempt to defend myself. "It's not what it looks like."

"Not like what?" he laughs. "Like you're sleeping with him to get back at me?"

Everything I could say sits on the tip of my tongue.

We're not even friends.

We're fake *friends.*

I'm entertaining his obligations, which are coincidentally people, because he doesn't want to be here, let alone be here with me.

He's only trying to help me not feel like this.

It would all be the truth, but I get it now—what Locke is trying to say. It doesn't matter what I tell Russ, he's not going to believe me. He'll believe what he wants to believe, which is that I'm on some petty road of revenge-fucking his rival.

And I'm quite certain there's more to that story that Russell never even confided in me about.

My phone chimes.

Hottie Icicle

Do you need help?

Russ scoffs and briefly turns to Locke. "Checking up on you?"

Locke's eyes don't leave mine, and I shake my head a millimeter.

Big girl pants, Maren.

"Russ, you're allowed to believe whatever you want because I don't think I can change your mind," I say, channeling my inner Locke. I think he'd probably sound harsher but it's all I have in me.

Russ cocks an eyebrow, anger flushing through his cheeks. "You know he doesn't do relationships or girlfriends, right? He'll get tired of *you* even faster than usual."

I blink back the tears that are trying to squeeze through. Okay, I lied. I need help. Russ knows how to strike where it hurts the most. When I frantically search for Locke, he's no longer at the table. Probably tired of sitting at the table by himself for too long and mad at me for leaving him. Maybe he escaped to the comfort of the bathroom to be alone in peace.

Russ' hand, which is still on my waist, pulls me into him slightly. I angle my head away and use his shoulder to try to push myself off him to no avail.

"I'll still be here though," he says quietly. "Lydia and I aren't serious. I made a mistake, and I'm sorry. You know we'll always love each other."

He's never going to let me go. He'll hover, bait me, lure me, chase me, only to discard me again and again—and I'll let him. Because being wanted and liked by someone wins out over everything else, even when it's fucked up.

Right as I'm about to let a tear break through, contemplating my fate or maybe accepting it, because I feel myself soften into him, another arm wraps around my waist so quickly, I'm two feet away from Russ before my brain can process the motion of events. Now, I'm wedged against a plane of warm muscle with no understanding of how I got here.

Russell's winning smirk falls, while my heart pounds against my sternum because I almost fell for the smoke and mirrors momentarily.

"I don't appreciate you touching her," Locke says as harshly as I imagined.

"What the fuck do you know?" Russ says like we're all just joking around. "She's *my* girlfriend."

With my body now against Locke's instead, I siphon every bit of energy I can from him. "*Ex*-girlfriend," I say, stronger than I feel.

Russ tips his drink toward me as if there's no difference in the two words and corrects his slip of the tongue. "Ex-girlfriend," he repeats and looks up to Locke. "And we aren't finished talking."

"You are," Locke says sternly. His lips brush my hair, and his voice is so soft I think for a minute he's communicating to me through my mind. "Just turn around. Do you need another drink?"

I can't see Locke's face but by the way Russ is staring above my head with hatred spearing from his pupils, I don't think either one has broken eye contact.

"Yes, please," I reply, letting out a breath.

My body has a mind of its own and sinks further into Locke as I turn away from Russ like I don't care that he's sitting there.

And I may not.

Because Locke's hand stays on my waist as I spin and settles on my hip.

I raise my eyes to his and imagine this is what all-consumed looks like. Dark, brooding irises never straying from mine longer than necessary. A body part always connected in some way when possible.

Locke would make me feel like *everything*.

"Another red wine would be great," I say breathlessly. I'm too close to his face, and he smells like leather and amber and fresh air. It must be something that costs a thousand dollars a bottle and laced with the magic of hypnotism.

Locke smiles, not fully, but just enough that his right dimple makes an appearance.

"Good girl," he says, his voice low and just for me, his fingers pressing into my hip bone before his thumb swipes over a row of the tiny holes in my dress.

My breath just audibly catches in my throat. The spark ignites below my belly button, and I have to shift even closer to Locke to dull the ache that now settles between my legs.

My body blooms with heat I didn't know it was capable of, a myriad of emotions running from head to toe like they're traveling along a lightning rod.

I'm almost ashamed that he's turned me into putty from two little words that I never knew could hold such weight against me. Besides, I absolutely should not lust after this man who is so hot and cold that he can't make up his damn mind about whether or not he wants to touch me.

But he looks so pleased with me, and he *is* still touching me, not to mention he's sexy as hell. I think I'd do anything he asked me to in this moment.

Also, I think I know now what I would want him to call me.

THE LINE
Locke

SHE HAS A PRAISE kink.

And I'd bet my Masters green jacket that she doesn't even know it.

Fucking hell.

What the fuck has Russell been doing? He couldn't even figure out what gets his girlfriend off?

I run a hand over my face and glare at him over Maren's head before he mouths a *fuck you* to me, which I ignore. I don't actually need to ask him the question because I know exactly what he's been doing—being a self-absorbed jackass. He gets up and slinks over to his table when the hostess tells him his party is here.

Say what you want about me being an asshole, but I'm not selfish. I put the people I care about above myself—which, yes, I can happen to count on one hand—and I notice things.

For instance, I noticed how Maren's breath caught in her throat, how she had to shift from one leg to the other to try to ignore how much my words affected her. I noticed that she looked at me with shock, lust, and shame behind her eyes before she quickly looked away.

Shit, the things I would do if she'd let me, if I'd let myself. I'd bring her into the back hallway, the coat closet, even the fucking bathroom and call her *my* good girl, compliment her like she deserves until she's begging and shaking and then begging again. Erase every fucking doubt from her mind that Russell put there.

To think, she doesn't even *know* how good I could make her feel just with words. This dress is so thin I can feel that she's not wearing any underwear, and she's probably wet from my unintentional little discovery—I should think about anything else right now.

My grandmother.

My upcoming tax return.

Alabama, Alaska, Arizona, Arkansas, California...

Presidents? George Washington, John Adams, Thomas Jefferson... this is what two years of college gets me.

But my hand is still on her. I don't really want to let go, even though I should, because I've already gotten a fix after trying so hard to stay away, and I want to ride the high. So, I simply will.

And fuck Russell Ashe. I'll make Maren forget he even spoke to her tonight.

"I'm looking forward to my peaceful, quiet, picture-free day tomorrow," I tease, sliding her newly deposited wine glass closer to her. She eases herself up on the now empty seat behind her and comes inches closer to my face. I run a hand down her arm.

"How far away do I have to stand?" she asks.

Fuck, if my fingers don't tense against her involuntarily before I break contact. "I have very good hearing."

"I don't believe you." She places a palm against my chest and tries to playfully push me backward, but I don't budge. "Did you even want to play golf professionally?"

"What makes you say that?"

"Things," she says and waits for my answer that isn't going to come. "Okay... did you want to graduate from college?"

"You ask a lot of questions."

"Just like I say a lot of words." The challenge in her voice rises at the end, throwing my own words back at me.

For someone who does both, she certainly listens well too.

"I never said that it was a bad thing," I tell her.

She bites her lip in thought. "I guess you didn't. Is it a bad thing?"

"No," I tell her truthfully.

She gasps and smiles. "You *can* answer questions."

"I can do lots of things."

Maren's ears go pink at the tone of my voice.

The woman sitting behind me gets up, so I pull the stool closer to Maren and sit back on the edge.

She tenses when she glances over my shoulder, eyes a mix of torture and worry, and I turn to see Craig has walked in, thankfully with his camera at his side.

I raise my hand and let myself wrap a palm along her jaw. "Focus back here. You're safe with me. I'll sue them if they air any footage of me."

She rolls her eyes like I'm joking. "You made the right choice not being a part of it."

"Forget it's there. And I *will* sue."

When she studies my very serious face, she nods, her cheek just slightly pressing into my hand like she's reassuring herself that I'm real.

I'll deal with Craig later.

"So, you really don't like golf?" I ask her playfully.

"I mean... no?" she says, unsure. "I don't know. I've never played. I've always just watched, sat in a golf cart. It's not that fun watching. What's your favorite part of playing?"

"It's personal," I say.

Her huff makes me laugh.

"Not like that," I add. "I mean it's literally personal. Most of the time, it's like I'm playing against myself if that makes sense. Always trying to beat yourself. No team that relies on you. And you can never reach perfection."

She nods. "That actually does make sense."

"What if I taught you how to play?" I chuckle.

"What? No!" she scoffs. "You're the last person I'd want watching me learn to play golf."

"Why's that?"

"I—" Maren hesitates then smiles sweetly, brings her wine glass to her lips, and says instead, "You know why."

"I do?"

"You're the best golfer, like... ever. Is that what you want to hear?"

"No," I challenge her, "I want to hear what you were initially going to say."

She sighs, almost as if she's about to melt to the floor, but she tells me anyway. "Your eyes kind of scare me."

I don't think she would be saying any of this if she wasn't on her third glass of wine. "I *scare* you?"

"Your eyes scare me," she says, tipping her chin up with confidence. "The way you look at me, I mean. They're really dark. And I'm scared of the dark. And they... they're almost black. The way you look at me is really intense." Her giggle gives away how nervous she is.

"It's fun to be scared sometimes though, right?" I ask her rhetorically, leaning in. "Then you feel proud and brave that you faced your fears." My voice is low, and I'm so close to her face, I can smell her shampoo. It's a mix of strawberries and peaches, and the thought of her in the shower flashes across my mind. She swallows, licks her lips, gives herself away—that she agrees with me but doesn't really know why. "And why are you always wearing those little golf dresses if you don't like golf?"

Maren flushes. "Because they're cute—because I like them, and they're comfortable."

"Because they're cute?"

She takes another sip, and somehow this is the sip that pushes her over the flirty line. "You tell me."

"Snarky, tipsy Maren is moderately cute," I say.

"Look at me going from mild to moderate," she jokes, scrunching her nose, "but stop calling me cute."

God, her freckles do something to me. I want this woman under me, on top of me, bent over for me.

"Maybe eventually I will," I whisper, leaning down until my lips hover just above the shell of her ear. "I know what you do want to be called now."

I crossed a line last night.

Though I don't know what the line was.

Fake friends to... fake friends I want benefits with?

A tiny part of me cares that I let this happen. This isn't what I set out to do. And a huge slice of me doesn't give a shit, which easily wins out when I see her sticking her tongue out at me and taking a step closer to me as Conrad and I find my ball on the fairway of the third hole.

She has on a black golf dress with these straps crisscrossing along the span of her tan back, and when she leans down to fix something on her white tennis shoes, her already short dress reveals the tight little shorts attached underneath.

I lift one side of my lip up at her in pretend disgust. Well, half pretend disgust because I can't hear her camera anymore, and it is nice. But I also want my face between those long legs.

"What is happening right now?"

"Mind your own damn business." I glare back at Conrad. "What's the slope on the green?"

He laughs. "I am. I just told you the slope, and you're too busy flirting with the photographer you half-hate to hear me."

"I don't hate her, and her name is Maren. Tell me again."

"You made *Maren* stand over there. One and half percent-ish maybe. Not a ton."

"I hate her camera," I argue. "She needs a tripod and an automatic button and she can stand as close as she wants."

Conrad smirks.

"You know what I mean. Is it going to spin back?"

"Yeah, probably some. It's too windy, so keep it low. Did something happen between you two last night?"

"Fuck no," I say, surveying my clubs. "What're you thinking? A wedge?"

"Nah, the seven. Something happened," he counters.

I consider his suggestion and slide the wedge out of my golf bag before I take a few practice swings.

I know deep down something shifted last night because I was this close to pushing her up against the side of my car, kissing her, and asking if she wanted to come back to my rental house. Conrad does not need to know that. Though I deserve a trophy for my self-control.

"You know how I get. How many yards are we out?"

"Hundred and fifteen, maybe. Locke, please do not fixate on sleeping with her," he lectures me.

Too late, I think.

I want to find out if her inner thighs are softer than her arms. I want to see how much she will let go. I want to hear what she sounds like when she moans my name. I want to teach her how to explore every fantasy she doesn't know she has. I want to fuck the name Russell out of her mind.

I want it so much that I need it.

Fixation is an understatement.

"Is this about Russell?" he asks.

"I don't give a shit about Russell."

"She does," Conrad drawls.

She wouldn't...

Conrad reads my mind before he taunts, "You're going to fuck it out of her?"

"She shouldn't," I stress. "He's been cheating on her since the beginning, and you and I both know it."

"She's too nice," he says. "Which means you of all people should stay away. She will not be able to keep sex and feelings separate, and you kind of have to work with her."

I ignore him, change out my wedge for the 7-iron, and swing the nicest hit. My ball lands on the green beautifully and rolls maybe eight yards from the hole. "Nice call on the seven," I scowl. "Stay out of my head."

"Gladly," he laughs and looks up from his notebook. "Gorgeous shot."

"Emmie's clapping for her daddy on TV," I joke. My heart suddenly drops to my feet as I frantically remember we're televised and feel around the collar of my shirt. "Shit. Are we mic'd up? I don't even remember."

"No," Conrad laughs. "I shot them down when they asked."

"God," I breathe out and relax. I could never live with myself if I blasted that over airwaves for someone to record and post on YouTube.

I'd be no better than Russell, who is waiting impatiently by the looks of his stance, for us on the green.

He gives us a sarcastically cordial, "Took you fucking long enough," when we reach him.

Conrad and I ignore him and put our heads together to discuss where my ball landed, which only infuriates him more.

"What are you doing?" he demands in his insufferable voice.

I look up. "About to chip in for a birdie. What are you doing?"

"What are you doing with my girlfriend?" he tries again like I didn't know what he was asking the first time.

We're going to do this little dance where we look like we're joking around, our voices light, so it doesn't actually look like we're pissed off at each other.

"Why do you keep calling her that?" I ask curiously.

"Is this about us?" He doesn't answer my question, but I suspect he's trying to keep her close, close enough that whenever he feels like it, she'll thankfully welcome him back with open arms, happy and blissfully unaware that he's manipulating her.

"Contrary to what you think, Russell, you hardly ever cross my mind," I say with a smirk.

"Stay away from her," he says, almost scared.

"Well, since you have zero control over me, I'll go on doing whatever the hell I feel like doing."

"You can't do whatever the hell you feel like doing with her," he sing-songs.

I blink. "Like you didn't?"

"She's not like that," he offers, looking like he's either about to crawl out of his skin or punch me. He settles for a smug smile instead. "I bet she won't even sleep with you. She sees you with your girl of the month every now and then."

"She also *sees* you now," I reply. "And I don't need your advice. One, my caddie doesn't pick girls out of the crowd for me. Two, I don't *cheat*. And three, she'll forget who you are the second my name leaves her lips "

"Bullshit," Russ laughs. "She still loves me, and she'll take me back when I'm ready."

"Maybe if you weren't so busy being an asshole, she wouldn't have outgrown you. You don't deserve her."

"Like you fucking do."

"I didn't say I did, but it's not my fault you didn't know how to keep her satisfied. You don't even know her." I shake my head and inspect the club I just slid out of my bag. I let my voice take on amusement. "Too busy with your side fucks to know how to get your own girlfriend off. You've always been careless."

I stand rooted when Russ flares with anger, forgets where we are, and takes a step toward me. "If this is about revenge—" Conrad slides in between us, cutting off Russell mid-sentence and making him step back.

One glance at Maren tells me she's been watching us and trying incredibly hard to read lips. Her face is covered in confusion, eyes worried, in disbelief that we're actually having a conversation that looks like two friends joking around that suddenly turned near-violent.

But I don't even know what I'm doing anymore.

I cross in front of Conrad and brush as close to Russell as I can without actually touching him. He's radiating hatred but has his look of fake camaraderie plastered on his face. My laugh comes out low.

"I don't give a fuck about you, Ashe, and eventually, she won't either." I give him my best dimples. "No one will care."

Which is probably his worst nightmare.

THE HOSPITAL
Maren

NOT SO BREAKING NEWS: Locke Hughes won the first tournament of the year and one point six two million dollars.

When I looked at the newspaper that was left in front of my hotel door this morning, my heart swelled with pride. One of the few pictures I took of him on hole eighteen sinking the winning shot ended up on the front page of the sports section with my tiny name beneath it: *Photo by Maren Murray.*

I'd pathetically imagined my mother opening the Florida newspaper and doing the same thing—smiling and running her finger over my name. But I don't think she follows golf at all. Instead, she's probably drinking her coffee on her front porch and online shopping for her grandson.

My dad did text me, though, with an iPhone picture of my picture, along with a "Nice!" and that brightened my day like he tends to do in his little ways. It's not both parents I've had to seek attention from my whole life.

They'd mentioned Russell's name about mid-way through the article. After his and Locke's weirdly cordial conversation, Russ had been flustered the rest of the tournament and fell behind to twelfth place.

His angry eyes and scowl followed me for days, hole after hole, but now, you'd think he was in love with me. Eyes sparkling, too much teeth when he smiles, shifting his good side toward the camera, always glancing to make sure I'm getting a good shot.

His voice doesn't even sound like him, not since the minute he walked into the children's hospital. It's all a PR opportunity for him.

The little boy in the hospital bed with stars in his eyes is looking at Russ, smile wide, cheeks flushed, with a neon yellow cast covered in names on his leg, and Russ is looking at me.

"Did you get some good ones?" he asks.

Instinctively, I look at the little screen on the back of my camera before I balk and lie, "Looks great."

Craig stands in the other corner, catching every second of our terse exchanges with his blinking red light, though I notice it's not focused on me nearly as much as it used to be.

I want to ask him if he erased the footage of Russ and Lydia on a wave of sympathy, if he 'lost' it, if the producer is going for extra shock value with the future season finale, or if they think we're going to somehow reconcile.

But mostly I want out of here. This room has become too small for anyone to fit inside with Russ' ego. I want the comfort of Locke's presence, which I never thought I'd say. Because I do feel safe with him, where I know the camera can't reach me, where I'm confident he goes out of his way just a tiny bit to make sure I know he has my back in our fake friendship.

Even if Locke has ignored me for the last few days, content that I'm standing an appropriate enough distance away from him, and likely mad at me for whatever happened between us four days ago at the bar, he doesn't make me feel like *this*.

Russ watches me go, stuck in place, as he plays *Sorry!* with the little boy who's idolizing him.

Back in the hallway, I press my back against the closed door and feel like not enough.

Not enough for anyone. All the time.

A blonde nurse shuffles by in her blue scrubs and eyes me like she isn't sure if she should call security or not—maybe I'm a crazed fan with my stalker camera slung around my neck.

I attempt my best smile, which I realize may look a little crazed. My heart feels like lead, and my head is about to float off from the anxiety.

I slip in and out of the next two rooms fairly unnoticed.

Landon, the young new golfer on the PGA tour with an infectious laugh and a boyish charm greets me enthusiastically before he poses for me with the smile of someone who has so much in life to look forward to, then goes back to the story he was engrossed in.

He's the golfer who's friends with everyone, who can say whatever he wants and get away with it. The one who goes out the night before tournaments and still manages to get up bright and early and play eighteen holes of golf despite being slightly hungover. His episodes on the reality show are always the most fun.

Bryan, the quietest pro-golfer I've met since I started this job, gives me a head nod and lets me take a few candid shots because he's doing a puzzle.

He's the golfer whose family travels with him, who goes out of his way to say thank you, and will typically keep to himself then disappear as soon as the day is done so he doesn't miss a minute with his children. His episodes always bring the sweet family aspect.

You pick up on things when you observe the same people for years—but you also become too complacent and miss other obvious things.

When I open the next door, Locke looks up from the end of the hospital bed, eyes dark. He's coloring with a little girl on the table they've wheeled in between them.

His eyes dart down to the camera I'm holding and back to me. One of his eyebrows twitches, so I let it fall against my stomach and dangle from the strap around my neck. I suppose I won't get into any trouble if Locke is missing from the line-up.

"Hi," the little girl says, startling me back into reality. She has on pink pajamas and is nestled under a white blanket. She and Locke have spread out two Disney princess coloring books across the table, and the crayons are stuffed in a cup at the edge. "Do you want to color?"

"Oh," I say, "hi."

I've forgotten how to talk to children, and I should probably work on that since I'm going to become an aunt soon.

"This is my friend Maren," Locke says. He pats the spot on the bed next to him. "Maren, this is Sarah."

I give him a look like *are we friends?* as I cross the room and plop down next to him. He just stares.

"It's nice to meet you," I smile. "What are we coloring?"

Sarah flips her pages back and forth. "Rapunzel or Belle?"

"I'm in a Rapunzel mood today."

Sarah furrows her eyebrows. "But your hair is brown."

"And it's not seventy feet long," I joke, "but I think we share a heart."

She rips the page out slowly and hands it over while she inspects my entire physique, sizing me up to see if I'm deserving of a precious *Tangled* sheet. "You're pretty though."

"Thank you," I beam, even though eight-year-olds call everyone pretty. "So are you. I wish I had red hair."

"I'm like Ariel." She holds up her coloring book to show me her *Under the Sea* picture.

Locke's coloring his prince's hair yellow. "John Smith? Fitting."

"Don't worry. I'll color his eyes black," he says without looking up.

I sit cross-legged on the bed, which causes Locke to break his concentration briefly to inspect my legs, and possibly more. There are shorts underneath my golf dress, but it seems to bother him anyway.

I pluck a golden crayon out of the cup and ignore my stomach curling into itself.

As mortified as I am for drunkenly telling Locke his eyes scare me, I'm equally as mortified that I'm turned on by them—and he knows it.

His voice, or maybe his choice of words, does something to me, and for a split second the other night at the bar, I thought from the way he was looking at me that he was going to kiss me. Or at least do *something*. And to top it off, I felt disappointed that we were interrupted by Graham telling us our dessert was at the table.

Especially now that he's back to wanting nothing to do with me.

I guess Russ isn't around to mess with his head and challenge him into vengeance.

Sarah's voice reminds me to stop looking at Locke's forearm tensing as he drags the crayon back and forth. "Do you color with your niece?"

I open my mouth before I realize she's talking to Locke.

"You have a niece?" I ask, raising my face to his.

"I thought he was your friend?" Sarah questions me like she's somehow caught me in a lie.

"*I* didn't say he was my friend," I tease.

Locke shrugs, head in his book, when Sarah shoots him an exasperated sigh. "We're co-worker friends. And no, she's only four months old. I mainly watch her while she sleeps so her parents can go on dates."

"I can start babysitting when I'm twelve," she says proudly. "And go on dates when I'm thirteen."

Locke laughs. "Don't rush it. Just stay a kid for as long as you can."

"That's no fun," Sarah insists, hard at work outlining her mermaid tail a dark teal.

A knock at the door has us all looking up to see a nurse in blue scrubs enter and smile at Sarah. "Let's get you unhooked," she says.

I try not to watch as the nurse dismantles everything and takes the tubes out of Sarah's arm.

"I need to pee," Sarah announces when she's free from the machine, and they both leave me and Locke alone. In this room. Together.

It's become unusually quiet. The kind that you listen to.

I try to focus on my drawing until Locke shifts, his thigh pressing against mine. "You want the brown crayon?" he asks, lightly running it down my thigh.

"Thanks," I say. My voice sounds too breathy, too affected.

When I take it out of his hand, he runs his palm up my thigh and ends with his thumb circling around my kneecap. He lifts his hand away from me only to come back again like he can't help himself.

His fingers lightly tease their way down my calf until I widen my legs just a millimeter. He travels back up, one finger this time, tracing a path on my inner thigh.

"Why the fuck is your skin so soft?" he whispers.

I don't have a chance to answer because Sarah bounds out the bathroom door, but how do you even answer a question like that?

Well, I exfoliate. Which I don't.

Neither Locke nor I move. My mind is partly focused on the tingling sensation that still lingers where Locke touched me, partly focused on my coloring, and partly still trying to make out a picture in my head of Locke feeding a baby a bottle, taking her for walks in a stroller, when I ask out of nowhere, "You babysit?"

Sarah curls back up on the bed, and Locke looks up to make sure I'm speaking to him. "Yeah."

My head goes back in my coloring page but only to hide the smile playing on my lips. Here's Locke, sitting in Sarah's room coloring a Disney prince, not wanting his photo taken to show off his good deeds to the world, and spending his weekends, when he's not playing golf, babysitting his niece—all while he seems to like the feel of my skin under his fingers.

Locke's still watching me. "What?"

"Nothing," I say, shaking my head with a laugh. "You were right. I don't think I know you."

"On purpose," he grumbles.

"I know him," Sarah says, rolling her eyes like I'm a ridiculous adult. "Locke visits me every time he's in San Diego when I have dialysis."

She drops her voice to a whisper. "He tells me secrets like he's scared of snakes and gets nervous waiting in line for a roller coaster."

"Sarah," Locke says sternly. "They aren't secrets if you tell people."

She scoffs. "You said she was your friend, silly. Friends tell each other secrets. My friend Mallory hides one of her brother's Legos that he needs under her bed and then laughs while he looks for it."

I'm not feeling anything I'd describe as friendly wafting off Locke, so I nervously look at my phone like I'm willing Camille to call me with a fake emergency until I come up with my own excuse. "I need to finish taking pictures of all the other golfers."

Locke stares again, and I'm so flustered I practically fall off the bed and trip over my feet as I make my way to the door. I gush over how nice it was to meet Sarah and how I will definitely come back the next time I'm in San Diego before I'm able to close the door behind me.

I hurry down to the end of the hallway and push open the door marked with a black stairwell sign. It's a few degrees colder than the already freezing hospital, but I stop and lean against the cement wall.

If you'd asked me months ago who the biggest asshole was, I'd have said Locke without a doubt.

Now...?

He regularly visits an eight-year-old girl and tells her his secrets. He answers her questions, and stays out of the spotlight, and he's an uncle. If I had to guess, I'd say he's probably a good one too.

I bang my head lightly against the wall trying to erase the feel of his inky eyes on me, his thigh pressing against mine, the fresh air smell that wafts off him when I get too close.

The door flies open minutes later, scaring me enough that I jump and gasp audibly when it hits the wall beside me.

Locke looks just as startled to see me, but he recovers quicker. His eyes flicker down my legs and back up.

I'm not sure how much time has passed because I'm solely focused on how close he's standing and how much he looks like he wants to eat me.

"Did I scare you?" he says intensely.

"Yes," I confess.

I didn't think it was possible but his eyes get darker, more intense than a second ago. He seems to watch my chest and my throat until he looks up. "Am I still scaring you?"

"Yes." Maybe minutes stretch until I hear myself add barely above a whisper, "But in a good way."

The way he settles his eyes on me is so laser focused I feel like he's welding me to the wall. Locke takes one step in, and I instinctually press my body against the icy cinder block.

He smirks. Then Locke slips my camera off of my neck, raises it to his eye, and snaps a picture of me.

I'm speechless, waiting for him to do *something*, anything, because I can almost feel how much he wants me.

Locke studies the picture he just took. "You are so gorgeous." He raises his head. "Do you know that? How pretty you are?"

I blink. I exhale. I shake my head an inch.

The only thing I want is to hear him call me pretty again.

"No one ever tells you?" he asks curiously.

He glances down at my lips, which I now can't help but lick.

Another shake of my head.

Locke lets my camera dangle from the strap in his hand before he gently places it next to his feet. "I can hardly control myself with you."

Heat blooms from below my belly button and winds down between my legs. My skin flushes, aching for him to put a hand on me anywhere, but even when he steps closer, it's like he steps as close as possible without touching me.

My hands work by themselves to grip his waist and pull him against me. His body is a furnace; tense back muscles, rigid lines between abs, and hard. Everything is hard.

He smiles, so fucking close to my mouth, when he places his hands on either side of my head then moves his face to the side so we're cheek to cheek.

"You have no idea how good I could make you feel without even touching you. By just saying the words you want to hear," he whispers. "I would take such good care of you."

"I believe you," I hear myself say. He knows whatever is going on in my mind, even though I don't know myself, because he sounds purposeful, like he knows exactly what he's doing.

"I don't think I'll be able to keep myself from not putting my hands on you though." One of his hands falls to my neck before his fingers skim the delicate skin below my ear. "I'm already addicted to how soft your skin is."

"Please keep touching me." My mind has dissolved and evaporated. I sound like I'm desperate, begging him for anything he'll give me.

His lips graze over the other side of my neck, and I damn near pass out. He groans, presses his hips into me, and practically holds me up with his thigh so I don't fall to the floor. He kisses me below my ear harder, using his tongue this time to taste me.

"Fuck," he whispers, sinking his teeth into my neck. His hands find mine, which are clawing into his lower back, before he raises them up together and pins them above my head. He pulls his shoulders back. "Look at you."

Obviously, I can't look at myself, but Jesus, if I'm not trying to somehow look even better for him.

I can't move with his weight pressed against me. His nose nudges mine.

Kiss me, is all I can think over and over and over.

"You want to be a good girl for me, don't you?" he asks huskily instead.

I nod, eyes locked to his. My heart is hammering against my sternum in pure confusion and lust.

"You've never explored how this makes you feel?"

I shake my head no. "No one's ever called me that before."

He smiles as I close my eyes. Immerse myself. All I want is more of his voice washing over me. "Fuck, Maren, I'll degrade you, and I'll praise you, and I'll worship you. Like you deserve."

My skin prickles as a wave overtakes my body from head to toe. I'll do anything to make this man happy as long as he admires me while I do it.

A whimper escapes my lips. "Locke, please."

Finally.

Finally.

His lips meet mine.

THE KISS
Locke

TIME HAS STOPPED. I don't give a shit where I am.

All I can focus on is Maren's pleasure.

I've been so fixated on fucking her, I don't care that I'm in a hospital stairwell. This is what obsessions do to you. Rational thought is out the window.

She tastes like honey dissolving on my tongue, seeping into my bloodstream.

"I would do anything to take you against this wall right now," I say into her mouth. She arches into me with a moan that goes straight through me. My hand travels down her waist, forcing her hips to grind against my dick harder. I mean it, *literally* anything.

Her kiss turns rougher for a second, begging for it, before she pulls back like she's surprised even herself with how turned on she is.

"Don't be ashamed," I whisper. "You can let go with me, Maren. You can be whatever you want; my good girl or my dirty slut."

Her eyes flash at the possessiveness of my words. "Call me yours again," she says shakily.

I'm at a loss for how she's never discovered this side of herself before, how no one has taken the time to allow her to explore how good this makes her feel.

She's flushed, practically panting with lust and need. "Please. Keep talking."

I smirk and let my voice drop low next to her ear. My hand sweeps down her side and up her dress. "You're going to be *my* good fucking girl. You'll look so beautiful with *my* cock down your throat. So beautiful with *my* cock buried deep inside you." I grind my palm against her clit. "This pussy will be *mine*. I'll tear you down like the whore you want to be, and then I'll build you back up like the princess you are."

She crashes her mouth back into mine, practically climbing me. I think I could make her come from my words and tone of voice alone.

It's rough, dirty, and all-consuming the way she kisses. The hesitation is gone. I'm matching her intensity because this is mind-blowing how good she feels pinned by my body weight. I could mold her into anything I wanted by simply saying whatever I felt like.

When I slink down to my knees in front of her, she inhales sharply. I run my hands up her thighs, letting my nose and tongue follow the path along her left inner thigh.

Her skin was made for me. I was right; it's softer here than the skin across her arms. It's so perfect that I want to ruin it with my handprints. I want to make it red and splotchy, give her pleasure from the sting.

"Now spread these long, pretty legs for me."

Her obedience earns her a smile with dimples. She's soaking wet through these tight fucking shorts. This is the most fun I've had with a woman ever and I haven't even touched her yet.

Another door crashes open. This time somewhere above our heads. Maybe two or three floors.

Clarity squeezes back through the cracks the sound created, and I suddenly remember where I am.

Whose legs my face is finally between.

We stare at each other, sharing heavy breaths.

Footsteps on stairs. Voice on a phone call.

I can't tell if they're coming down or going up, and I have thirty seconds at most if it's down.

Maren loosens the grip she has on the roots of my hair.

"Shit," I breathe out, but I can't help myself. I run a hand over her shorts to feel how wet she is for me. How close I was to tasting her. How close I was to letting myself spiral out of control. My mind is all over the place, and I'm not sure what I'm doing anymore or why I'm doing it. "This was a bad idea."

"Locke."

Maren says my name like she's searching for me, wild and out of breath.

I rise to my feet, and she just watches me go.

THE MOTHER
Maren

IN NINTH GRADE, CAMILLE and I took an internet quiz to find out how kinky/vanilla we are.

I thought I was paste—the plainest vanilla. Not even vanilla bean. It told me I liked my vanilla ice cream with a cardboard cone.

And it's not that I'm some inexperienced woman who saved herself for the man she loved. I've been having sex since my first awful high school experience, with boyfriends and flings alike. Things were good, got even better—it's just always been... regular?

Well, look at me now, random internet quiz. Turns out, I might be more adventurous in bed than I previously thought because, according to Google, I have a praise kink.

I never knew two small words—good girl—could open up this entire new world for me.

The only problem is I don't know where to go from here. I haven't seen Locke in over two weeks, and I'm not about to make some dating app profiles just so I can tell a man to call me his good girl. Which also makes me realize, there's something specific about Locke that makes me come alive because I throw up in my mouth when I think about Russell calling me that.

Locke wasn't at the tournament in Pebble Beach last week or Scottsdale this week.

I've gotten exactly zero texts or calls from Hottie Icicle.

And I think I saw him speed away on a golf cart when I got here this morning to drop my camera equipment off at the club.

I'd say he was avoiding me if I also didn't think this was his entire personality at the same time.

Maybe I'm not cut out for the no-strings-attached sex with the sexy but emotionally unavailable man—kink or no kink. I still have a heart, one that desperately wants the all-consuming love… but I also kind of want to experiment with my newly found sex drive.

I can't get Locke's deep voice out of my mind. Sex for me in the past had always been rather quiet. Now my body wants to do everything and anything just to hear Locke talk to me like that.

I don't know if I should be thankful or embarrassed, maybe it's a little bit of both. But I've definitely been overthinking.

My phone dings as I'm locking up the closet.

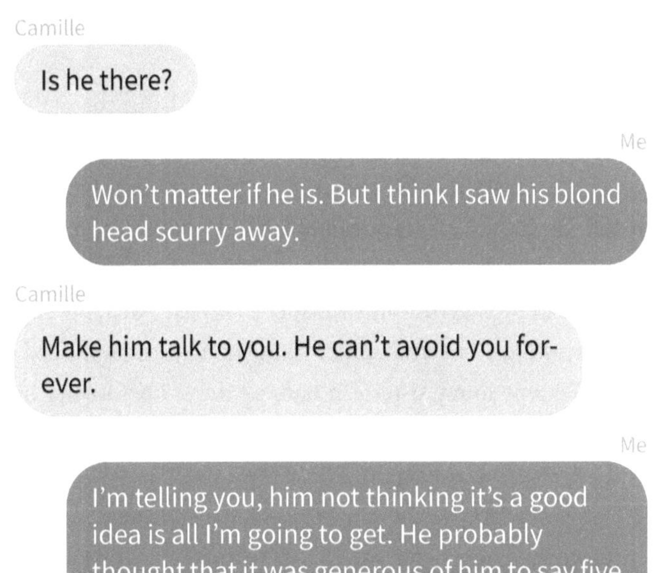

As I walk out to the parking lot, I stuff my phone into my purse without bothering to wait for Camille's reply.

I don't need Locke's explanation, and he obviously isn't the best communicator, so I don't expect him to want to talk to me. I know how he feels.

He inadvertently discovered something about me, and he wanted to have sex. But in the middle of a hospital stairwell was the last place that should have happened, and he's thankful he got reminded how much I talk and how much I feel and how much I ask questions and how much we see each other before it went too far. There's nothing more to it.

I throw my purse into the passenger seat and slip the key in the ignition, but my car rumbles and goes dead.

My day goes straight to shit when I try three more times and each time it sounds like my car is squealing from the depths of hell.

In a moment of sheer nuttiness, I punch the steering wheel before I lay my forehead on it gently and whisper to myself. Well, my car.

"I'm sorry. I didn't mean it, and I need you to be okay. I need to go find an apartment so my sister can have all the sex before her baby is born and she becomes a mommy zombie. Just give me a win. I love you, and I'll never hit you again. Please start."

I close my eyes, pray to the saint of engine mechanics, and turn my key one more time only to get such a low guttural churning sound that I think the engine might fall out from the bottom of my car.

I groan and scream, "Fuck!" at the same time I lift my head to see Locke standing directly in front of my car.

My face flushes immediately, and I hope there's somehow a reflection bouncing off my windshield that prevented him from witnessing that. Maybe if I'm really still he won't even notice I'm sitting here.

He rolls his eyes after a second. *I know you're in there*, he mouths.

Right, the entire golf course heard my traitorous car.

And I can see you, he adds.

I scream another *Fuck!* in my head.

"I'm just going to get an Uber," I say after I open my car door, stand, and stretch in that way you do when you're uncomfortable and you just need to make your body move, which always turns into the most unnatural thing ever.

He blinks. "You're not getting an Uber."

"I've got things to do. Lots of stops. It will take a while," I say, waving a hand and going back in for my purse.

He waits patiently while I dig around in my glove compartment, my center console, under my seat. I check some random knobs, even though I have no clue what they do. I can't think of anything else to do to stall.

"Done?" he asks, amused.

"Yeah," I mumble as I unlock my phone to see if he'll finally leave. I can't afford a million Ubers anyway, so I'm going to shamefully have to call my little sister to pick me up in her nice new BMW.

"If you think I'm letting you get in some stranger's car to drive you all over the city, you're insane."

I pick my chin up and challenge him back. "It's not like they're going to murder me."

"I wouldn't let you take the slightest chance."

Coincidentally, I'd probably take the chance on someone murdering me before inconveniencing Locke.

"Let me?" I scoff, then promptly blush at the thought that I was asking him to call me *his*, turned on by his possession of me, when he had me pinned against a wall and his erection pressed against me.

God, don't look at his crotch, I think as soon as my eyes hit the zipper of his pants.

Locke's eyebrow dips, one dark eye narrows below it. "Besides, we need to talk."

He turns like he expects me to follow him—which I do because that paints one hell of a compelling picture.

Locke Hughes wants to talk.

Not that I particularly want to talk about it. I can't even keep myself from melting into a puddle of embarrassment when I harbor my own thoughts, so I have no idea how he expects me to say words out loud about this situation.

His car is large and black, and I have to practically climb into the front seat.

I'm delighted to find seat warmers, which Locke quickly condemns me for. "It's not that cold outside."

"I like my butt toasty. And if I'm going to sit in this car, I'm going to get the perks."

Locke smirks. "Where do you need to go?"

"Oh," I say, "home is fine."

I'm not about to bring him along to look at the cheap apartments I can afford. I can't imagine what Locke's house looks like. He just got one of those huge checks that you hold up for the cameras, and it had two commas in the number.

"Quit lying," he says, starting the car. It makes a nice loud but smooth sound. Probably a V8. Something where a hundred thousand dollars alone lives under the hood. "You said you had lots to do. Such as...?"

I sigh. "Remember my sister is having a baby?"

He nods.

"Right. So, I need to move out. She and Parker, her husband, have let me stay with them long enough. I was going to go look at some apartments, but I'll call the landlords and reschedule."

He stares straight ahead, maneuvering out the parking lot and onto the main road. "Which way to the first one?"

"I'm not letting you chauffeur me around to the crappy places I might live."

He glances at me for a little too long that I almost want to tell him to keep his eyes on the road. But I know *that* wouldn't be very much appreciated.

"Give me the address to the first one," he insists. "You will probably need me as back up in case you don't stand up for yourself. It will be a good lesson in how not to give a fuck and gain some confidence."

My mouth forms an *oh*. "Are we still doing that?"

"I *want* to, Maren. Are you embarrassed to bring me to these places?" He's not really asking, because he knows that I am, so I don't bother answering. He scrunches his forehead up as he types away on the screen in between us. "Address?"

I cave and ramble off the address from the ad I saw. The landlord is expecting me in ten minutes, and the robotic woman tells us we'll arrive at our destination in twenty-four. Hopefully he doesn't take that to mean I'll be late on rent too. Also, it's twenty-three minutes too long to spend with Locke in a car.

"How was Pebble Beach and Arizona?" he asks.

"Fine," I say curtly.

He stops a little too abruptly at a red light, his hands a little tense on the wheel. "Did something happen?"

"Nope. Uneventful." Which it actually was. Craig and company seem to think I'm now boring, and I like it this way. I get in what little obligation I have per my contract, but there's nothing fun about me anymore so I'm sure they won't even air it. "Where were you?"

His grip relaxes. "Home. Spent time with my niece, Emmie. Played golf. Stayed away from cameras."

"Why didn't you go?"

I sit on my hands and look out the window when he doesn't answer. Of course, I take that to mean that *I'm* the reason he didn't go. Maybe that's self-centered of me though, and I'm overthinking it like always.

You shouldn't care, I remind myself. *I can't control his feelings, and we're adults who kissed and made a mistake.*

Locke seems to sense where my mind has strayed. "I'm playing in fewer tournaments this year. Conrad just had a baby, and I want him to be able to be with her. Traveling all year is tough."

I smile at how sincere he sounds—like I just got a real answer, like somehow, I earned it. "You don't want to play with another caddie, do you?"

He shakes his head. "Absolutely not. And I can afford to not play every damn week. I'm calling it the year of less, but it might just be the rest of my life of less." Locke winks at me. "Don't tell Graham that though."

That wink goes straight between my legs in a thundering roar only I can hear, and I've forgotten how to form thoughts. I clench my thighs, willing my body to settle down.

"But," he goes on, "I do owe you an explanation."

I whip my head back around, but Locke is calmly merging onto the interstate.

"We don't have to talk about it," I say hurriedly.

"I know I... don't say a lot of words, and I know that you don't actually believe that, *and* I know you've been giving a big shit about it for two weeks."

Two weeks and one day, but who's counting?

"You don't know me," I say, scrunching my nose.

Locke's eyes fall to the motion and sweep over the bridge of my nose, inspecting my freckles, before he snaps his attention back to the road. "Look. Russell and I have a history. I know you assume that now. We used to be friends and some college stuff happened a long time ago. This thing between me and you, I couldn't have you thinking that I was trying to get revenge on him by fucking his ex-girlfriend."

I blanche. "Nice."

Though I *am* thinking that would be more than nice—Locke's voice saying gruff things in my ear. I like the rough edges and the blunt cuts, the way he makes it sound primal.

"Sorry, *sleep* with his ex-girlfriend," he corrects himself, and it loses its luster. "I don't lose any sleep over Russell anymore, but I don't want you questioning my motives and not knowing what happened between me and him. I would never use you like that. Like I said, I'm too much, and I'm already a little too..." He chooses his next words carefully. "Preoccupied with you. So, we're mature adults, friends who kissed. I think that's a better place for us, and I'm not looking for a relationship, or maybe I just can't be in one. You don't seem like the kind of girl to..." He doesn't finish that thought.

As much as I want to badger him, pepper him with endless questions, I bite my tongue. I think you get more with Locke by being patient. I can respect that he puts golf first, that he's closed off, that we're not compatible.

I can also ignore how much he makes me forget I have a brain because I could just lean over and give him a blow job while loving every second of the filthy words he would call me. I'm not sure I know myself anymore.

"Hey, who said anything about mature? I'm not thirty yet," I joke.

Locke laughs, slides his arm across the console, and grabs my thigh. His fingers squeeze between my legs. "Sorry," he rushes out like I've electrocuted him. "Friends who also don't touch."

"Friends who don't touch," I repeat, even though I feel like he plugged himself into me.

Brain. I have a brain. Capable of rational thought, though it doesn't feel like it when we fall into a weird silence for the next ten minutes.

"Take a right here," I say just as the car's voice tells us to take a right at the stop sign.

Locke studies his little screen as he turns, us as a little yellow triangle on the map with street names zigzagging back and forth. Then he looks up out the windshield at the building half a block down.

For once, I can read his face: he's judging me.

I'll admit it looks a little run down. Paint is peeling off the sides of the brick, and the stairway in the front is littered with trash. The street looks almost deserted, and there's an empty lot across the street that looks sketchy. But it's all I can afford really.

Still, he doesn't say anything—just parallel parks as I gawk internally at how hot he makes it look to turn a steering wheel and glance over his shoulder.

His frown is still present while he gets out of the car and follows me up the stairs.

"I texted him, so I hope the landlord waited for me," I say.

Locke doesn't respond but what he's thinking is all in his eyes: *I hope he didn't.*

I stop in front of the white door with a gold 5A above the peephole. There's dirt caked into it, but I can clean it, add a cute doormat, and make it mine.

Thankfully (I guess), the landlord opens the door when I knock. He's tall and lanky with no smile. Bags hang from underneath his eyes like he hasn't slept in days.

He grunts in greeting, gives Locke a head nod, and his greasy brown hair falls in front of his eyes. "Morning," he says, pointing to himself. "Henry. This is it. About seven hundred square feet. Take a look around. I'll wait in the kitchen."

He steps back to allow us to enter and stands off to the side in front of the '90s refrigerator.

I immediately regret this terrible idea. Locke has probably never even laid eyes on an apartment in this price range. It smells wet. As I step into the small living room, I'm questioning if they've cleaned the gray carpet since the last tenant moved out and if it's actually supposed to be white. Maybe Henry will let me rip it up. I'm sure I could YouTube how to DIY it.

Locke follows me, close on my heels, as I amble around the small living room thinking of what to say before he veers off to the first door on the left. I stand in place and do a three-sixty turn before I follow him in and find him staring at the dirty white wall.

"Maren," he says, voice deep.

He's looking at a giant grayish-green spot of something on the wall that's climbing up and spreading across the ceiling like it's crystalizing.

"What's that?" I ask.

Locke's shoulders visibly tense as he traces the pattern back down the wall with his eyes. "Black mold."

I step closer to the wall and peer closely at it. "It doesn't look black."

He reaches out with lightning speed and pulls me back practically by the neck. His forearm drops to my collarbones, and I'm flush with his entire body.

"Are you crazy? Don't get that close to it."

"We're touching," I say.

He holds me tighter against him to make a point. "You're not living here."

"I don't have many options."

"Here isn't an option," he says, grabbing my arm and leading me back out through the inch-long 'hallway' to the kitchen. "Henry, there's black mold in the bedroom."

Henry startles, his face going pale, because Locke's voice is what I'd describe as nastily angry.

Locke doesn't give him a chance to respond. "You need to have that cleaned before someone moves in here." He opens the door and practically shoves me out. "Don't think I won't call the city to report it and inspect it. And I'll absolutely be checking up on you to make sure it gets done, Henry." His tone isn't lined with a threat—it's all threat.

When he steps outside and slams the front door in Henry's face, my mouth gapes.

"Don't look at me like that," he scowls. "You were not going to breathe that air for another second."

"You didn't have to be mean," I say, following him down the stairs. "I definitely can't live here anymore, or Henry will treat me horribly."

"Too mean to the landlord putting people at risk? Good. And yes, I did. Otherwise, he won't fix the problem." Locke opens the passenger side door for me in a weird show of chivalry. "Next," he says, slamming the door.

Next isn't any better. Locke won't even let me see the actual apartment after I get out of the car and a group of twenty-somethings loitering in the hallway harasses me.

The one after that he drives by and doesn't stop since he doesn't like the neighborhood.

"Locke," I say, exasperated. "I'm running out of options."

"Where did you live before you moved into your sister's?"

I stare at him.

"Before that," he adds.

"I checked," I sigh. "I can't afford it anymore. My landlord raised my rent as soon as I moved out and that was years ago. It was even more than I imagined it would be."

"What'd you do with the money from your little show?"

"It's not *my* show," I say, even more exasperated, "and I paid off my student loans on top of a little present for myself in the form of a camera. Now I need to fix my car, which will probably break again, so I'll have to buy a new one, and the last time I checked I didn't get a check bigger than my wingspan a few weeks ago. I live on a photographer's salary, so *these* are my options, Locke. I'd appreciate it if you'd stop judging me and help me by not ruining every place we look at."

"I'm not judging you," he says softly, "but I also can't live with myself knowing you're sleeping underneath black mold or getting hit on every time you step out your door." He looks around skeptically when we pull into the parking lot of my last option. He gives me a pained look. "I'll try."

Locke keeps his word and does try. This one isn't as horrible as the others. There does seem to be a lot of people coming and going when we get out of the car, but the apartment is fairly clean.

There are some projects I can attempt to make it better, and the kitchen actually has shiny new appliances.

He sticks his nose in every door, inspecting every inch of the place, checking under the sinks for leaks, and testing every hinge on the doors.

"It's not so bad, right?" I whisper when he steps back into the living room. I motion to the sliding glass door where a potted plant with nearly dead pink flowers inside is hanging from the edge of the roof. "It has a balcony."

"It's loud," he says, pointing to the wall where we can hear the neighbor's television and shouting and maybe something else we shouldn't be listening to. "But it doesn't smell. If you're okay with it, I'm okay with it."

I smile and clap my hands. "Okay, a win."

"Okay, let's go sign the paperwork," Locke says with a grimace in his smile that doesn't look convincing.

He trails behind me when I walk out the door and run into a woman who just emerged from my next-door neighbor's door.

"I'm so sorry," I say, stepping back into Locke's chest. His arm snakes around me, holding me to his chest tightly, back in protective mode over this tiny woman whose arms are so scrawny she wouldn't be able to punch a piece of paper.

She sways, eyelids heavy, and waves me off nicely but in a tired and slow way of doing it. I'd peg her as early fifties, but the long years she's lived have etched themselves into her face. Her dirty blonde hair is gathered in a low, messy ponytail, and her dark brown eyes do look kind, but with a far-away look, like she's out of it.

"That's okay, swee—" Her eyes fly above my head in a look of shock. She immediately shrinks. "Locke?"

"Hey, Mom," he says harshly.

I can now feel his heart racing against my back in double-time. The plane of his body is one hard contraction of muscle.

Her eyes go even wider. "What're you doing here?"

"We were just leaving."

His voice makes me hold tight to his thighs, like I'm unsure what his mother is capable of.

Locke is brushing past her so quickly with me in his arms that he's as close to carrying me as he can be without actually carrying me. I'm not sure my feet are technically touching the ground, and I'm fuming and squirming in his iron grip.

When we reach the car, he places me in the passenger seat like I weigh nothing and closes the door before I can say anything.

Locke leans his back against my door, his shoulders rising and falling sharply.

"Mom? *Mom*?!" I shriek as soon as he opens his own door and slides behind the wheel. "I thought your parents were dead!"

THE HOUSE
Locke

"I KNOW YOU DID," I say after a minute. I still haven't started the car, but my mother isn't going to follow me, thank fuck.

"You lied to me," Maren says angrily.

She's cute when she's mad; eyebrows pinched deeply, and a scowl that could rival mine. And I think I've finally seen that part of her, a part I almost feel lucky to be experiencing because she's comfortable enough to show me.

I run my hands down my pants. "I did not lie to you. You assumed, and I never bothered to correct you."

"Whatever," she huffs. "You don't owe me any explanations. We're not friends. Can we go back and sign the papers now?"

I shake my head. "You're not living here."

Maren groans when I start the ignition. "What the hell do you mean? You said it was okay, and this was the last one I found in my price range. The alternatives are even shittier than this, and I'm sure your mega-mansion has warped your reality of other people's realities."

An idea pops into my brain, and I start to pull out of the parking space before she can sprint out of the car.

Her voice rises in confusion and irritation. "Your own mother lives here, Locke. It can't be that bad."

"She doesn't live here," I tell her. "Considering I pay her mortgage, I know where she lives."

Maren sits back and crosses her arms like she's daring me. "What does that mean?"

I go still, drive through a green light, merge onto the interstate, and head back north. It's been at least five minutes since she asked me that question.

Nothing in me wants to elaborate, but I do, because over my dead body will Maren be living within a ten-mile radius of that.

"You're not living next door to my mother's drug dealer."

I've rendered her talkative little mouth speechless. Fuck, how badly I'd like to render it speechless because she's choking on my cock, but that ship has sailed. I pull my eyes off her lips.

In a split-second decision, without any further thought other than I need to protect her, I say, "You're coming home with me."

"What?" she splutters, recovering from her shock. "No, I'm not."

"You are," I insist. "I live in a 'mega-mansion' and have a guest house that no one has ever lived in. You will never see me. It's separated from my house by a pool and a golf course."

She laughs. "*You're* the insane one."

"I am completely in my right mind when I say that I will not let you live in any of these places, and if you think I'll lose this argument, you'll quickly realize I'm not fucking around. My house doesn't have black mold. It isn't in a bad neighborhood. No one will try to grope you. And you won't be living next door to daily drug deals."

"Locke," she starts, twisting her waist to face me, "I'm not *living* with you."

"You'll be *living* by yourself," I clarify. "Technically next door, but I guess it's still further away than that really."

Maren sits back. "I cannot afford whatever your house looks like."

"That's cute you think there's a rental fee."

"I'm not living in your mega-mansion for free. I'm a big girl, and I don't need your help."

"Name your terms," I say. "I don't give a fuck. You have thirty minutes to figure them out, and once we get there, I won't have to convince you."

I'm done talking. She can see for herself that I will not be jeopardizing her health or safety when I have an entire house that has sat empty for almost six years, and once she does see it, she'll be hard-pressed to say no.

MAREN'S TRYING HER BEST not to look out the window when we pull up to my iron gate, but curiosity is getting the best of her.

She looks at her lap when it opens slowly, refusing to watch as we wind down the long, paved driveway lined with palm trees.

My white house, mostly reflective windows from floor to ceiling with a black roof, appears to our right, but she still doesn't look. She waits until I pull around to the back, past the pool, which she can have to herself, past my six-hole golf course on our left, which she could use but probably won't, and stop at my guest house, that looks like a miniature version of my house, at the edge of the water.

Maren steadies her breathing and peers out the window. "It's two stories," she says. Her eyes flicker out over the small waves. "And waterfront."

"And it's all yours," I reply.

It's perfect for her, really. One loft bedroom, one bath, triple the size of the apartments she was looking at. She'll agree if I could just get her inside.

"Nope. This is crazy," she says. "Take me home—to my sister's."

I smirk as I slide the key around the gold ring and place it on her thigh. "I'll do no such thing." She stares at it, still sitting on her hands, so I look up through the windshield. "It's furnished."

She sighs. "Even more of a reason to take me home, so I don't mess up your furniture."

My mind instantly turns dark at how much we could mess up the bed. I rub my lips in anticipation like I have a smile that isn't there that I'm trying to wipe off my stupid face. What I really want to say is something that will make her wet for me, but if she's going to be living here, I'm going to have to be on my best behavior.

I set a timer on my watch and challenge myself to get her inside the house in under five minutes.

"King bed. The sheets are comfy. Best espresso machine. There's a balcony that overlooks the water. There's a remote that controls everything. The shades, the television, which pops up from the end of your bed, the fans, the lights... I'll build you a darkroom."

That last one earns me an amused nose scrunch. She's going to have to stop drawing attention to her freckles if I'm expected to be a gentleman.

Four minutes and seventeen seconds. I wish I had an actual darkroom to entice her with. I try my real smile instead.

"This isn't fair," she says, eyeing my dimples.

"I don't really give a shit about fair." Not when it comes to her. I cock my head toward her window and pout. "Look at my pool I never use."

"No." She fails. Three minutes and forty-four seconds. Her eyes brighten a little, I assume imagining herself tanning in those chairs. She averts her gaze to the dock where my boat is docked with its cover over it. "What else do you not do?"

"Live here and find out."

Maren leans over to inspect my wrist. "Why do you keep looking at your watch?"

"I'm playing a game," I say coyly.

She studies the watch face, not picking up on what I'm doing, then rolls her eyes. "*If* I live here, I'm paying you rent and signing something."

"Fine."

She picks up her chin, the sun hitting behind her in a halo. Two minutes and fifty-eight seconds. "I want it to say that you can kick me out any time. I need a contract that has all the stupid legal stuff I don't understand. I need your list of rules, like do I have to take off my shoes? Am I allowed anywhere in the yard? Can I use that pool? Can I touch that boat? Are my friends allowed over? Which I guess is just my sister lately. How much noise can I make? Can I take pictures?"

"Done," I chuckle. "And you can do whatever the fuck you want to do. You live here."

"Not yet. I need time to think of other demands, and I need to consult my sister," she retorts. Maren narrows her eyes. "Are we just going to sit in the car like children?"

"*I'm* not," I say, knowing full well she won't either. "I'm thirty." I'm halfway to the front door when I hear her car door open.

"Stop being a pain in the ass and just go inside," I say when she stops beside me and shifts back and forth on her feet.

She glances at the key in her hand before shoving it into the lock.

Thirty-seven seconds.

I can't help myself, and I'm already hard, thinking about her showering in my, well, *her* bathroom. I want her thinking about me when she sees that bed. When she's lying down tonight, drifting off. I won't touch her, but that doesn't mean I can't have fun.

"That's my good girl," I whisper over her shoulder.

Her head almost whips back, but she catches herself. I can still see the smile she's trying to hold back through her hair.

THE LEASE
Maren

The door swings open.

If Locke wants me hot and bothered, walking around his house with wet underwear just for the fun of it, he's succeeded.

I gasp as soon as I take a step inside.

Everything is white with black accents and glass on glass on glass. My eyes land first on the curved glass staircase to my right. A sleek white sofa sits in the middle of the living room in front of a huge flat-screen TV.

The kitchen is open to the left with a granite island bigger than my old bedroom. I count six acrylic bar stools lined up along it.

And the far back wall is—shockingly—all glass, two stories high.

Living here must be like a permanent beach vacation without the sand. No wonder Locke just wanted me to come inside.

"Who would ever willingly leave this place?" I say.

"Exactly," he deadpans. "Where should we build your darkroom?"

My eyes scan the room. It could definitely fit one.

"I haven't said yes yet," I argue as Locke's watch starts beeping. He moves a little too quickly to silence it. My mouth drops open. "Were you *timing* me?"

"Technically, I was timing myself."

"To see how fast you could get me inside?" I guess. "And you won?"

He smirks. "I always win."

"You do, don't you?" I say slyly as I brush past him to survey the kitchen.

His eyes follow me intensely, like they're full of questions, while I run a hand over every smooth, white surface.

"If it means anything, it's not like I'm always trying to. I just can't stop myself until I've—" He cuts himself off so abruptly I stop walking and turn around. I hit my hip against the corner of the island and wince. Locke swallows, his throat muscles working to bury his next words, his eyebrows furrowed deep with confusion, before he leans a hand on the island. "Well?"

"Well what?" I ask, dizzy from the whiplash, before I realize he's asking me if I like the house. "Oh. I don't know. It's almost too nice."

He takes a step into me, his fresh air and leather scent surrounding me, and says sternly, "You need a place to stay. I have a place to stay. Accept my help."

Without breaking eye contact, his thumb finds my hip bone on the first try to soothe the pain that's pulsing through it.

"I don't know if it's a good idea," I say hesitantly, mostly because I can't stop imagining what he looks like without a shirt. I'm already a step closer to him, and I don't know how I ended up here.

Locke places a hand to his chest where I'm staring. "I'll be on my best behavior."

I nod—certainly not wanting to be on *my* best behavior. "I need to talk to Camille."

This is crazy. This is *really* crazy. Also, it's crazy that this entire house has never been lived in. What a waste.

He steps to the side and holds his arm out. A smile stretches. "Take the stairs up to the bedroom. It's even better up there. Text me when you've decided."

Don't touch him, I tell myself, sliding by him in the tight space between the sink and island.

While my phone rings, Locke exits out the front door, and I climb the staircase.

When Camille answers, balancing her phone on her stomach and her face all up in the screen, she scrunches her nose and examines my background. "Where are you?"

I pan the phone across the first floor so she can get a good look. "I'm in Locke's *house*," I whisper like he can hear me. Maybe he can because I would assume there are security cameras in here, and he's probably watching me on an app or something. I hear his car start as I sit on a step midway up. "Well, guest house, I mean."

"No fucking way!" she screams and shimmies her boobs at me. "Maren, what did you do?"

"I didn't *do* anything," I say. "I'm still dumbfounded how I've ended up here. He wants me to *live* here."

Her eyes bulge, and she drops the phone. The screen goes black when she says, "Back way the hell up and tell me everything. You said he was avoiding you like a few hours ago."

"I don't know. I don't think he was." Camille comes back into view with a chocolate chip cookie in her hand. She takes a bite and waves at me to continue. "My car wouldn't start, and I was supposed to go see all those apartments, and he brought me because he refused to let me take a taxi like an annoying man."

"A swoony man," she interrupts. "He's protective and didn't want you to get murdered."

I roll my eyes. "Not that I could afford it anyway, but I didn't want him to know that, and he lured me into his car with promises of a 'talk,' and I'm a sucker because it's Locke and Locke doesn't talk. So, he's driving me around West Palm Beach, and he's finding things wrong with all the places."

"They were shitty, weren't they?" she lectures.

"Of course, they were shitty, but that's beside the point. I didn't need him to tell me, I already knew, and he's giving me his opinion anyway."

"Like a swoony man," she interrupts again. "He's sticking up for you."

I roll my eyes again. "Then I've finally got him lukewarm on one, and..." I trail off, realizing that his mother's situation—whatever that might be—is something that Locke obviously holds close to his chest. "And of course, he finds black mold in the bedroom, so I'm out of options. Now I'm sitting on the stairs of his guest house, and he's negotiating the terms of my lease—which happen to be 'do whatever the fuck I want.'" I take a deep breath. "What do you think?"

"I think I need to see your bedroom to decide."

I stand, flip the camera around, and climb the remaining steps. We both gasp at the same time.

The modern king-size bed to the left sits in front of a black accent wall and the sun is starting to set, bringing in a gorgeous blend of pinks and purples across the room.

"Fuck yes," Camille says delightfully. "When do I move in?"

"I don't know what to do with myself," I admit, falling on the bed like an angel. I sink. "Wow, this bed is soft."

"Did you get your talk he promised you?" she asks.

"Yes," I sigh. "I told you it wasn't a good idea. He didn't want me to think he was using me to get back at Russell for something that happened between them. Before you ask, I don't know what it was. And he acknowledged that I'm a relationship girl and he's a fuck-buddy guy. Oh, and I can't forget that golf is more important than everything combined in the entire world. So, yeah, we talked. We're mature adults. We're friends. The end."

Camille nods. "So mature."

"Do any of us ever mature?" I joke. "I still feel like I'm figuring myself out. I don't think my thirties are going to be any different."

"Figure it out while you live there. Also, if your car is broken down and you're stranded there, at least sleep on it. Locke is too much of a gentleman to drive you home anyway, and you're not welcome here tonight." She winks and yells off to the side. "Parker! Change the locks!" Her eyes go molten, I suspect in response to something sexual Parker has done off camera. I'm tired of being in their way, all up in their space. They deserve at least tonight.

"Goodbye," I say.

She grins. "Good*night*."

I let my phone drop beside me as I make an Egyptian cotton five-thousand-thread-count sheets angel. Then I pick it back up and text Locke.

Me

One-night trial.

Hottie Icicle

You're so good at making me happy. I'm proud of you.

Ugh, if I don't melt into the bed thinking about Locke's deep voice repeating those words into my ear. I'll probably dream about pleasing him.

I think if I sleep here, I'll never leave.

When I wake up the next morning, my car is sitting outside, newly washed and sounding like it has a brand-new engine. On the hood sits my lease.

One page. One paragraph. Written below a letterhead that reads Carmichael, Berry, Franklin, and Powell.

I can't help but laugh. Locke has already signed it above his printed name along with David Carmichael, Attorney at Law. There's a blank line waiting for my signature. I squint to see if he printed this off the internet as a joke, but no, it's completely official.

Except for what Locke must have forced an actual lawyer to type out and sign: Maren Murray, the alliteration, can live in Locke Hughes' guest home and do whatever the fuck she wants. Locke Hughes can kick Maren Murray out anytime he feels like it, though he will never do such a thing. Maren Murray can write Locke Hughes checks that equate to whatever she was paying when she previously lived alone, but Locke Hughes will never deposit them. If any other confusing legalese arises that Maren Murray does not understand, her opinion will always be correct.

It's been three weeks since I signed my name on the line, wrote out a check for the deposit, first month's rent, and an estimation of my car repairs, and dropped everything in Locke's mailbox.

The first week, I was back in California for half of it while Locke skipped another tournament. The second week I was off from work while Locke played in the tournament in Mexico.

He'd come in second, but Landon won his first PGA tournament, which was pretty exciting. When I watched the highlights on television, Locke shook his hand and clapped him on the back, and I think he did it because he was happy for Landon—despite his face looking unemotional.

The only evidence that Locke lives next door is the occasional light I've seen come on, or the television glow from what I assume is his bedroom. He parks in the garage, so I never know if he's home or not.

When I knew for certain that he was over a thousand miles away in Mexico and not spying on me from one of his enormous reflective windows, I felt comfortable enough to roam the backyard—if you can call it that. It's more of a vast expanse.

My front yard is the second hole of Locke's six-hole golf course that winds along the outer edge of his property. His pool had been calling my name ever since I laid eyes on it, but I had to wait until I was sure he wasn't home to feel okay enough wearing a swimsuit and traipsing around like I was on spring break.

The one thing I wasn't prepared for with living here is the loneliness.

When your core group of friends is rooted to your ex-boyfriend, you're usually the one who gets left behind. And when your best friend/sister is about to have a baby, she and her husband are marathon dating before they're too tired for shit like that.

So, one might be desperate enough to call their mother just to hear a human voice.

And desperate enough to fake enthusiasm when she answers the phone with, "Hi, Maren, sweetie. Oh, Camille told me all about your new house. Is this my invite call?"

"Hey, Mom. And soon," I promise, making a mental note to yell at Camille for I-don't-know-what-yet. "I've been trying to get settled in."

A small laugh slips out at the thought of my mother meeting Locke. I wonder what some of the first words out of her passive-aggressive mouth would be:

You've always lived alone in this huge house?

Why golf? No, I can't say I watch it. It's boring. I've always preferred football.

A smile would make your face so much more handsome.

She sighs. "Of course, I'm sure you'll invite me when you're ready. Speaking of invitations, I can't believe you'll be thirty in a couple of months. Seems like yesterday I was giving birth to you."

"All eighteen hours of it," I say before she can. Usually, she makes it seem like I should feel bad and take responsibility for my unborn fetal self.

"Eighteen and a half," she laughs. "But how are you feeling?"

"About?" I question her, despite knowing exactly where she's going. To hell if I'm not going to make her say it out loud.

"About turning thirty."

"Fine," I say. "I think it's going to be the same as twenty-nine."

"Sure," she says, "but I'm sure it's scary starting over. Thinking you were with the man you were going to marry, and now you're single."

"Thank you," I say, immediately regretting that I picked up the phone. "I always welcome the reminder."

"Sweetie, don't be sensitive," she says. "We all get old."

"I'm not old, Mom," I insist. "And I don't want to marry someone who doesn't love me. That's not too much to ask."

She hums in response somewhere between agreement and condescension. "How's your job going? Anything interesting or new?"

"Sadly, no. It's men still swinging golf clubs. But I like it enough. After Camille's maternity shoot, I was thinking I might start doing that in my free time."

"Don't do anything rash, Maren."

"I wouldn't," I stress. "It's just an idea. I still need a pesky little paycheck and health insurance and a 401k. I don't know. Forget it. It's just a dream."

Her chuckle scrapes along my eardrums. "I'm only looking out for you. I wouldn't want to see you make a huge mistake like quitting your job."

"I know," I sigh.

She sighs harder. "What?"

"Nothing, Mom. I'm not a child, and I can make my own decisions. I know I need money to live."

"I'm trying to give you advice because I love you."

And she does. In her own way. But that way, I'm starting to see, has shaped the person I've become. No wonder I'm a people pleaser. No wonder I have a praise kink.

"I know," I say, softening. "I'm sorry. I'm tired, but I promise I won't make any stupid decisions."

My phone buzzes, and I pull the phone away from my ear to see Locke has texted me.

Hottie Icicle

> My family wants to meet you if you'd like to come over for dinner.

I shoot off my reply, happy to have anything other to do than converse with my mother over my age and profession. I'd accept an invitation to sit on a transatlantic flight in the middle seat next to a screaming baby right about now.

"Oh, Mom," I say hurriedly, "I have to go. I have plans with a friend."

"A frien—"

"I love you," I say, cutting her off and hanging up before she can play 20 Questions about my fake friend.

THE DINNER
Locke

"WHY WOULD YOU PUT it that way?" Elise asks over my shoulder.

"Because it's the truth," I say, putting my phone down next to me on the couch and covering it with my hand. "And stop reading my texts. I'm a grown man."

She pinches my cheeks in a way only she could get away with before hugging me from behind. "She is all alone over there, Locke. It's the nice thing to do. And sure, you've never brought a girl home in your life and now one is *living* here, so excuse me if I want to meet her."

My phone buzzes underneath my hand. Maybe it's a little too quickly how fast I go to read it.

Maren

I would love to. Should I get ready and come now?

Me

Any time is good.

I can feel Elise's smile against my head.

"We're not dating," I clarify for the millionth time.

"I know," she says, patting my chest once for each word I've repeatedly told her. "She's just a colleague living in your guest house. You said it yourself you haven't talked to her since she moved in. I only want to make her feel welcome."

"Conrad," I say, "tell your mother to behave."

He looks up at us from where he's playing with Emmie on the floor. "It's your own fault for telling her Maren was even living back there."

I scoff under my breath. What was I supposed to say when the first thing Elise asks me when she walks in the door is whose car is parked in front of the guest house and why are there lights on?

Conrad already thinks I'm insane for letting Maren stay, but he doesn't really know how it happened. I think he sympathizes with my irrational need to protect her—though I've never fully understood it myself. He knows I've been staying away from her and that I'm trying my best to keep her out of my head. She's been here for three weeks, but I haven't gotten a chance to speak to her. She won't come out of the house when she suspects I'm here, and the one time she thought I was gone, I had to remove myself from the window because I felt like a stalker watching her sit on my dock taking photographs of passing boats.

Leaving Maren alone is best.

When she knocks, everyone quiets down to annoyingly watch me walk out of the room.

I can see her through the window standing on my front porch in a dark blue dress with skinny straps and her wavy hair curling over her shoulders. It would help if she'd stop wearing so many goddamn dresses that are short and show off how long her legs are.

She smiles brightly when I open the door.

"You didn't have to come around to the front," I tell her.

"I felt weird," she says, smoothing out the front of her dress. There's nothing there except nerves.

I quirk an eyebrow. "Didn't you read your lease?"

She springs her head up, green eyes bright. "You have a sense of humor under there, don't you?"

"Und—"

"Maren!" Elise cuts me off and brushes past my shoulder. She gathers Maren into a hug, and I'm suddenly acutely aware that Maren is still standing on the porch because I didn't invite her inside. "I'm Elise, Locke's aunt. We're so glad you could come."

"I'm so glad one of you is a hugger," Maren says, swaying back and forth with her eyes on me over Elise's shoulder.

Elise breaks away and ushers her into the living room. I follow like the odd person out.

Elise introduces her to my uncle, who stands and bear hugs her in his booming and overpowering-but-silent way when she sticks out her hand to shake.

Maren doesn't seem to mind when she's practically picked up off her feet and giggles. "Locke was raised by two huggers."

"I'm Phillip," he laughs. "And of course, we're going to hug you. We've been waiting to meet you all evening."

I refrain from rolling my eyes. They didn't even know she existed hours ago, but they're already all in on their delusion.

When she's back on the ground, she turns to Conrad. "Conrad, right?"

"It's nice to officially meet you." He waves a hand toward Blake and Emmie lying on the rug. "This is my wife, Blake, and our daughter, Emmie."

I wonder how she feels in a room with my family, all eyes on her, but Maren doesn't miss a beat as she plops herself on her stomach next to Blake and side hugs her.

"It's so nice to meet you, Blake," she gushes. Then she turns on a cooing baby voice for Emmie. "Look how cute you are."

Emmie lifts her head in the direction of Maren's voice and babbles, her pink cheeks shiny and blue eyes bright.

"She's getting so good at tummy time," I say without thinking. Everyone slowly turns to stare at me as I sit on the couch, including Maren, who is smirking over her shoulder like she can't believe that just came out of my mouth. I clear my throat and stand before my ass has barely grazed the seat. "Yeah, I can't believe I just said that. Do you want a drink?"

"Just water, please," Maren replies.

I can hear Blake and Maren cooing at Emmie as I grab a glass in the kitchen.

While I'm filling up the water from the refrigerator, Maren walks through the wide entryway that separates the open kitchen from the living room.

"I didn't get to thank you," she says, leaning her elbows down on the island. My willpower is shot instantly as her breasts swell and form a deep groove that I swear I only glance at for a millisecond, but I can't be sure.

"For what?"

"For the lease and my car. I wanted to tell you in person, but then I didn't see you and it felt like too many days had passed to call or text without it being awkward. I'm trying not to feel awkward. So, thank you. But you haven't cashed my check."

"I'm beginning to think you're not taking your lease seriously." I slide the water across the counter. "Also, you're avoiding me."

"You're avoiding me," she counters and brings her water up to her lips in a futile attempt to hide her smile. "What happened to mature adults?"

I watch her throat as she swallows. I watch her lips as she licks them. My mind is only in one place—a stairwell in a hospital.

When our eyes meet, her body skips like there is a blip in the matrix. Then the oven timer beeps just as Elise walks into the kitchen like it's resetting the universe.

Of course, she'll be the first to pounce. "Maren," she says, putting on oven mitts, "where are you from?"

"Outside of Orlando," Maren replies as she pulls out a bar stool and slides onto it.

The smell of the roast that's been cooking for hours fills the kitchen when Elise opens the oven door.

"A fellow Florida girl." Elise smiles. "I lived in Tampa my entire life, but we moved near here to help with Emmie when she was born."

Maren matches her smile. "I love that. I'm sure Locke is happy to have his family close too." She motions to the bowl of lemons, bag of sugar, and black juicer. "Can I help make the lemonade?"

Elise considers it and nods, only so she can trap Maren in the kitchen to pepper her with questions. "Did you go to the University of Florida?"

"Nope," Maren says. "Florida State for photography. Well, no, that's not true. *Technically,* I majored in business, then I'd take all these photography electives that didn't count toward my degree at all, but I like to joke that I minored in it. My mom was thrilled, and I racked up some nice student loans."

Her eyes fall on me briefly as I walk out, but this conversation is not one I want to be a part of. Nothing good can come from getting to know more about Maren.

My skin has been buzzing for weeks, like I'm having a withdrawal from the contact of her body against me everywhere, and it's finally somewhat bearable.

I've never had such a strong reaction to a woman before. The others were like downers, dulling my brain, but Maren, she's an upper, speeding up my nervous system. I don't know if it has to do with my irrational protection of her or her praise kink or what, but I do know she makes me feel like I'm high.

One minute later, my plan doesn't work when Conrad and Blake decide to go sit on the porch swing with their drinks while I sit on the floor and flip through a picture book for Emmie's viewing pleasure (I also happen to know that a baby's eyesight gets better at four months).

Phillip stays in the recliner, invested in the college basketball game.

And fuck the modern, open kitchen—why don't people want privacy anymore?—because I can hear them clear as day now.

"—was never my passion. I actually want to be a lifestyle photographer. Capturing the little moments is what makes me happy."

Elise cracks up. "You hate golf?! But you take pictures of golfers for a living!"

"I know," Maren giggles. "My brother-in-law got me the job. He's a personal doctor for a few of the players on the tour. Do you play?"

"I dabble. I picked it up when I suggested Locke should try it. It seemed like the perfect sport for him to channel himself into, so it became our family thing. Of course, within a few months, Locke made it not so fun for everyone else when he was pulling ahead by ten-plus strokes, but he still appeases us and waits only a tiny bit impatiently to finish each hole."

I roll my eyes to myself as I point out the pink pig on the page and make a low oink sound. Emmie stares, her little blue eyes full of baby disparagement.

"Don't judge me," I whisper. "I'll teach you how to play golf, and I'd never be impatient. You're the only person I'd ever consider teaching, so you should feel lucky. Plus, you'll be better than all of us."

Emmie bats the book out of my hand, and after I pick it up, I have to orient myself back in their conversation.

"—honored to take photographs of you and Emmie. I could never charge you."

"Does this weekend work?" Elise asks. "We could swing back by here. Take them outside in the backyard."

"I would love that," Maren replies. I can hear the huge smile that she must have plastered across her face in her voice, and she can't hide how happy she sounds.

"You have to charge people if you want it to be your job," Elise teases.

Maren drops her voice to an exaggerated whisper. "Locke won't cash my checks so we're even."

"Fine, then I will recommend you to all of my friends," Elise says.

"Thank you! I'd love that. I've been wanting to do some family portraits in my spare time. It's not practical and will never happen, but I do wish it could be a full-time job for me one day. My sister is having a little boy in a few months, and I took some maternity photos of her if you'd like to see them."

I steal a glance.

Maren is leaned over the island, her dress riding up a few inches and the bottom of her ass *just* hidden from view. Elise is hunched over looking at the phone between them and admiring the pictures with *ohs* and *ahs* and *beautifuls*.

"She looks just like you," Elise says.

I already know Maren is more beautiful. Her sister doesn't have the same freckle pattern or the same shade of brown hair.

Maren turns her head so quickly that she catches me staring at her.

Alarm bells ring in my head. I shouldn't touch her, *and* I shouldn't look at her.

My mind and body are rewiring themselves. I *know* I shouldn't, but I can't exactly make myself stop.

THE GOLF CART
Maren

I FRANTICALLY LOOK AWAY.

Every time our eyes meet, sparks burst and singe my skin everywhere from the thought of his lips on mine. They aren't very good for smiling, but they are far better at other things, and I can still feel the brush of them against my neck, like a searing hot brand.

He must feel it too by how quickly he averts his eyes at the same time.

He lives here. I live here... but over there.

Best behavior, I repeat to myself. *I have a brain.*

"Locke," Elise calls, "bring Emmie in here and help with the green beans."

I bury my head in my lemonade-making station and pretend not to watch him in the living room as he picks up Emmie. From my peripheral vision, he *does* smile at her when he lifts her into his arms.

Even if I don't look at him, it's hard not to be very aware of his presence. First, he buckles Emmie into her highchair, then wheels her next to the island, where he starts trimming the greens beans on his cutting board.

He murmurs at Emmie through the whirring of my juicer, explaining everything he's doing to her like he's an instruction manual.

I let my eyes wander for split seconds when I know he's not looking.

It's amazing watching Locke in his element. He's always so sure of himself, but in his own home with his family, there's something about him that seems more at ease. Like maybe one layer is missing, the layer that he uses to protect himself from the outside world, and he can breathe better. I wonder how many layers he has.

"So, real photography?" he asks out of nowhere.

I look up from where I'm focusing extra hard on opening a bag of sugar to find Locke tossing green beans in olive oil. His eyes stay trained on the bowl.

"Yeah," I say, amused. My brain ticks up from the excitement of knowing that he'd been pretending that whole time like he wasn't listening. "But it's all *real* photography."

His eyebrows raise like I've answered life's deepest question. He dumps some garlic in his metal mixing bowl before I pour the sugar I measure out into my pitcher and use a long wooden spoon to stir.

"Locke has always hated having his picture taken," Elise laughs. "Even when he was little."

His smirk pulls out only to the left, and he whispers, pretending he's responding to Emmie, "It's exposing, isn't it?"

Elise smiles and rolls her eyes toward me as Conrad and Blake enter the kitchen laughing.

They fall into a conversation amongst themselves about Emmie eating solid foods.

I try to soak in what I can for my upcoming appointment as the best aunt, but I'm so distracted by Locke's movements, I keep watching him when he turns away.

The way he pulls the plates down for everyone. How he sets the silverware on top of each napkin. When he pours my lemonade into everyone's glasses.

His forearms tense. His scent wafts.

We sit down next to each other at the dinner table, whether it's on purpose or not, I can't tell.

I've never wanted something so badly for myself before, but how do I ask for it?

AFTER DINNER, LOCKE INSISTS on driving me back to the house so I don't have to walk in the dark.

He's quiet as he weaves along the golf cart path. It's almost pitch black out from underneath the lights of his back porch and pool, and I must have forgotten to leave any lights on in the guest house because we're traveling further into darkness.

"Locke?" I whisper on a wave of courage. I can't be imagining the way he looks at me. Or I hope I'm not.

"Hm?" he replies.

"I was thinking... could we just be mature adults who also touch?"

"What?"

"What if I don't care if you use me? If you want to revenge-fuck me to get back at Russ for whatever, I don't care."

"Maren," he says, his hands gripping the steering wheel harder. "I don't want to revenge-fuck you. And I told myself I wasn't going to touch you, especially now that you live here. I'm running on my last synapse of self-control."

I only hear one thing. "But you do want to touch me, right?"

"Of course I want to fucking touch you." He might break the steering wheel off.

I wrap my hand around his forearm and tug it into my lap. My legs open an inch for him, where I place his fingers against my inner thigh. He lets it happen. This is happening.

That alone took most of my courage, but I have to dig deep for more. Stop freaking out. I'm just going to have to come out and say it.

"I googled my..." Kink? Fantasy? Sexual preference? I can't say any of those words out loud. "I googled my thing. And I read about it. I *know* you know. You figured it out before I even did." Deep breaths. Deep breaths. "I imagined it was your voice saying what the internet says I'd like to hear." His jaw is clenched to stone, but his fingers are trailing lightly along my inner thigh as he tries to focus on the pathway in front of us. "I want to hear you say them for real and help me explore what I like. I'll keep my emotions out of it. What if I want to use you?"

My question hangs in the air all the way back to his guest house. His hand remains on my leg, caressing my thigh like he's savoring it, like he's missed it. After he parks the golf cart on the other side of my car, blocking us from view of his house, I let out a breath.

"Are you going to make me beg?"

He shakes his head and rubs his free hand over his face. I hear a muffled, "Shit."

I deflate. This was *such* a bad idea, and it's my fault for fantasizing that Locke would ever agree to this. He may want to have sex with me, but not enough. I'm too much and never enough, like always.

"Forget it," I hurry out. "I live here. I talk too much and ask too many questions. I've never had a friend with benefits. I know. Just... never mind."

His grip on my leg tightens, stopping me from getting out of the golf cart, and he looks at me with such intensity that his eyes are darker than the night surrounding us. "I think you'd look fucking beautiful on your knees begging me."

My body immediately pulses and wants to drop to its knees for him, but in a motion that both of us initiate, I'm suddenly straddling his lap.

Locke kisses me lightly on the lips then trails down my neck. "I know that was hard," he breathes against my skin, "and I'm proud of you for asking for what you want."

It *was* hard. And fuck, if I'm not melting at the acknowledgment that I never get in any other parts of my life.

His lips back on mine feel electrified, and I've been missing them every second for weeks.

He pulls back to watch his fingers play across the upper curve of my breasts until they drop to my hips and grind me over his hard-on.

"Shit," I whisper at the same time he growls, "Fuck."

"I'm going to ruin these pretty thighs." He presses his fingertips into my inner thighs and claws his way down them, I assume leaving four marks along each because it hurts in a good way. "Tell me if I say or do anything you're not into. Say no." I nod, but he pushes me. "Use your words. Do you understand?"

"Yes, I'll tell you."

I'm glowing as he gathers my hair in his hands, and his lips find their way back to mine. He bites my lower lip as he slips the straps of my dress down my arms and tugs the top of my dress down to my waist.

My nipples are already hard, but the breeze over the water sends shivers straight from them to between my legs. Locke pinches them between his thumbs and index fingers.

He moans into my mouth, pulls back, and widens his legs. "I'm going to show you how good I can make you feel with words. Get on your knees for me."

Hearing that surprises me, though this is what I want. Maybe it's the surprise of realizing how the tone of his voice could control me, because right now he sounds sweet. I didn't think Locke was capable of sweet.

I slip down his body, still topless, and position myself in between his legs. There's just enough room for me to fit, but if I lean back too far, the steering wheel jabs into my back.

He tucks my hair behind my ear as I rub his erection over his pants. My mouth is watering at the thought that it will be full of his cock in a matter of seconds and how lucky I am to somehow be in this position. Locke is letting me in in a really small way, and I'll take whatever I can get.

The metal button of his pants slips out easily, and I zip them down. He raises his hips so I can tug his pants and boxers down slightly.

My eyes widen when I take him in my hand, proud of myself for doing this to him, making him this hard. I let my thumb memorize every curve and vein, how he feels in my hand.

"Are you overwhelmed?" he asks softly, watching me.

I can't comprehend his confidence, the confidence I don't have. "A little."

"Good," he says. "Everything is for you, not me, because you deserve it all." His voice snaps from sweet to rough. "Now, eyes on me. I want to see how pretty you look with my cock in your mouth."

I lick him from bottom to top before I wrap my lips around him, *for* him, because every fiber in my body wants to show him I can be pretty; that I can be enough for him.

He's warm, and I can feel him pulsing against my tongue. I use my hand and mouth in a steady rhythm until I've gotten used to his size. I let my saliva run down him when I take him deeper, and he groans. I'm so wet I'm squirming in the small space, trying to find a release that doesn't exist.

Locke places a hand on either side of my head as my mouth works over him. "I know you can take it deeper than that, Maren." He pushes up with his hips. "Breathe for me."

I listen, taking a breath through my nose as I open my throat and take him to the point where I'm just about to gag. He holds my head there, but I push myself, because I know how much he'll like it when I try harder for him, and force him farther down my throat. I choke and splutter, spit running from my mouth and tears welling in my eyes.

"Good girl," he whispers, sliding a hand around my neck and squeezing gently. "Listen to those pretty sounds you're making when you're my good little slut."

An unintentional but appreciative moan escapes from my full throat, and my thong is soaked. I'm realizing I've never been that 'slutty' in bed before, but I *love* being a slut for him and, even more so, being rewarded for it. It's like I can take back that word, rewrite it and make it mean something different to me, a good thing, a positive thing—I like sex, and I'm willing to do things with Locke that I'm not okay doing with anyone else. I feel good about myself. Powerful. This is mind shattering, and he hasn't placed a hand on me.

He seems to sense what I'm thinking when I come up for air. "Look what you're doing to yourself. So turned on for me. Touch yourself and feel how wet you are."

My heart pumps into my throat as I slip a hand up underneath my dress and into my thong.

The touch alone sends a jolt ricocheting through my body, and my fingers are coated.

Locke watches me wriggle on my knees, trying to get any sort of friction in the tight space. He brushes his thumb across my cheek. "One finger in," he demands.

"God," I whimper as it slides in easily. This isn't nearly enough, but I have no room to move. A frustrated moan slips out when Locke starts playing with my nipples, and I can't widen my knees between his feet.

He smiles like he knows. "Shh. Listen to how wet you are," he says, running a thumb over my lips and dipping his head to kiss my neck. "Two fingers."

I bite my bottom lip, trying to hold in the deranged sounds of pleasure I want to make as a second finger fills me.

The slick sound coming from between my legs is half humiliating and half hot as hell, so my skin is searing for two completely different reasons.

He nibbles playfully up to my ear. "I can feel you blushing. Is this a no?"

I shake my head.

"Words," he insists and bites me.

"No, it's not a no," I whisper, the blush running deeper. "I love how wet you make me."

"Own it then," Locke says, pulling back. "Watch. Watch how beautiful you look fucking yourself." He pushes my head down, forcing me to watch my frantically moving hand tucked into my thong. My hips try to buck, and I can feel it dripping down my thigh. I feel the sexiest I ever have in my life, like I really am beautiful when I'm wildly out of control and letting go.

"Fuck, Maren." Locke starts to stroke himself. My eyes are stuck watching his huge hand move slowly up and down, imagining how good he would feel inside me. "You're desperate for more, aren't you?"

"Yes," I moan. "I want more."

"Tell me what you want."

"I want you," I whisper. "I want you to fuck me and admire me for letting you use me."

"Well..." Locke smirks. "This is all you're going to get tonight."

THE HIT
Locke

SHE GROANS IN ANNOYANCE.

I've had over a month to fantasize about what I'd do to Maren if I allowed myself to go this far. I'll deal with my own hang-ups later, but when a woman asks you to help her explore her fantasies, you don't say no.

So, no, I'm not going to let her come tonight, because what comes next has been playing on repeat in my head, and it's going to be the best kind of torture for her. I want her wet and uncomfortable, squeezing her legs together every time she thinks about how good I can make her feel, and wondering when the next time she'll have me like this is, because I know exactly how I'm going to fuck confidence into her.

"So needy already," I tease her as her fingers pick up speed in protest. I grab her wrist and pull her hand up to her mouth. Her fingers and hand are glistening from how wet she is. "See how good you taste."

Her eyes pop to mine, and I know instantly she's never done this. I wait for her to use her words and say no, but she looks more ashamed of how into it she is than turned off by it.

How Maren can be this embarrassed when she's fucking perfect the way she is, is almost insulting. No man has ever taken their time with her.

And fuck, if I'm not dying to have the taste of her on my tongue, so I try a different approach.

I lean in and bring her two fingers into my mouth, sucking them clean and holding back the groan of pleasure. The possessiveness that rips through me is coursing through my veins, controlling every move and thought I have.

At this point, I already want her fantasizing that it's me whenever another man touches her in the future. I'll make sure they could never fuck her as good as I can.

I hover my lips over hers. "I said, come see how good you taste."

This time my voice comes out so demanding, I hope I didn't scare her, but the hesitation she had before is long gone. Everything is back to a rough and dirty kiss when she presses her lips to mine in a frenzy.

My tongue slips between them, sharing the sweet and salty taste of her, and I moan into her mouth uncontrollably. It's so fucking good; I may just decide not to let another man ever taste her again. I remind myself I'm sadly not spending my night with my head between her legs and pull back.

"You're doing so good," I tell her.

She smiles, eyes locked to mine. "I want to taste you," she whispers.

These little breakthroughs of boldness have me reeling, and I'm about to come all over her face and tits before she even has the chance to suck my dick again.

Maren drops her head and takes me into her mouth deeper than before as I gather her hair in my fist. I close my eyes and will myself to last a few more seconds as she works her mouth up and down. I've never been so turned on in my life.

"Fuck, you're so good at sucking my cock," I say softly, looking back at her. I run a finger lightly over the freckles dotting her nose. "It's going to be our little secret that you're a whore on her knees for me—and only me."

She digs her fingers into my thighs appreciatively and the slightest smile forms around the edges of her full lips as she picks up speed.

Her green eyes sparkle happily back at me when my legs start to shudder, and I press the back of her head down, holding her in place, as I come the hardest I ever have in my life. I wrap a hand around her neck to feel those muscles work as she swallows. She's doing so well letting me coat her throat, that I can't seem to stop coming from the thought alone that she's loving it.

Even after I go still, she's smiling, proud of herself, and licking me again just for the aftertaste. This woman is so sexy, and she doesn't even realize it.

I slip two of my fingers in her mouth and bring them back out to drag them over her nipples. Her breathing slows as I slip the straps of her dress back up her shoulders.

"Is that what you wanted?" she asks shyly, sliding back up my body into my lap. "Was that good?"

Good doesn't even begin to cover it.

"You're incredible, Maren, but I need you to do one more thing for me to make me happy."

She nods. "Anything."

"Don't touch yourself or make yourself come when you're alone." I kiss her forcefully and selfishly slide two of my fingers into her. "I have plans for you."

Fuck, she feels so good. I curl my fingers to give her the slightest bit of pressure and wish I could sit her down on my cock right now to feel her wrap around me, but I know it will start to seem suspicious how long I've been gone.

Maren lets out a shaky breath before she moans my name and her back arches involuntarily.

A new gush of wetness runs down my hand. She's probably aching from how badly she needs the release. I pull my fingers out, the animal in me becoming too much as I run them over her lips and force them into her mouth. She's surprised for a second how deep I press before she naturally lays her tongue flat and breathes through her nose, but I don't care. I want her to taste herself for hours, not able to get me out of her brain, and I will drive my point home. "Taste that? That's for me. No one else. Your pussy is mine. And I'll say when it comes."

Maren nods. "I promise I won't," she says obediently, sliding her tongue along my fingers and causing my heart to skip a beat.

"Whose good girl are you?" I whisper affectionately.

"Yours, Locke."

I've unlocked something that I know is fucking dangerous. I can feel my brain tingling from the rush of chemicals.

One hit and I'm already in too deep.

CONRAD IS THE ONLY one to look at me for longer than a second when I come strolling back in through the back door.

He follows me through the living room and into the pool room, shutting the door behind him.

"Fuck it out of her?" he asks amusingly, picking out a pool stick off the wall. "I thought you said you were going to keep your dick in your pants."

"Not your business what I did or didn't do."

He watches me rack the pool balls and laughs. "You look flushed."

Yeah, I just got the best blow job of my life, I don't say. Conrad can assume whatever he wants. He's used to the way I am and will piece enough of it together himself without me telling him details.

"It's hot outside," I say. My break lands a red stripe in the corner pocket.

"Right. February." Conrad gives me silence while I put away the nine and the thirteen but miss the twelve. He leans down examining his options. "She's different from the women you usually spend time with."

"No shit," I laugh, unsure yet exactly how to feel about this.

My tongue rubs the roof of my mouth, tasting her over and over. If my entire family wasn't spending the night, I'd be at her doorstep as soon as they left. She's that intoxicating.

But then again, I want her going out of her mind by the time I have my way with her again.

"So you're playing with fire. Have you heard from Casie?" Conrad asks, pulling me from my daydream.

"No." I realize it's my turn, but I'm uncharacteristically off my game tonight when I miss my shot. "Come on, Conrad. You know it wasn't anything worth talking about. She and I got exactly what we wanted. You know she didn't give a shit about me."

He leans on his pool stick and surveys the table. "Maybe because you purposely hang out with girls you know won't?"

"Don't start your psychoanalyzing bullshit," I laugh. "You're not my sports psychologist, and it's not that deep."

"No?"

"Girls that want deep don't want me. The girls who want me want the lifestyle I bring them. In fact, it's simple. They don't really want to talk to me. They want the gifts and the trips and the boat and the private plane. When they realize I won't give them the spotlight, they move on. I don't really want to talk to them. I just need someone to keep my bed warm sometimes. Win-win."

"Which is exactly what Maren isn't," he says, like I haven't thought of that. "She's still hung up on Russ of all people after being cheated on. She doesn't want the spotlight. Plus, you don't even like talking to me. You really think she'll be able to just have sex?"

I raise my eyebrows, watching him line up his shot. "I do, actually."

"Is she a groupie in disguise? Bouncing around from golfer to golfer?" Conrad hits the cue ball cleanly and lands his purple ball in the side pocket. "Please don't tell me she's fucking you to make Russell jealous so he wants her back."

I clench my teeth. Maren isn't thinking about Russ right now, that's for fucking sure. "I don't think that's what's on her mind," I tell him.

"So, she's going to want to talk," he says. "And get to know you. Then what?"

"She already knows about my mom," I say, raising my voice to an angry pitch. "So what?"

Conrad spins on his feet. "You told her?"

"Yeah, we ran into her when Maren was looking at apartments. I wasn't about to let her live where my strung-out mother does god knows what. So, that's why she's here, which I know you were wondering. It's not just hiding her away from Russell and that reality show. I told her a personal detail about myself, and yet, she didn't catch any feelings for me."

He hesitates, letting his shoulders drop. Then he picks up the blue chalk and rubs the end of his pool stick with it, deep in thought.

"Did you tell her about you and Russell?"

"No. She knows we have a history and that it doesn't involve her."

His scoff makes me grip both of my hands around my pool stick harder.

"Why the hell do you care so much anyway?" I ask.

He pauses. His eyes look softer than a second ago, but he shakes his head, coming back from whatever he was thinking. "Man, I just thought it was a bad idea. She's not as strong as you, and Russell did some awful shit to her. Just like he did some awful shit to you." He sighs, eyes meeting mine. "I don't want you to hurt her like that."

"She's a big girl, Conrad. And fuck you. I'm not going out of my way to hurt her, and I think I just heard you compare me to Russell Ashe. *I* tried to protect her, and you know it." I throw my pool stick on the table. The sound bounces around the room as I turn and stalk out into the kitchen, where I lean my back against the island.

A few seconds later, I hear Conrad's righteous ass take the front stairs to go up to bed, where his wife is waiting for him.

Once upon a time, he was right there next to me, fucking every girl he laid eyes on and hurting some of them—until he laid eyes on Blake.

And I'm genuinely happy for him to have found love. They're devoted to each other, but we don't all get so lucky.

I know I don't have the kind of personality that a woman hanging around me wants long-term. I know what I'm good for, and I keep myself in my lane of women so no one gets hurt.

Maren knows what she's signing up for, and it's not *me*. She'd probably take anyone. I'm not someone she wants falling in love with her.

"Locke."

I jump and turn to see Elise tucked up on the oversized chair in the dark with her Kindle glowing in her lap.

"I didn't know you were awake," I say, flicking my eyes toward the pool room. "Did you hear that?"

She shrugs. "You two were being loud."

"Right." I run a hand through my hair. "I'm sorry. That was, uh… nothing."

Her smile is illuminated by her screen. "Listen, Locke, I know you don't want girl advice from your aunt, but I *do* know you better than anyone. If you would let yourself open up, you might be pleasantly surprised sometimes that it's okay to be vulnerable and that it's okay to intensely feel for someone. Not all obsessions are bad. And just so you know, Maren watches you when you're not looking as often as you watch her when she's not looking."

There's no way to tell my aunt it's because Maren wants to use me to fulfill her sexual fantasies—or do they make a card for that?

She stands and makes her way to the stairs, pausing at the doorway to look back at me when I say, "Hey, Elise?" I don't tell her nearly enough. "I love you."

THE PRESS
Maren

THIS USED TO BE my favorite tournament every year. Familiar faces. Familiar surroundings. It was easy to feel comfortable.

But something doesn't feel so comfortable anymore. More eyes are on me than usual. I'm not blending in to the room full of reporters. Men keep stopping to smile and tell me hello.

One of the two women at this press conference is giving me a catty side-eye, and I'm trying to remember if she knows Russell and what I could have possibly done to her.

I haven't seen or heard from Locke since I floated into the guest house last night high on an endorphin rainbow, and I've been nearly out of my mind since.

It's funny that a few weeks ago I felt suppressed and depressed over Russell Ashe, and now, Russell is an afterthought and Locke Hughes' balls have been in my mouth. How the hell did I get from point A to point B?

I wonder if he's finished practicing yet or hiding in my photography closet avoiding this crowd. The thought sends blood up to my cheeks and down between my legs.

I could slip in and slip out in under three minutes and leave satisfied based on how incredibly and constantly turned on I've been in the last twenty-four hours.

Locke knows what he's doing to me, but I don't want to touch myself because I can be good at following his directions, and I know whatever Locke is going to do to me will be one thousand times better.

He could just push me up against the wall in the dark...

"Maren," a reporter, based on the media badge around his neck, says.

I snap back to reality and blink into his squirrelly face. "I'm sorry. What did you say?"

"We missed seeing you in Mexico." He winks.

"Oh," I say as he turns away. "Thank you?"

My co-photographer Jeffrey ("No, not Jeff, Jeffrey"), who's been taking professional golf shots since before I was born, glances at me, and with a smirk, goes back to looking through his viewfinder.

"What was that about?" I ask.

He stares first, then rolls his eyes. "Probably something to do with your relationship."

"People still care about me and Russ?" I huff. "*Why?*"

I don't even seem to care anymore. Is this what sex does? Well, the kinky friends with benefits kind? Because I haven't had a second to fit Russell in on top of my thoughts about Locke.

"Not him," Jeffrey says amusingly. "The other one."

"What oth—" My scoff comes out too forced. "Locke and I aren't in a relationship."

"I don't really care," he chuckles. "Not my business. These people, though, want the scoop."

"There is no *scoop*, Jeffrey. They never cared about me before when I was with Russ."

"Locke is very different from Russ. Locke won't tell anyone anything, so they need to pry. Anyway, like I said, don't care." He turns to take some candid shots as two golfers walk into the room and take their seats at the long table. "I did just order this amazing lens. Check it out."

He steps aside slightly to let me look through his camera so I can geek out.

"The sharpness is excellent. Awesome autofocus. I can't wait to take it birding," he tells me.

"Birding? Is that a modern slang term for birdie?"

"Birdwatching."

I smile, eyebrows raised. "I *love* that you love that."

"Don't look so surprised. It's fun," he laughs.

My phone buzzes against my thigh in the little pocket of my shorts.

Hottie Icicle

Flirting with older men? Are you into calling me Daddy?

I look up to see Locke sitting at his spot at the end of the table, nodding at a production assistant and fooling with his microphone. I think he's joking, although I have no way to really tell through text message—it's just something I feel. After thinking, I decide it does nothing for my body.

Me

No, I don't think so. Are you volunteering as a test subject?

Hottie Icicle

I *am* thirty you know.

Me

Soon you'll be into birding just like my boyfriend Jeffrey.

Hottie Icicle

> Too late. I do that with him occasionally after I practice.

Me

> You bird watch? Who are you?

Hottie Icicle

> Don't look so surprised. It's quiet. No talking involved. And Jeffrey knows how to keep his mouth shut.

As if on cue, a reporter in the crowd asks Locke the first question cheerfully. "Home course, Locke. How are we feeling?"

Locke stares at him like he's an idiot. "I don't know how you're feeling."

The room collectively murmurs in various laugh levels.

"Of course," the reporter says before humorously correcting himself. "How are *you* feeling? I imagine you've played this course the most out of all in the world."

"Never counted," he replies, shrugging. "I guess."

"And Russell, you were out here yesterday putting and chipping. How are the greens treating you this week?"

Russell launches into a long-winded response about how they're slow right now, so I take a look around.

One glare from the only female reporter here reminds me that the entire room seems to be *aware* of me.

I probably shouldn't be texting Locke in the middle of a press conference in front of so many people who will put two and two together, but whatever.

Me

Hottie Icicle

> Do you realize everyone here assumes we're in a relationship just like I told you they would?

Does that matter? They thought the same thing weeks ago when they were incorrect and we'd hardly ever talked.

Me

> Oh my god. They're still incorrect. Or are we officially fake-dating???

Hottie Icicle

We will never be fake dating. Get the idea out of your pretty little head.

Me

> And why does Miss Tight Bun hate me?

Hottie Icicle

Because we used to hook up sometimes, and I didn't want to sleep with her in Mexico.

"Back to Locke," a man to my right says when Russell finally finishes his novel. "Same question for you. Russell says the greens are playing slow. How are you feeling about them this week?"

I zone out when Locke says something about how he's preparing for the course and what his strategy with Conrad will be.

I pretend to take a few pictures until I find the profile of Locke's sometimes hook-up. She's incredible close up. Tan skin, sleek dark hair, and model-worthy cheekbones. She definitely knows how to contour, while I slap some bronzer on my cheeks and pray it looks like I know what I'm doing.

Her tight black dress shows just enough cleavage, and she's crossing her legs back and forth that end in gorgeous four-inch heels. Her shoulders are pulled back, exuding straight confidence I only see on celebrities.

I can't see a single flaw, even with my lens, and the stark contrast between me and her is unnerving. She's all black cat vibes—mysterious, slightly villainous, could probably really bitch someone out with zero remorse and could absolutely fuck someone and keep her feelings out of it. She looks like she'd dominatrix the shit out of a man. I wonder if that's what Locke is secretly into.

Russell gets another question before my phone buzzes again.

Of course, I don't believe him, but a reporter just asked Locke what club has been his favorite lately.

"Hold on," Locke tells him impatiently and drops his head to focus back on his lap.

His message pops up a minute later, but it feels like an eternity in a silent room with a million pairs of eyes watching Locke, who looks like he doesn't have a care in the world.

> You don't realize how sexy you are. Your little freckles drive me insane. I love that I just discovered that those tiny shorts under your golf dress have pockets. You gave me the best blow job of my life, and I've been obsessing over you every minute of the last twenty-four hours. And longer than that. So, no, Maren, Miss Tight Bun does not compare to you, and I won't stop until you believe it. I'll have you naked and panting on my bed in a matter of hours, where I'm going to drill it into that gorgeous head of yours.

"Am I interrupting?" the reporter jokes.

"Yes," Locke says, "but please, continue."

I'm too stunned to move. To think. My heart is beating wildly in my chest, unable to return to baseline until the next six questions Locke has been asked are answered.

BACK IN THE COMFORT of my closet, I fold my tripod up and lean it against the wall before I detach my lens from my camera and crouch down to lay them both in their respective slots of my black camera suitcase.

When the door opens, I expect to see Locke coming to tell me his meeting is over, but I find Russell looming over me instead.

His blue eyes are deep, wild looking.

"What do you want?" I sigh.

He crosses his arms. "You won't answer my calls."

"Yeah." I fake gasp. "I don't want to talk to you."

"Whatever you're doing, it's working. Dating him, fucking him, *living* with him?"

"I'm not doing anything," I seethe, sitting back on my calves. "And how do you know where I'm living?"

"You thought you could both show up here this morning in the same car and people wouldn't talk?" He crouches too, lowering his voice to pillowy soft. "I'm jealous out of my fucking mind, Maren. Is that what you want? Is that what you want to hear? That I want you back? Because I do."

Weeks ago, I would've fallen into his arms and cried tears of happiness. I would have been happy for the earlier "girlfriend" Freudian slips. I was that pathetic, but not anymore.

"Well, I'm sorry, but I don't want you," I say before I change my mind. "Actually, never mind. I'm not sorry. I just plain don't want you back, without the 'I'm sorry.' Because I'm not."

His eyes hold steady on mine until they drift down to my waist and back up. "It's just sex for him," he says plainly, his eyes flickering over me as if I'm a disgusting fleck of dust.

It's just sex for me *too*, I correct him in my head, and technically, we haven't even had sex.

I pretend like I'm Locke at a press conference. "It's not your business if we're having sex or not. Maybe I am. Maybe I'm not. I don't owe you anything, and I certainly don't have to tell you what I'm doing in my personal life or who I'm dating or where I'm living."

"Maren, it's *me*," he says, tone sincere like that alone should sway me. But I don't see him the same way anymore. "This entire thing has made me realize how crazy things were getting. The camera always filming us, nothing was personal anymore. Maybe I let it get a little bit into my head. Opened up my life too much."

I laugh and cough out a deep scoff at that, but Russ curves a hand around the back of my head.

"I bought you a ring, Maren. Before you moved out. I wanted to marry you, and it was going to be filmed for the show." He smiles softly, and his blue eyes hold onto me with purpose. "But now they can film us getting back together. We can get back to that place, be in love, engaged, married. I've only ever wanted that with you."

Tears burst out of me. Those same eyes used to make my stomach flutter—while they looked at every other girl. I'm not sure this man has ever truly cared about me, and the realization is crushing. He used me just to use me—just because he could, because I was there at his side smiling and trusting him. And I think he wanted to marry me because I went along with whatever he said, ignorant enough to let him get away with whatever he wanted.

"I'm not getting back together with you," I manage to say in a blubbering whisper. "Locke or no Locke."

I don't even know why I'm crying—maybe it's for the version of me who was too weak and fell for this.

He slides his hand across my thighs and lowers his voice, laced with concern. "You know his mom is a drug addict. He's probably addicted to something too. I don't want you living there. Come home."

"You're disgusting," I say, pushing his hands off me.

"I'm looking out for you."

My back straightens, but I'm still whispering. "No, I don't think it's about me at all. You want to take me from Locke just to say you won."

Russ narrows his eyes. "What did he tell you?"

I open my mouth to tell him it doesn't matter just as the closet door opens.

Locke's eyes fall on me first, bounce to Russ crouched down in front of me, and then back to me in panic, assessing my tear-stained cheeks and the situation he's just walked into.

I jump when Locke lunges and yanks Russ up by the back of his shirt. "What the fuck are you doing, Russell?"

"Get off me, asshole," Russ hisses, throwing elbows as he's dragged out the door. "There are people watching us. Craig is *right* there."

Locke lets him go outside the doorway, and Russ immediately starts fixing his polo shirt while I sit in shock.

"I'm not doing anything. I was having a conversation with Maren that doesn't involve you," Russ says, staring down Locke.

Locke lowers his voice so deeply it sounds as dark as his eyes. "I fucking swear to god if you talk to her again, I will go to jail."

Then he steps back into the closet with me and slams the door behind him.

THE HISTORY
Locke

My brain is searing, fire lighting along its pathways. I can't remember the last time I've seen red like this.

"I'm sorry. I shouldn't have gone to that meeting and left you alone," I whisper, dropping to my knees in front of Maren and brushing my thumbs over her cheeks, her freckles. "What did he do?"

She shakes her head and sniffles. "It doesn't matter. I don't want to waste my time thinking about him."

"It does matter," I insist, but she shakes her head again. "You can tell me."

"I don't want to talk about it."

Respect that, I tell myself. I can't push her to talk when I don't even talk myself, and we're not in a relationship. She doesn't owe me anything.

"Can I turn off the light?" I ask.

The darkness will make this easier, more comfortable for me. I don't want to have to look her in the eye when I explain what happened, and I don't want her to be able to see my face. This is hard enough without the bright white lights over-saturating this tiny closet.

Her eyebrows pinch, but after a second, she nods like she gets it—gets me.

After I stand and flip the switch, we're surrounded by pitch black. I step carefully and feel my way around the room until I've found the back wall without shelving. I sink down against it before I fumble around, searching for a body part of Maren's I can grab.

When I've found her arm, I tug her gently. "Are you scared? Come here."

She's breathing heavily, trying to get her crying under control, but when she finds my lap and straddles me, she buries her face into my neck and whimpers.

I hold her until her breaths become steady, and then I let out a heavy breath of my own.

"In college, Russell and I were friends," I start. Maren's body tenses, but I rub my palms along her thighs reassuringly. "Or I thought we were."

"You don't have to tell me," she says into the crook of my neck. "I promise, and I understand why you keep so much to yourself."

"I want to, Maren," I insist. She melts into me and nods, so I continue, "I was a sophomore, he was a freshman. We were even roommates the second semester. I told him about my mom because I mistakenly thought I could trust him."

Maren hugs me tighter, because she knows exactly how that feels—trusting Russell Ashe when you didn't realize you shouldn't. But she stays quiet, giving me the silence I need.

"I didn't realize he hated me, resented me for being better than him. I think it started when I was selected as captain over him. Anyway, months later, he borrowed my car one night and drunkenly hit a parked car. I didn't know until the next morning when I got called into our coach's office to watch the footage of my car smashing into another one, backing up and running over a sign, and then taking off."

"Locke," she gasps uncontrollably.

I find the ends of her hair cascading down her back and twirl it around my fingers in comfort.

"It's okay," I assure her. "I told my coach that I was home sleeping, that I wasn't driving, but refused to tell him who was. I wasn't about to rat Russ out."

"You should have," she sniffles into my neck.

I chuckle. "That's just not me, but naturally, as my roommate and best friend, Russ was called in next. He didn't waste any time throwing *me* under the bus and telling them that I was probably an alcoholic or high on something like my mother. My coach didn't believe him, but there was no proof of anything—just my word against Russ'. I had to take a drug test, which came back clean, so I was allowed to stay on the golf team on probation, but I lost my scholarship."

"How did you not end up in jail then?" she mutters under her breath.

"That's not even the end of it," I add, squeezing her closer. "Russ knew how poor I was, that I needed every scholarship I applied for to stay in college, so he started applying for the same ones and cheating in school to win them. He wanted me gone, didn't want to compete against me since he hardly ever won. He knew I didn't want to play golf professionally. After the year was up, I decided I should just go pro for the hell of it, pay for my family to live, make enough money for the rest of my life, even though that was never the plan. I wanted to be the first in my family to get a college degree."

"Locke," Maren sobs. Her tears have been soaking into my polo. "I'm so sorry."

"I promise I don't regret it. I'm happy." I laugh. "I have an extremely addictive personality which turns out to be great for professional sports. I channel my obsessive energy into winning, and I can pay for my mom to go to rehab however many times it takes for her to stay clean. She's tried twice already, so I'm just waiting for her to want a third chance. I like my life, and yes, I'm a closed-off asshole, but it's better that way."

"You're not an asshole," she says. Her tears fall faster against my skin. "I'm ashamed I loved him, that I didn't know who he really is. How could I have been so blind? I can't believe he treated you that way." She pauses. "I feel like I'm in shock."

The room falls silent. I listen to Maren breathing, feel her chest rising and falling against mine. My mind twists back and forth wondering what she's thinking, how she's processing all of that, as she hugs my waist and runs her fingers over the notches of my lower spine. She's the first person outside of my family I've ever told the story to, but I'm not sure she'll ever realize that.

"Thank you," she whispers eventually, "for telling me and trusting me." She kisses my neck lightly. "Will you take me home now?"

AFTER OUR EYES HAVE adjusted to the bright lights of the country club and then the brighter sun outside, Maren sits in the passenger seat of my car and stares out the window.

Her face is still a little puffy, and she wears a slight frown as her eyes scan the passing trees and houses.

Maybe I made a mistake telling her my and Russell's history. I never want her to doubt that I'm not in this to get back at Russell, and I have no idea if she believes that I moved past it a long time ago.

In hindsight, we shared a way too intimate moment, and I made myself incredibly vulnerable. Even more disturbing is I'm thinking about her reaction, her own vulnerability that I want to see, and craving more.

I can't help but keep glancing at her brown hair curling over her shoulder. Her teeth nibbling at her bottom lip. Her hands stuffed under her thighs.

My body is buzzing with the need to touch her. All while I wonder about every question I won't ask her, because women don't want a man who is addicted to them. They want a man who loves them.

We stop at my gate for me to punch in the numbers on the keypad, and when it swings open slowly, Maren takes a deep breath in through her nose and leans her head against the window with her eyes closed.

She has a small smile playing on her lips. I hope my house feels safe for her, that she loves it here, that she's breathing in the fresh air breezing in through the open window because it calms her.

When we pull into my garage and the door starts to close behind us, the room slowly turns dim.

Maren is still sitting there with her eyes closed.

"How old are you?" I ask, breaking the silence.

She opens her eyes slowly and swivels her head toward me. "Twenty-nine," she says with a bright smile.

It's not much. Just the tiniest bit of information. But I feel a thud against my sternum, and I want to feel it again.

"What's your middle name?"

"Ruth. After my grandmother."

"When's your birthday?"

"May second."

"What's your favorite color?"

"Yellow."

I nod. "Just curious."

She unbuckles her seatbelt and lets it slap back against the side of the car before she climbs into my lap. Unlike before when her hips were straddling me in the closet, this time they're desperate. She bears her weight into me, and I feel myself sinking like quicksand, molding around her, trying to claim her. I want her somehow inside my body like my own personal drug.

"You're allowed to be curious," Maren whispers breathily, wrapping her hands around my neck as I grip her ass hard under her dress. Her kiss that comes next is light. "Make me forget."

THE GOLF CLUB
Maren

LOCKE OPENS THE CAR door and slides us both out. He doesn't even bother shutting the door because he's too busy kissing me back harder.

We're frenzied, nails digging into each other, tongues pressing into each other's mouths. Moans and grunts slip between us as he navigates us through his house.

My back hits the banister of his stairs. His shoulder hits the doorframe of his bedroom.

When he throws me back against the pillows, I pause to take in his room. This feels monumental, like I've made it to some marker that qualifies me to see it.

I angle my head upside down to stare at the white abstract painting above his headboard. The ceiling is so high it seems like an optical illusion, and the black canopy bed is connected at the top in a modern open square. To my right there are large French doors, which I assume open into a bathroom, and to my left sit two low chairs in front of the biggest pane of glass I've ever seen.

It's exquisite, but there is no way he decorated this. I'd never imagine Locke as someone with a canopy bed.

"I bought it furnished," he says, voice low, watching me from the end of the bed.

I'm suddenly very aware that Locke somehow managed to get my golf dress off down to my waist between the car and here, and it's blindingly bright. I start to cover myself with my hands.

"Don't do that," Locke says gruffly. "Arms above your head."

I listen, although it's not fast or unhesitant enough for him based on his look of annoyance.

He steps up against the end of his bed, grips my dress bunched around my waist, and starts tugging. "You're going to feel as sexy as you actually are when I get through with you, Maren."

My dress goes down my hips and causes my legs to fly up in the air when Locke pulls it down and off my body completely. He lets it fall to the floor next to his feet, but his eyes never leave mine.

Part of my brain doesn't want my legs to fall open and be this exposed for someone who has never seen me naked, but the majority of my body fights that thought. Since last night, I haven't had a moment to calm myself enough to not be turned on, and I want him to touch me desperately, no matter what it takes.

Locke smirks, closed-lip and not enough to make his dimples appear, but enough to make his devilish look send a shock straight to my clit.

"Do you normally go commando under your dresses?" he asks, voice gravelly, "Or were you hoping I'd find you today in the photography closet and fuck you?"

"Both," I whisper, widening my knees.

He's still clothed, just staring at me, but the crotch of his pants is pulled out tight. "Wider," Locke says.

This time my obedience earns a hum from deep in his throat as he slinks to his knees. He grabs my thighs and slides me closer to the edge of the bed.

Locke licks two of his fingers and runs them over my clit. The cold sensation snaps through my blistering hot core like a slingshot. I gasp when two of his fingers enter me.

"This pussy is perfect," he says, eyes never straying from between my legs. "I wish you could be inside my brain right now. See how perfect you feel. How warm and tight you are." He pulls his fingers out slowly before he sucks them into his mouth. I whimper at the loss. "How good you taste. I would give up every single thing I have to be inside you right now."

"You can be," I huff under my breath, "without giving up anything."

Locke shakes his head. His palm rubs over me, two fingers go in quickly before he pulls them out and stands to hover over me. "Repeat after me," he says, running his fingers over my lips. "'My pussy is perfect.'"

I've never called or thought of my vagina as my pussy in my life. But something about thinking about it this way makes my *pussy* pulse, fire violently rushing down my core.

"My pussy is perfect," I whisper.

He smiles, this time with dimples, then presses his fingers into my mouth and praises me, "Good girl."

I moan around his fingers as my veins ignite.

"Have you ever been edged before?" he asks, dropping his face into my neck.

He kisses his way to my boobs and circles his tongue around each of my nipples.

Every time I suck in a breath, Locke looks me in the eye and does it again, like he's making sure he got it right, memorizing my body. Every curve, every dip, every notch, every blemish. The intensity is every bit as... intense as I imagined. What made me ever think this would be a bad idea? Because Locke Hughes *notices*. He learns and keeps learning, and he demands perfection from himself.

He bites my hip bone. "Focus."

"How can I focus when you're looking at me like that?" I ask breathily and shake my head. "Except for the last twenty-four hours, no, I've never been edged."

Based on his stare, he likes my answer. "Do you want to be?"

I pick my head up to look down my body at him as he trails his fingertips along the inside of my thighs.

"I don't know," I admit, but the thought intrigues me. "Do I want to be?"

Locke doesn't answer me. Instead, he lowers his face into my pussy and licks me once slowly with a flat tongue.

"Fuck," I gasp, my hands flying down to braid into his blond hair at the same time my hips arch. Every inch of my body needs his tongue back on me.

He resists my attempts to get him to make contact again, then smirks, eyes like charcoal, and drags his tongue across his bottom lip like he's savoring the taste of me. "I'm going to have trouble stopping myself, but yes, I think you want to be. I'll make you come so hard you'll think you passed out. But we're playing by my rules."

"Which are?"

"Simple. Repeat after me." I wait for him to elaborate, but he just watches me when I bite my lip. "Yes or no?"

"Yes," I say like I hadn't already decided the moment his tongue met my clit that I'd do anything for this man.

I swear Locke's eyes lighten for a split second as he breathes against me, "No one has ever made me as happy as you make me."

Fisting the sheets, I try to keep my heart from fluttering by pressing down against the mattress. He doesn't mean it literally, it's just a game. A kink.

His mouth is back on me, tongue swirling, slowly at first before he picks up speed and inserts his middle finger. Thanks to my night and day full of sex dreams, I've been wet since I woke up.

He sucks lightly, causing me to take a sharp breath and grind against his face. He breaks contact like it's painful for him.

"I'm so beautiful," he commands.

I scrunch my eyebrows, thinking he's talking about himself, until I remember the rules. A blush starts in my cheeks and travels down my neck and chest.

"I'm so beautiful," I say shyly.

Locke pierces me with his eyes as his fingers pick up speed, curling into my G-spot. I know exactly what he wants.

"I'm so beautiful," I say again with more conviction. The blush subsides as the wave builds, and I swear my body loosens. "I'm beautiful."

"Louder."

"God," I groan as my orgasm starts to build. "I'm beautiful!"

And then everything comes to a halt when Locke pulls back.

For a minute, I forgot what we were doing. The momentum was almost past the point of no return, and every muscle in my body is vibrating.

Slowly, I come down from the short high, breathing heavily. Locke watches, cued into my body like he's learning a golf course. He kisses my inner knee before nibbling his way closer, where he bites me harder and then sits back to admire the little crescent shapes that must be indented on my skin.

"What?" I ask him while a smile plays around on his lips.

"Mine," he whispers, licking his bite mark and making his way back between my legs.

I run the tip of my index finger over the little marks. "Yours," I whisper back.

'Just sex' is fun. Maybe the most fun I've ever had.

The sun catches a set of golf clubs in the corner and reflects around the room. And the first thought that I have is one I could never say out loud.

I throw my head back when he sucks again, lightly at first. His tongue is hitting a perfect rhythm, and I'm already seeing stars behind my eyelids after five seconds.

"Locke," I plead when he adds a finger.

"Look at you," he says, pulling back. The thumb of his other hand presses and circles my clit. I've reached a point where I would do anything to chase this high, and my hips are being downright shameless. "You're fucking gorgeous when you let yourself go and take what you want. 'I'm gorgeous.'"

"I'm gorgeous," I moan so loudly I surprise myself. I *feel* gorgeous—and wet, but I have no time to be embarrassed about that right now. I can mostly only feel gorgeous, like I'm radiating beyond my control.

Locke groans against me when he forces himself to stop. "I can't wait to see how you look when you finally come."

My head spins from the quick climb, pressure building everywhere, and then the subsequent free fall into nothing. "This is torture," I smile.

My eyes land on the golf clubs again, and I blame my raging, slutty mind. I'm becoming depraved, and it simply took no time at all.

I look back at Locke when he kisses my other knee this time, sinks his teeth into my thigh a little harder. Then he slides up my body to kiss me.

"You're so fucking wet," he says into my mouth as we share the taste of me. He runs his fingers lightly over me, slowly dipping one in and out like he has all day to make me suffer. "Tell me how sexy you are."

"Shit," I breathe, arching into his hand when he picks up speed. My fingers dig into his bicep. "I'm so fucking sexy."

I sound wild and confident, like I know exactly how sexy I am, and any man that sees me like this is the luckiest person to ever grace the planet.

Locke crushes his mouth to mine, finger fucking me until he decides I've had enough.

My body is aching, pulsing, deprived. I've never needed a release so badly in my life, but I've never loved being denied something more because I know how rewarded I'll be in the end.

When he lifts himself off me, my eyes can't help but fall back on his golf clubs.

"What do you keep looking at?" he asks curiously, turning his head.

I shut my eyes. "Nothing."

When I open them again, I can't tell where Locke's pupils end and his irises start. His voice is so low and deep in understanding, he sounds animalistic. "Tell me what you want."

He couldn't have possibly figured out what I was thinking that quickly... could he?

"Words, Maren," he presses.

God, he *knows*. He knows what I'm thinking, and I don't know whether to be humiliated or proud of myself.

"How many golf clubs do you own?" I ask.

One of his eyebrows hitches in surprise, but his voice comes out teasing. "That's what you were thinking?"

I nod sheepishly, but I can feel my ears warming.

"Hundreds probably." He gestures toward the black bag. "This is my favorite set. I usually only use it in the biggest tournaments."

"Oh," I say.

He crosses his arms. "Didn't we already establish that you're not a very good liar?"

"Possibly."

"God, I'd be so proud of you," he says, smiling, "if you told me what you are really thinking."

My ears turn hot and itchy, but I take a deep breath. "I want to be a dirty slut."

"How dirty?" he presses further.

There's no way he will do anything without me giving him consent, but I can tell I've made him happy just thinking it, by wanting something that is kinky and submissive and possessive. He's stroking his erection over his pants like he can't help himself.

"I want to come on your golf club," I whisper.

Locke smiles, taking a step toward the bag leaning in the corner and slides one out. He holds the handle up in front of his face before his eyes focus back on me. "You're such a perfect whore for me. Full of surprises. I've never done this before. Have you?"

I shake my head no. My heart jumpstarts at the thought alone, that he's into it. That he's going to give me what I want. My legs widen an inch.

His laugh comes out hoarse and throaty. "Your pussy wants to come on my golf club and then watch me play with it tomorrow, doesn't it?"

I nod, and Locke steps to the edge of the bed. He slips two of his fingers inside me, then runs them over the handle of his driver, making it glisten.

"You're going to be taking pictures of me tomorrow as I swing this and think about how hard I made you come with it inside you."

The anticipation is driving me mad, but I nod like a good girl. Everything is mental. The thought of him playing with it in the tournament tomorrow. That it will be our secret. How he'll always look at that golf club and think of *me* and how good I was for him, how proud I made him. Locke Hughes, the number one golfer in the world, fucked me with his golf club. I think I could get off on just the fantasy alone at this point.

I'm so laser focused on every move he makes like he's doing it in slow motion.

He places the end of it against my pussy. I squirm against it as he just holds it there, his eyes glued between my legs. "Such a good fucking girl begging me."

I moan in pleasure and rub my clit against it again. Locke drops back on his knees.

"So fucking wet," he says, letting the tip enter me a centimeter before he pulls it out. "Tell me if it hurts."

I think I'd welcome the pain like pleasure. "I will," I say.

He presses it further, filling me, and my mind goes black for a split second before bursting into colors that I didn't know existed.

THE THRILL
Locke

"THAT'S THE HOTTEST FUCKING thing I've ever seen," I say, watching it slide in and out of her dripping wet pussy.

I'm about to come in my pants from the sight alone, from knowing how far her thoughts can go, from how willing she is to please me. I think I'm the only person who has discovered this, and I'm going to get hard thinking about this moment every damn time I tee off for the rest of my life—every time I think about how she's moaning as I pump it in and out of her, how much she loves it, and most importantly, that it's *my* memory only, and no one else's.

I lean down and swipe my tongue over her clit. Maren moans my name so loudly, the room starts buzzing.

"Fuck," I say under my breath. It's slipping in and out so much easier than I thought it would. Something so new and chaotic, that I've never experienced before, is ripping through my body. I add my thumb, pressing little circles into her clit. "You own me, Maren. This perfect little submissive cunt may be mine, but you fucking own me for the rest of your life."

And I might mean it. Because I will literally never forget this.

She sounds delusional. Her eyes roll into the back of her head as she grips my white sheets so hard her knuckles almost match.

"You own me," I tell her.

"I own you," she moans back.

"Whose good girl are you?"

She doesn't answer. At least, I don't think she does since nothing coming out of her mouth is coherent, and I'm not entirely sure she heard me.

"Mine," I answer for her. "Show me how good of a slut you are."

Her back arches up off the bed.

"You're amazing," I tell her. "Absolutely perfect. You deserve to be worshiped. And you know it."

I replace my thumb with my tongue because she is going to come against my mouth *and* on my favorite golf club.

Her legs start to shake, and her entire body is jolting in waves of pleasure. I don't think I've ever made a girl come as hard as she is right now.

"Keep coming," I coax, rolling over her clit faster. "Don't fucking stop."

Her hands switch to my hair, lacing into it and pushing my head down harder. This woman is so greedy for me beneath her little sunshine persona that I'd give her anything she asked for if she forever let me be the only person who knew. The flood of chemicals in my brain wants her. And only her. Over and over.

I hear my name in between a jumbled mess of letters and a few curse words, as she grinds her hips, chasing the orgasm, and then she jolts one last time before she goes completely still.

After a minute of me caressing her inner thighs, trailing my nose and tongue along her soft skin, she raises her head. "I think I passed out."

"Probably," I chuckle, rising to my feet and scooping her up off the bed, "from dehydration."

She looks wide-eyed at the enormous wet spot on the bed where she was just lying. "That's your own fault."

"I love it," I groan into her neck. "I want it there every night, and I'll take full responsibility."

I open the French doors to my bathroom as Maren clings to my neck with her legs wrapped around my waist. My shower sits behind the freestanding bathtub and a wall of glass. I place her on her feet on the black tile inside before I turn on the water and raise the temperature on the thermostat.

My shirt comes off first, and Maren immediately starts running her eyes over every curve of my torso.

"*You* have a *tattoo*?!"

I lift my arm to look at the little golf tee that sits in between two ribs. "Stupid, drunken team decision when we won the championship my freshman year. It's so cliché; a pro golfer with a golf tattoo."

"I like it." She reaches out and runs a finger over it. "And I like knowing it's there now."

Her fingers switch to my rib cage, then my abs, pressing against the ridges of my body, before she unbuckles my belt and yanks my pants and boxers down together. She smiles when she wraps a hand around my hard cock, and I step into the shower with her.

"Finally, I have you naked," she says, green eyes sparkling. "Why are you so hot?"

I raise my eyebrows as I squirt some shampoo into my palm. "And cold?"

"You're not as cold as I thought," she confesses before she turns and leans against my chest.

I lather the shampoo and rub it into the top of her head. My dick rests against her lower back, so she stands on her tippy toes to run her ass along it. I hum into her ear as I reach for the bar of soap over her shoulder.

Maren hums back when I run my soapy hands across her breasts, stopping to play with her nipples.

My hand travels down her stomach and circles her belly button before I hold her tight against me and clean her thighs.

"You're just going to get me dirty again," she breathes.

I bite the cartilage of her ear. "True."

I'm like a cat playing with a mouse—the thrill of dragging it out is a reward, all pleasure centers of my brain heightening, but in all honesty, I also know something different is happening to me.

It's chemical. I feel it.

On my skin. Along my veins. In my mind. In my racing heart.

Maren lathers soap in her hands and then turns around to clean my neck, chest, and abs.

When she's done, she slowly sinks to her knees. I run my finger over her freckles as she runs her tongue over the end of my cock.

"Tongue out," I demand, grabbing her hair at the back of her head by the roots.

I trace her upper lip before I press deep into her mouth. My knees immediately weaken from the feel of her warm throat, and she digs her nails into my hips.

Every memory of last night flashes through my head, but this time Maren remembers every little move that made me groan.

"Oh, *fuck*," I say through gritted teeth when her tongue does something across my balls that I can't describe, and I almost come. I've been practically edging myself all day too. I tug her hair gently, bringing her to her feet. "You're too good at that."

She smirks, voice low, as I pull her head back to make her look me in the eye. "I love having your balls in my mouth."

Before I can register what I'm doing, I push her roughly against the glass, causing the walls of the shower to vibrate from the thump. Maren smiles—one I've never seen before, almost wicked, like she's proud of herself for making me lose control—and hitches one leg over my hip.

"Maren, you're dangerous," I say harshly, kissing her neck. I bring her arms over her head and press her wrists against the glass as she grinds her pussy against me. I get tested all the time and haven't had unprotected sex since high school, but I'm about to throw that out the window in less than a second for her.

"Please, I need you," she whimpers. "Birth control, and I got tested."

I pull back an inch to look her in the eye. "I've been tested recently. I would never do anything that I thought would hurt you. You know that, right?"

"I know. I trust you."

She *trusts* me. My brain is a prism of colors, electricity buzzing along every nerve, when I pull her other leg up and slide into her.

The way she feels warm and tight around my cock could physically end me. I'd fuse myself to her if I could—I can't pull my lips off of hers, and how will I be able to walk around like normal, spending wasteful minutes not being inside her. I'll crave it like the need to breathe.

"Locke," she gasps into my mouth when I pull out slowly and slam back into her.

With my forehead resting against hers, I do it over and over, each time taking her breath away. My own lungs can't keep up from how perfect I feel inside her.

"I was wrong," she says with a smile. "You are so much fun."

I've never seen anything more beautiful. The way her full lips curve, and the way she sinks her white teeth into the bottom one. Water droplets drip down her skin in zigzag paths, and her hair falls in wet clumps. She traces my collarbones with her fingertips, pressing into my rib cage and dragging her nails across the grooves of my abs like she's mesmerized by my body. Her hips match my rhythm, pulling me in deeper.

"And you are *mine*," I whisper, driving myself balls deep. "Look at you, how perfect you look taking all of my cock."

Her legs tremble. Her fingernails sink into my shoulder blades. "More," she pleads.

Maren hovers on the edge, moaning through the start of her orgasm and begging to be thrown over.

"Tell me what you are."

"I'm such a good girl," she breathes, green eyes stuck to mine. "I'm only your good girl. And I look so beautiful when you fuck me."

Her hand slides down my arm before she grips my wrist and brings my hand up to her throat.

I wrap my fingers around her tiny neck gently, but she shakes her head, tightens both her hands around my forearm, and whispers, "Use me."

"Fuck, Maren." My fingers press, constrict. "You're a fucking pleasure to use." She smiles, opens her mouth, but just slightly, from the thrill of having her airway blocked off. Her eyes are wild and playful. I can feel her orgasm building throughout her body as my cock rocks into her so hard I hope it hurts her to walk tomorrow. That way she'll be thinking about me every time she takes a step. Every time she sits. My entire body starts to tense. "You're going to look even more beautiful with my cum dripping out of you."

My knees almost give out when she moans my name and comes on my cock, squeezing around me tightly, her entire body shuddering against the glass.

I follow right behind her, every one of my nerves juddering and rolling in a wave of pleasure I've never felt. I groan into her neck as we catch our breath.

We just stay here silent with the water splashing around us. Her fingers twist in and out of my hair, my cock still deep inside her. Our chests heave up and down in sync, trying to regain normalcy.

"God, Locke," she whispers underneath an airy giggle as I brush my lips over her jaw, down her neck. "I like this."

I can't wipe the smile I know she can feel against her skin off my face.

Whatever is happening to me scares me.

Because even after the high slowly fades, my first instinct is to reply, *I like you.*

THE TEE
Maren

LOCKE IS CURRENTLY SMILING at me with dimples, which turns into a smoldering smirk, as he pulls his driver out of his golf bag—*that* driver.

The sky today is cloudless, the perfect day for golf but sadly, not photography.

I don't know who I am anymore, but I like this girl.

I feel sure of myself. *Confident.*

Conrad seems to be keeping an extra eye on me, but more out of curiosity, I think. I'm standing far enough back that I know Locke can't hear my camera, and I've gotten good shots of him along with the young new golfer Landon, his partner on the course today.

Who knew this would be this hot? Us being the only two in the world who know what happened last night—how I willingly give myself over to him to please him, and in return I'm really the powerful one. It's on my terms. I never realized sex could make me feel like this—or maybe it's the not caring that's rubbed off on me. I can't be entirely sure.

It surprises me how deeply I trust Locke. But I guess that is what kinks are about—trust. He has looked out for me repeatedly, every step of the way, and always seems to have my best interest at heart. He would never do anything that he thought would harm me. And even when I think he doesn't notice me, I'm starting to think he actually does.

His body is always angled in my direction, even when his head isn't. He fiddles with a tee in his pocket while he looks for me after we walk to each hole, and when he finds me, he settles.

I'd even go as far as saying that Locke's a little jealous based on his double take when Landon sidles up next to me.

But Locke can't be for long as he steps up to tee off and transforms into his serious golf-above-all-else attitude. The crowd whoops and claps behind us before falling quiet to give Locke the silence he expects.

Landon is all smiles as usual, exuding that fake confidence young people sometimes project. He gets as close as he can to me, whispering under his breath. "Make sure you get my good side, Maren."

"I did," I laugh-whisper back. "Besides, I can make any side your good side with angles and light."

Locke takes a few practice swings. I wait behind my viewfinder.

"What do you like to take pictures of when you're not working?" he asks, still barely audibly.

"People," I joke, "not playing golf."

I decide against this lens and choose my longer range camera draped over my right shoulder and take one quiet picture of Locke in his backswing. With that golf club that I'll forever think about.

After he finally tees off, the crowd noise rises and someone yells, "Get in the hole!"

Locke sidles over to the rope the crowd is contained behind. He pulls a golf ball out of his pocket and signs it with a permanent marker a little boy is holding out before handing it back to him. Locke says something I can't make out, and the boy jumps up and down ecstatically.

Landon smirks and lets out a long, "Borrrring," before he looks up at the sky. "It's weird how perfect it is today when there is supposedly a hurricane on the way."

"There's a hurricane on the way?" I ask back at a normal decibel.

It certainly doesn't look like it. The blue that stretches across the sky is deep and bright and steady, all one uniform color like nothing could disturb it.

"Yeah," he chuckles. "You're from here, right?"

"I am," I say slowly.

My phone buzzes against my leg. As I slide it out of my little shorts, I find Locke staring at me with a tight grip around his driver, and his thumb running over the top of it.

Hottie Icicle

> Who should tell him how hard you came on my golf club last night?

Me

> I don't even think he's old enough to drink.

"Are you prepared?" Landon asks, pulling my attention away even though a scathing fire has been lit inside me. "Or are you evacuating?"

"No idea," I laugh, "considering I just learned this information."

Anxiety spikes. I wouldn't want to be caught by myself on Locke's huge piece of property with no electricity. It would be dark for metaphorical miles. Locke would be states away in a matter of hours thanks to a private jet, and I'd be fumbling around for a birthday candle if I could manage to break into his house. He probably doesn't even own a birthday candle.

Me

> Are we prepared for this hurricane I didn't know was coming?

Hottie Icicle

> Yes.

When I look up, Locke shoves his phone back in his pocket in a display of finality twinged with anger that makes me itch with discomfort.

He huddles close to Conrad so they can discuss whatever the hell golfers talk about... I assume golf strategy.

I shouldn't be texting him while he's playing in a tournament. He needs to focus, and I need to chill out before he thinks I've developed deep-rooted, never-quite-erased feelings for him.

Then I realize *he* was the one who texted me first.

I slip my phone back into the pocket under my dress, willing my body to stop overreacting. It's not fair of him to be mad at me, so I'm not going to worry about it. I'm minding my own business, and not being clingy, so he needs to realize I'm the one keeping boundaries since this doesn't come easy to me.

I take a few photos of Landon teeing off and then focus my attention back on him when he's done and sidles up next to me again. We turn together to make our way down the fairway.

"Where do you live most of the year?" I ask.

"Scottsdale," he replies. "I trade the hurricanes for heatstroke."

I light up. "I love it over there! I went to the Grand Canyon last year, did the whole helicopter tour."

"Amazing, isn't it?"

"God. The whole thing made me feel so incredibly small and inconsequential." The almost unexplainable colors and vastness splitting the world like an enormous crack run through my head, along with the wild horses I saw running through the woods hundreds of feet below us out the huge helicopter windows. "Don't even get me started on how much I loved Sedona. I've never seen anything like that growing up here my entire life."

"Man, I would've loved to take you there earlier this month. Maybe next year," Landon says, then at my face of surprise (I'm assuming), he laughs at himself. "Sorry, you and Russell are still seeing each other?"

"Oh," I say. "No. No, nothing like that. We're not together anymore."

Suddenly, I remember that Russ was sitting next to me in that helicopter last year, and not one image that ran through my brain a second ago involved him. He was there though, holding my hand with his unfaithful one, kissing me with his wandering lips, experiencing it all beside me, and yet it was almost like I forgot he is... alive, existed, my ex. For just a split second.

Landon smiles. "So, you're single? We could grab drinks tonight if you're interested." My eyes involuntarily cut to Locke who's about ten yards in front of us, and Landon's good-natured laugh returns. "Now I thought *that* was a rumor."

"It is." I laugh right back, wondering how you defend yourself against what is being said about you, when you don't know exactly *what* is. The truth, I surmise. "I'm very single, and honestly, I think I'm going to stay that way for a little while. I'm very flattered though."

Internally, I'm amazed that this twenty-year-old would even be interested in me. He could get anyone.

"No worries," he says. "I totally understand. If you ever want to hang out just as friends, I'd be down, though. This traveling thing gets lonely."

I have no idea if he's telling me he's down to hook up occasionally, but I brush it off. "I'd like that."

He flashes a smile at me, all boyish features and charm, and I try to imagine myself sleeping with him. Maybe I'm into the age gap. Maybe I'd get a thrill from this young guy thinking I'm hot. I picture him calling me a good girl, and while I bristle slightly at the thought, it doesn't resonate as much. I almost hear it like he says everything—as a joke.

There's something much more captivating about Locke. The way he looks at me like he's searing through my clothes. That manly thirty-year-old *something* that I can't put my finger on.

The way his broad shoulders sit like he's completely comfortable in his own skin. The way he struts down the fairway with one hand in his pocket. That white baseball hat that casts a dark shadow over his face. The gruff manliness combined with the glimpses he shows of just a little something extra underneath.

I can't remember the last time I wanted to burrow beneath a man's attitude so badly and find out what lies beneath the surface, find the real layer.

But I think peeling back to the real layer is even more dangerous.

THE FAIRWAY
Locke

CONRAD LOOKS UP FROM his little book as we walk down the fairway. "What's wrong with you?"

"Nothing," I scowl, even though I feel Maren and Landon behind me like an earthquake. Their conversation drifts toward me, and Maren's little giggles feel like knives into my chest.

My hand is balled into a fist in my pocket.

He shoots me a leveled look when we stop and find my ball, then swivels his head to Maren, who's behind us looking at me curiously, and Landon, who's checking out Maren's ass.

"I told you not to sleep with her," he sighs. "It's been what? Less than forty-eight hours? Let me guess, she's already professed her love."

"No, still just sex."

For her, I don't add, and there's certainly no way for me to come out and say, *I'm fucking addicted to her.*

She insisted on going back to her house last night, all in the spirit of being fuck-buddies, which left me alone in my bed staring at my ceiling fan and wishing she was beside me.

Not somewhere I want to be when I'm in my head, coming down from the high and already itching for another hit.

Now, I'm standing here like a shell of my former self, jealous of some kid talking to her, texting her while I'm in the middle of a professional round of golf, and worrying that she will get scared of the dark if the lights go out at her place—on top of watching her look like a confident little ray of sunshine that makes me so proud I want to push her up against a palm tree and fuck her back into submission.

"Well," Conrad starts, "try not to *talk* to her."

"She slept in her own bed last night," I say. "No talking."

Except for before, where I'm spilling my secrets to this woman in a pitch-black closet while she cries into the hollow of my neck.

I *knew* this would be a bad idea. I'm too close already—to everything and everyone involved, her especially.

"No more talking, anyway," I clarify.

Immediately, I regret it when Conrad cocks his head and holds up a hand to block the sun in his eyes. "What does that mean, 'no *more* talking?'"

"It doesn't mean anything," I say.

He squints. "What'd she do?"

"She didn't do anything." The anger swells momentarily—she's done nothing to deserve hate from Conrad. "Get off her fucking back."

Conrad seems surprised for a split second before his eyes clear. "I'm guessing you shared something else about yourself then." He searches my face, reading it like only he can do. "Locke," he says slowly. Almost like a question. Like so much hangs on my name.

When he doesn't continue, I say gruffly, "What?"

"Nothing." More searching my face for god knows what. "Do you think maybe you should tell her?"

"Are you insane? She will think I'm insane."

"You think?" He shrugs his shoulders up and down in a wave motion. "She might not."

I inspect where my ball landed, survey from here to the green. "Can we focus on this little round of golf instead of my sex life?"

"Then quit looking at her," Conrad quips.

I can't, I think. *It's almost impossible.*

Like a moth drawn to a flame—to their death.

Maren's in yellow today—her favorite color. It's not even tight, just sort of flowy, but I already know she's got shorts attached underneath. Her white tennis shoes with a light blue stripe look brand new, one lace about to untie. Her hair is in a messy knot on top of her head, but she still has a light pink scrunchie on her right wrist. Her two huge cameras are slung over each shoulder, and she keeps switching back and forth, though I have no clue what makes her choose one over the other, and now I desperately want to know. I want another piece of her. All the pieces, I'd hoard them like a fucking lunatic.

But mostly, I'm pissed at myself for noticing every little damn thing.

"Just be my caddie," I mutter angrily, "and tell me golf things."

"Golf things? Okay," Conrad says slowly under his breath like I've lost my mind. "So, if we're two oh four, let's hold it with the wind."

I lean down and pinch a few blades of grass between my thumb and index finger before I let them go in the wind. They fly back toward my stomach.

"See the pin," Conrad tells me, consulting his book. "You've got twelve feet behind it."

"Seven-iron, you think?"

"Yeah, I like that," he says, sliding the club out of the bag and handing it to me. I take a few practice swings. "Feel it."

"I'm thinking I aim for the camera there," I say, holding my club out toward the cameraman I can see in the distance. "Try and cut back right just a bit."

"Love it." Conrad's face is buried in his little book before he looks up. "Yep. I'm good with it if you're good with it. Love it."

I set my feet, take two practice swings, and then step forward. The club vibrates perfectly in my hands when it hits the ball, and I know before I look up that it's an amazing shot.

The crowd claps, a man whoops, and I do my best to shut it out after I give a small wave. Transforming into the nice, genuine, grateful golfer for two seconds.

As Conrad gathers my golf bag and starts to walk down the fairway to the green, I hang back.

Maren watches me take off my glove while she approaches with Landon, and I don't miss how something so seemingly simple turns her on when she has a hard time tearing her eyes off the motion.

"Nice shot," she says brightly. "I got a good photo of it."

One hardened glance at Landon and he takes the hint. His head dips to acknowledge that he's bowing out.

She gapes as he walks away. "Did you just have an unspoken man conversation?"

"I don't know what you're talking about," I say, cocking my head to the side.

Maren scoffs amusingly and walks beside me. "Yeah, okay."

Running a hand across her lower back, I graze the top of her ass just enough to feel the curve under my fingers as I say, "But yes, I'd prefer if he didn't stare at your ass."

Her eyes glint when she looks up at me, and she bites her tongue playfully. "Someone's a little jealous, but don't worry—my ass is yours at the present moment."

"Someone's a little confident," I tease. "I like it."

She laughs. "Do you think I won't be as attractive to you when I'm confident? Like a girl who's only hot because she doesn't realize it. And then when she does realize it, all the magic is gone. That's when you'll get tired of me."

"No," I say, dropping my voice. "It only makes me want you more. Because only *I* know how much you like to spread those pretty legs for me."

I step in front of her and continue walking backward. She sucks in the smallest breath, bites her bottom lip, as my eyes dip down from her waist to her calves.

"Locke, don't turn me on right now."

I hum disappointedly, letting my eyes linger between her legs and getting hard picturing her sitting on my face. "I like you in yellow."

Then I change the subject. "So, I was thinking... even though you don't like it, you did say you wanted to learn. I'm going to teach you how to play golf."

THE LESSON
Maren

"THIS IS A WORSE idea than all of mine combined," I argue when I whiff the golf ball for what feels like the hundredth time. "How do you make this shit look so effortless?"

My hands ache, and we've only been at this for thirty minutes since day one of the tournament ended.

When I lean my club against my legs to stretch them, Locke takes a few steps closer and gathers my hands in his before he starts massaging his thumbs into my palms and down my fingers. My bones creak.

I try not to make a big deal about it so I don't spook him, but his rough hands feel warm and massive in a good way.

"Some people say golf is the hardest sport," he chuckles, pressing into the pad of my thumb. "You're doing well for your first time. Don't be so hard on yourself."

"What about hockey though?" I tease. "You think you could cut it on skates?"

"Maren, we live in Florida." Locke smiles with a playful look in his eyes. "But I have played before."

I almost let out a satisfied moan when he works his thumb along the outer edge of my palm, but I manage to only roll my eyes. "Let me guess, you're amazing?"

He laughs—a deep sound, one that crinkles his eyes. "Hell no. I couldn't stand for shit the first day I tried."

"I'd pay money to see that."

"But that's what's great about sports," he says, pinching my skin. "Keep practicing, or in my case obsessing, which is what I did the entire vacation I spent with an NHL friend in Boston a few years ago. He had to drag me off his ice rink, and if I'd had a week or two, I could have at least put up a fight." He pauses before his voice drops. "Would you like me more if I played hockey?"

I shake my head no, not sure what is happening, as Locke brings my arm up while holding eye contact that simultaneously scares me and melts me. Then he kisses my wrist tenderly. The low hum that follows from deep in his throat flip-flops my stomach violently.

"Give me a few weeks, and I can practically do anything," he adds. "So, do you want to quit?"

"No," I say breathlessly, my heart racing and trying to jump hurdles. "I don't want to quit."

He lets my arm drop to pat me on the ass. "Attagirl."

I pick my club back up as Locke nudges my foot with his, putting it into position. I can still feel his handprint.

"Let me see your grip," he tells me. I line my hands and fingers up like he showed me. "Remember, not too strong or weak. You want neutral. It will help with the soreness when you get it right."

I loosen my body and bring my club up.

Locke watches affectionately before he tips his chin toward my left arm. "That arm a little straighter. You don't want a baseball swing."

I fix my arm and try again, hitting the ball this time, but it still shanks off to the right.

"Better?" I say, shrugging.

"Better," he beams. "You're a quick learner."

After I've finished hitting an entire bucket of balls, most of them shanking far off to the right, I turn back to Locke. "It feels so unnatural. I have no idea how you hit it hundreds of yards."

He smirks. "That sweet spot."

"Must you have a little name for everything?" I ask, jabbing the top of his feet with my club. "Sweet spot, eagle, mulligan, cabbage, chili dip. It's nonsensical."

He grabs it out of my hand and pulls me into him with his arm around the back of my neck. His chuckle lands in my hair. "I didn't invent golf."

"I still blame you," I joke.

"What else do you blame me for?" Locke brushes my hair back to plant his lips below my ear. When his lips part slightly, his tongue swipes across, tasting me. My legs go weak from surprise, my vision tunneling as I stare at the blue sky.

"Calling me a good girl."

"You're my little sweet spot," he murmurs into my skin.

"Locke," I whisper hesitantly, even though one of my hands immediately goes to his waist, wishing his shirt wasn't tucked in, and the other finds his free hand and laces with it. "We're in public."

He squeezes my hand, pulls me harder against him when I look up at him. He blinks, eyes never straying from mine, and runs a thumb over my lips, first the top, then the bottom.

Without bothering to look around Locke whispers, "There's no one out here, but I don't really give a shit," before he kisses me.

Strong hands braid into my hair. Tongue teases mine.

My heart starts to float.

I don't give a shit either, I don't give a shit either, I repeat in my head, trying to secure it back inside my rib cage where it firmly belongs.

SOMEHOW, LOCKE HAS MANAGED to convince me to get on a golf cart and venture out into real golf territory after I was able to not whiff an entire bucket of balls.

Okay, maybe partly because he picked me up by my thighs, wrapped my legs around his waist, and *kissed* me before throwing me into the seat next to him.

"I'm not ready for an actual course," I groan.

"Practice course," he corrects me. "I'm not taking you out on the course where we're currently playing a tournament."

"I don't think that makes any difference."

"It's completely different," he says without a hint of irony.

I go to roll my eyes but find the edge of his lip shadowed in humor. "Let's talk about this sense of humor you've got buried deep, deep down."

Locke keeps his eyes on the golf cart path, his mouth shut, face blank. And I know in my bones he's messing with me.

"I have a proposition for you," I say slyly.

He snorts. "Fake dating?"

He's not laughing, but I still say, "Laugh all you want. It would have worked. People would fawn over you if you cared about PR," because I know he is in his head.

"That shouldn't even be a thing, and I have no idea why anyone would actually need one." That low, throaty chuckle finally pushes out of his mouth. "But I'll admit, you would have been the fucking best fake girlfriend."

I shift closer, cross my legs. "Thank you," I drawl playfully. "I would have. I'm very... compliant." I smirk when Locke sideways glances, the tone of my voice causing his face to blank, like his mind stumbled. "Now, while I play these practice holes, you're going to take my picture."

I tap the top of my camera bag that sits between us on the floor with the bottom of my foot.

Locke's eyes heat as he traces the bag, then my foot.

Then my leg.

A century passes inside of a split second before he stops the cart, sweeps a warm palm up my shin, and bends at his waist to press his lips into the top of my knee.

Just when I think he's going to protest, his dimples divot deeply when he straightens and pulls me two inches into him so our thighs are flush.

"I'm going to take the shit out of your picture," he says.

He will, since he demands perfection from himself, and my chest blooms with something that feels like pride before he's even had his first lesson.

Locke pulls off the cart path at the first practice hole and patiently watches me unzip my camera bag and snap a lens onto the body.

"Why do you hate having your picture taken so much?" I ask him.

"As much as I'm seen," he says, "I don't like to be seen. If that makes any sense."

I nod. He continues.

"And I don't know why anyone would want to see me, even a picture." He laughs. "I don't even like looking in the mirror. I know what's going on in my head, and I know how I feel, and when I look at myself, it always seems fake. I've had my picture taken more than enough, without my consent, for a decade. What do you love so much about it?"

"For me, it's about the memories," I explain. "You think you'll remember the little things, but time passes, people forget. A picture, though, can spark the feeling you tried to preserve, bring it back."

"I like that. Those are the pictures you want of yourself, the ones that hold love. Not the ones of a crazy fan snapping a blurry camera picture of you buying toilet paper."

"Celebrities," I tease. "They're just like us."

"We're worse," he jokes, then holds out his hand, smiling. "Now... come on. Teach me about this thing."

"First," I say, twisting the camera away from him, "you need to learn about aperture."

"Aperture," he repeats.

"Do you want the background of your photos to be clear or blurry?"

He thinks, looking out over my shoulder. "Blurry."

"I approve," I tease. "So, your aperture needs to be wide. It lets in more light by opening the diaphragm." I wait for him to make a joke, but his eyes lift to mine, all the lines of his face etched in serious concentration, waiting to hear my next explanation. I angle the camera's screen toward him and turn the dial to show him how to set it. "It's measured in f-stops. The lower the number, the higher the aperture or the hole in the lens that light is coming through. This camera is an f/2.8, which means that's its minimum f-stop, and it goes up from there."

"The lower the number, the better the pictures?" He smirks and holds out his palm impatiently. "Just like golf."

I hesitate, hovering just above his outstretched hand. Part of me wants to lecture him more, explain every little piece of the camera, instruct him on how to use every setting and dial, how to time the photos. I could talk for hours.

But Locke reassures me, "Trust me, I got it."

So, I place my most prized possession in his hand and slip out the golf cart.

The clubs Locke borrowed from the shop for me look like the matching women's set to his. I slide my driver out from the black bag in the back seat and step up to the tee.

Locke watches my movements intently and steps around me in a long arc. He raises the camera to his eye.

I open my mouth. Close it.

He peers around it with a wink. "Pretend like I'm not here."

Well, that's physically impossible. I constantly feel like I'm holding a candle close to my chest when he's within eyesight. Maybe even when he's not. Just a running thought across my brain, and I'm suddenly a human heating pad.

After I place my ball on the tee, I concentrate on Locke's instructions: how to hold the club, how to angle my body. I take a deep breath and close my eyes to calm myself. The last thing I want to do is completely whiff the damn ball and have Locke catch it on camera.

When I finally swing, I know I at least got that right, because it feels awkward as hell holding my one arm so straight to 'keep the baseball swing out' like Locke told me.

My ball doesn't even slice *that* far to the right.

"Shit," Locke mutters. Whipping around, I see he's looking at the screen. "I took it too early."

I squash the smile that wants to push through my lips. His voice sounds so concerned, determined.

"Do it again," he adds.

And only because I'm so nice, I appease him eight more time before he's satisfied with his photograph.

I know before he even says anything based on his wide blooming smile that he's finally reached what he considers perfection.

"I could do this all day," he says, eyes dark. He doesn't look away from the camera, almost like he's stuck. "You're so beautiful." Then he pops his head up and uses a free hand to wave me along. He traces my body with a hardened look. "I get why you love this so much. Keep going."

He sure knows how to motivate a girl. Because now all I want is to play every single practice hole. Three times—even though I look ridiculously silly because it *is* my first ever lesson. Just so he can take my picture.

After Locke buckles himself into the driver seat back in the parking lot of the country club, his hand immediately finds my thigh.

His fingers skim my inner thigh as both of us stay silent.

I try to concentrate on anything but his warm hand. Anything to distract myself from the feeling of how much he seems to *like* having his hand on me, almost like he can't help himself.

Until out of nowhere, he says, "Tell me about your mom."

When I glance at him, he gives me a small reassuring smile without looking at me.

"What do you want to know?"

"What is she like?"

I half laugh, half scoff. "That is a complicated question."

"I figured," he says. "But I'd like to know, if you want to tell me."

"She's nice," I say. Locke squeezes my thigh gently, urging me to continue. "Or at least she can be sometimes. But she's also a lot of other things. Critical. Passive aggressive. She tends to make everything about her."

He nods. "Does your sister feel the same way? What's her name again?"

"Camille," I say, "and yes, but she handles it better than I do. She's the confident one, remember? Camille stands up for herself and doesn't let my mom push her around or guilt trip her into doing anything she doesn't want to do."

"Maybe she's that way because of you," Locke muses.

I laugh. "Maybe."

"Parents are harder on their first child," he insists. "You're like the guinea pig."

"What do they say about the only child?" I joke.

His laugh comes out a little too low, a little too morbid. "I don't think I had a typical only-child experience."

I place my hand over his and play with his knuckles. I have no clue if he'll elaborate, and I have no clue if I actually want him to or not.

Things are shifting. We're wading into personal territory—territory I'm not sure why we're navigating. It seems dangerous, almost like we *care.*

Which I do. But I tell myself I don't.

But only a beat passes, and then he decides to test the slope of the hill, this new terrain we've found ourselves on, like I actually coaxed him with my silence.

"My mom and I got into a car accident when I was three. I don't really remember it, but she hurt her back and was prescribed opioids. Things spiraled from there. Sometimes my mom was great. Happy. Stretches would go by when she showed up for my games, when she cooked dinner, read me a book before bed. And then there were other times when she'd be so strung out, she couldn't walk straight. She would be passed out on the couch or disappear for a few days when I got older. I took care of myself, did the laundry, cleaned the house, took the bus by myself to and from school. It took a while for my family to realize what was happening. I was so secretive, didn't want anyone to find out about my reality. And I didn't grow up in a nice house in a nice neighborhood like you thought. But underneath all of that, my mom is truly the sweetest woman. Just like Elise. They were close growing up."

"And your dad?" I ask.

"He left shortly after I was born, wasn't ready to be a parent," Locke explains. "Which didn't stop him from trying to reenter my life after I became a professional golfer. So, I do tend to shut people out, because it's easier to let people think of me as an idea, because it's not always *me* they really want."

"Locke," I say, my hands suddenly clammy.

My armpits are sweating more than they did when I was golfing, but Locke doesn't let me finish, doesn't let me express that I now feel like I've been using *him*.

Instead, he hushes me as he pulls through his gate. His hand roams up my legs, wraps around the back of my neck, when he parks in the garage.

The air turns thick, sudden need pulling at us.

He smiles at me, full dimples on display, before he leans over the console and kisses me gently.

Locke exits the car and waits for me to do the same in the darkened garage.

After I open the door and cross in front of his car, he says, "You look all sweaty from your work out," before he removes his polo in a quick, fluid motion, exposing every line I wish I could run a finger over. "Let's go jump in my pool I never use."

I laugh, heart hammering, as Locke slips my yellow straps down my arms and pushes my dress to the ground around my feet.

He kisses his way back up my body, starting at my knee and ending at my boobs. Then he turns and throws open the door that leads to his backyard, flooding the orange sunset through the garage.

"It's too cold to swim," I protest, following him as he walks through the door.

Locke shakes his head. "It's heated."

I hear his belt buckle clink before he slips it out of his belt loops, drops it on the path, and turns to face me.

First his button is loose. Next his pants and boxers are at his ankles. Last, he kicks them off.

He's already hard. I'm already wet. And we're staring, taking each other in like we've never done this. Like we've never been naked in front of each other. Like we're seeing each other for the first time.

"What are we doing?" I whisper.

"I don't know," he whispers back.

He takes half of a backward step, close to the edge of the pool, and I instinctively take one forward. Locke takes that as some kind of signal and reverses his motions to scoop me into his arms and jumps into the deep end. I can't even squeal because I have to take a deep breath.

Underneath the water, I wrap myself around him. Our hands are everywhere. Soft places. Firm places.

When our heads break the surface, Locke holds me against him and swims to the shallow end.

He swipes my hair out of my face for me after he's able to stand.

"Hi," he smiles.

"Hi," I smile back.

His kiss on my lips is light. I wouldn't be able to tell someone what is happening if they held a gun to my head. Are we friends? Are we more than friends? Are we dating? Are we fucking?

The lines are blurred. Then just like that it quickly snaps back into place.

"Will you come with me to a charity dinner on Sunday?"

Right. Our arrangement.

He's using me too.

If he doesn't feel bad about it, then I shouldn't either. Caring is overrated, right? We're both getting something out of this, complete with amazing bonus sex.

"Of course," I reply, throwing my arms around his neck. "I'll be sure to talk an extra lot."

Locke buries his face in my hair, licks across the skin beneath my ear, bites my collarbone.

"The only thing I want to hear come from your lips right now is my name."

He walks us to the edge of the pool and wedges me against the wall. He removes my hands from his biceps, but I tighten my legs around his waist. His hands grip my hips hard, forcing me to stop grinding my pussy against his cock.

"Locke," I whine.

Locke chuckles and bites my lip hard. His tongue soothes the sting. "Not like that, Maren. You're going to moan it. Scream it." Like I weigh nothing, he lifts me and sits my butt on the edge. "I stare at you in your little golf dresses all day and the only thing I can picture is my face between your legs." He bites my kneecap. "Spread and show me."

When I obey, the deep groan from the back of his throat is so low that I almost didn't hear it. "Locke," I whisper, less bratty, more needy.

"Relax," he breathes into my inner thigh. "Lie back and let me show you how much I appreciate you."

"Locke," I beg, now all moan before he's even touched me.

I gasp as his thumb runs over my clit before he pushes it into me. I lean back on my hands, because Locke won't accept anything less.

"How could anyone not praise you? So wet for me all the time. Such a good listener. Just begging to be fucked."

I nod and breathe out. When Locke teasingly licks my clit, my hand wraps around the back of his head to apply pressure, forcing him to bury his face.

He only smirks and lets me—his eyes, latched to mine, are the darkest I've ever seen them. It's like he's drilled into mine and refuses to look away.

Out of all the places in the world Locke Hughes could be, he's here, eating *me* out like he can't get enough, getting *me* off like he wouldn't rather be anywhere else.

I have no thoughts. I'm mesmerized, watching his tongue work, feeling every one of his enthusiastic groans tremble through my legs. Every feeling I have, I hone in on, trying to experience them all at once, catalog them. I'll miss it when we're no longer doing this.

My hips arch repeatedly as I ride his perfect tongue. His two fingers press against my G-spot, and the pressure starting to build is so intense that it's almost uncomfortable.

"Locke," I moan, halfway between euphoria and hesitation. My entire body is trying to fight what is happening.

In all my kink googling, I now have extensive knowledge on things I didn't before, and I know exactly what Locke is trying to do. How I feel right now is exactly how most people described it. Though it intrigues me, the unknown is a little scary, and no one has ever taken the time to get to know my body that intimately.

"Relax," he says, pulling back an inch.

I squirm. "But I think I'm going to—"

He covers my mouth with his hand, smothering my words, and picks up speed with his other. His voice comes out like steel. "That's what I want, Maren. If you want it, let go and fucking soak my face. I want you messy. I want you all over me. I want you in every single way I can have you. Now relax, baby, and make me happy. *Take. What. You. Want.*"

My entire body responds like it's no longer connected to my brain. I'm putty, melting under his touch, molding against his mouth. Shaking, messy, gushing putty. And the internet is right—this is fucking incredible.

I'm holding his face tight against me as I grind unapologetically, practically drowning him as I scream his name, and he's loving every second of it—which only makes me come harder, longer.

Maybe I like to be dominant just as much as I like being submissive because I'm drunk on power.

Maybe good girls can have both.

THE EX
Locke

"Spend the night with me," I say, scooping her almost lifeless body into my arms after I push myself up out of the pool.

The sun is just about to disappear below the horizon, and it will look beautiful from my bedroom window.

Maren nods into my chest and clings to my shoulders.

When I make it up the stairs and into my bedroom, I dry both of us off with a towel before I slide my comforter back and deposit her into the middle of my bed.

I climb in next to her, and she hitches a leg over my waist and nuzzles back into my chest, smiling to herself and drunk on pleasure. "Have you ever had a girlfriend?"

"Yeah," I say, twirling my fingers through her hair, "in high school. Gwen Stevens."

"What was Gwen Stevens like?" she asks.

I laugh. "Out of my league."

"Hm," she hums. "I don't believe you."

"I was hopelessly in love with her all through middle school."

"She didn't know you existed?"

"No, she knew," I say, rolling my eyes. "She ignored me."

"Well, what happened? You grew a foot? Or did you become a junior golf champion? No, you got contacts and your braces off, and suddenly, she realized you were hot all along?"

I pull her across my body and pinch her ass. "You think I'm hot?"

"Yes," she sighs. "You think you're hot. I think you're hot. You know I think you're hot. We're all in agreement."

"I like hearing you say it. Especially when you get feisty."

Maren crosses her hands on my chest and rests her chin on top. She scrunches her nose, and those tiny little brown freckles make my stomach drop. My pinky runs over the bridge of her nose, making me wish I could somehow feel them.

"So, how did you win over Gwen Stevens?" she chuckles.

"I didn't even know at the time really," I admit. "I didn't care about her anymore. I was so focused on golf freshman year. And then sophomore year, my mom tried to get clean for the first time. I was naive, of course, thinking this was it. She'd go to rehab and stay sober. Be my mom again. Elise paid for it out of her retirement, so it also makes me happy that I can now take care of my entire family. They don't need to worry about things like that anymore."

I pause, knowing I'm saying too much, but I can't find it in me to care enough to stop myself. Maren doesn't even seem bothered, unlike every other person besides my family I've ever watched fidget uncomfortably.

"Anyway," I say, "at a party sophomore year, Gwen was suddenly into me. Out of nowhere. Looking back, it made sense. I'd been hooking up with girls from other schools, keeping my lives separated. It was so much easier that way. I never had to see them or open up to them. They didn't know much about my life, and I didn't care about theirs. I think Gwen saw me as a challenge for the first time."

Maren cocks her head to the side, studies my face with furrowed eyebrows, then chuckles out, "What'd you do? Challenge her right back?"

I can't keep the smile off my face. I can't keep my hands off her body, they just roam everywhere. "You think you know me?"

"Yes," she says slowly, ears pink, before she recovers confidently. "At least, I think I'm starting to."

"I'm an asshole sometimes," I confirm, squeezing her thighs before I hesitate, wondering how much I should share with her. But every part of me wants to be honest with her and that wins out. "An asshole who is always trying to win a game—challenging myself, playing with my food, cat and mouse. I get off on the thrill, addicted to the adrenaline. It's a mystery why I never wanted to play golf past college because it's everything I love. Though I've matured *some* since high school, I think it just runs in my blood. My mom's dad was an alcoholic who drank himself to death before I was born."

Maybe I haven't matured that much, because here I am, doing the same thing—adrenaline courses through my sick, twisted veins now from the anticipation that my dick will be buried inside Maren whenever I decide I want to. I've been hard since we got out of the car. All I have to do is kiss her, and she'll appease me. And yet... I'm still talking, still dragging out this feeling.

Or maybe it's the talking flooding my brain with dopamine. At this point, I'm not even sure. Maybe I'm challenging her to think less of me. Daring her to put an end to us.

Before I ruin it. Before Maren sends me into a spiral—one she won't want any part of.

But fuck if her smile doesn't make my stomach twist. I love how kind she is to everyone, how she shines for everyone else, but still has a fight in her that she doesn't want you to see, that makes me feel lucky when I do.

Maren lifts her chin so she can skirt her hand to my rib cage and trace my tattoo with her fingertip. "That doesn't make you him or your mom," she whispers.

"Maybe not, but I made Gwen work for it, pushed her to make the first move, because I never would. No matter how badly I wanted her, the buzz I got from seeing how far she'd go was fun. It's funny though because I knew she didn't really want *me*. She wanted to say she had me. She wanted me because she thought I'd go pro.

"And sure, eventually I let Gwen have me. She was my first crush after all, and I'd take her on any terms. Then I became so consumed with her she broke up with me because I was too much, too obsessed with her. I talked about my mom, my family, stupidly thinking that my mom would never relapse. I lost the mystery she was chasing, which I've dealt with for a decade now. It's hard for me to trust people in the first place and being a professional athlete makes it even harder. Women see me as a lifestyle. They want to be the one I fall in love with, but none of them actually want *me*. They see what I have, what I can give them, and I'm the little inconvenience they have to accept to get it. Luckily, I don't care enough, and I don't want to share my personal life with people, so it works for everyone for a while. It taught me what I'm good for though, and it's not relationships."

"Locke," Maren says softly, "you're worth so much more than that, than all of the things you own, no matter how well you can hit a golf ball. And maybe some girls don't want that but some women do—the head over heels, I can't think straight, I'd do anything and everything just to kiss you right now, she's *mine* type of love. Some women know what it feels like to always come in second place."

I sweep her hair back and lift my shoulders off the bed to kiss her. "Is that what you want?" I ask, rolling us over and pinning her to the bed. "Someone who's obsessed with you?"

Her green eyes pop as her pupils contract then expand. She nods, her breathing heavy underneath me like she's trying to push back against me.

I can feel her pulse racing in her wrists above her head where I have them in a tight grip.

"Put your weight on me," she asks.

Taking the weight off my forearms, I let my body drop further onto hers as I slide my cock into her.

She moans out my name. I've never felt anything more perfect, heard anything more beautiful, seen anything more gorgeous.

Everywhere—my heart, my brain, my nerves—is shot. Blackened and deadened from the sudden shock.

"How can anyone not be obsessed with you?" I whisper into her neck.

She nibbles on my earlobe, bites it, before she gasps when I push myself into her fully. "More," she pleads, digging her nails into my back.

Like I'm playing a role: the guy who gets her off on her praise kink.

To her, I'm the guy who doesn't mean the things he's saying. To me, I can't explain it because I've never felt this way before, but I do mean it. Even if I don't understand it.

I press my forehead against hers. Our eyes are an inch apart, and there's nowhere else to look. "You don't even know, Maren. I would do anything for you. The lengths I would go to keep you happy and safe and loved, keep you coming on my dick every night." Her legs shake. A *fuck* falls out of her mouth under her breath when I slam into her as deep as I can. "You feel how good you fit around me? You're a fucking treasure. You're out of my league. I mean it when I tell you you're *my* good girl, and it would be a fucking privilege if you were obsessed with *me.*"

I kiss her hard. She kisses harder back.

We're trading groans into each other's mouths until we're both coming together, sweaty and wild.

It feels real, raw, and for a second, I think I see the same feeling in her eyes blazing back at me before it quickly goes out.

THE SESSION
Maren

I STEP BACK AND admire the now light-yellow accent wall of my old room—I mean, my nephew's room.

We've been painting for hours, and my arms hurt after lifting a paint roller above my head on top of carrying two heavy cameras all day.

"This is the perfect shade," I smile.

Camille nods in excitement. "I knew it would be." Her shoulders fall when she looks at the crib, which is in a million disassembled pieces in the corner. "Now this crib, on the other hand. How long do you think this will take?"

"Suspicious that Parker is conveniently out of town when this thing arrived," I tease. "What do doctors even have to travel for work for?"

"Right." Camille narrows her eyes. "That orthopedic surgery conference he booked a year and a half ago. He *knew.*"

"We shouldn't have promised this room would be done when he got back, even though we've been procrastinating. What's another couple of months?" I joke, crouching down and picking up an L-shaped tool. "What is this?"

"Pliers?" she guesses. "Oh, an Allen wrench."

"Okay," I say, sitting back on my heels and mimicking how I assume it's used. "I can twist."

Camille sits on her new trendy brown pouf and spreads the five-page (front and back) instructions out across her belly. "Find piece A."

My eyebrows pinch at her bossy tone. "Is this the dynamic we're going to have?"

"I can't twist," she says, imitating me sarcastically, "or I'll hurt baby boy."

I roll my eyes as I search for a light brown piece labeled with an A sticker. "What's the latest name list?"

"Finn, Noah, and Parker Junior."

"I still like Finn," I pout.

She smiles. "I think Parker Graham Blanchard, Jr. is going to win. I like thinking he'll be just like his daddy."

"What if he doesn't want to be a doctor?" I question her.

"He can be whatever he wants to be. We'll support him no matter what."

"Good answer," I quip.

Camille isn't going to fail at motherhood, just like she doesn't fail at anything else. Not that our mom did, but she doesn't support photography, my passion, or anything that makes me happy in general. I wish I knew why because I think it would help me understand her better. But I don't think I could ever gain the courage to ask. I'd be afraid her answer wouldn't satisfy me.

Holding up the long and skinny piece A like a trophy, I ask Camille, "What does it connect to?"

She tuts like I'm an idiot. "B." I search the pile in silence for a minute until she asks, "What about your photography business?"

"You're my only client," I say, "and it wouldn't be a good look for my one review to be from my sister."

"You need a website," she says.

"I dunno." I shrug. "Maybe. I'm taking photos of Locke's aunt and his niece tomorrow evening."

"Maren!" Camille gasps, eyes bright. "That's amazing. Why didn't you say anything?"

"Let's see how it goes first. She's just being nice."

"She's not just *being nice*. People aren't just *being nice* when they tell you your photographs are fucking good."

"I'm not naive," I groan, fitting my new B piece that looks like a slat for the bottom into the first set of holes in A. I start twisting away with my Allen wrench. "I want people that don't know me to tell me."

After I've screwed every slat into piece A and set aside the bottom of the crib, Camille joins me on the floor to help me find the side railings.

I try to ignore the buzz of a text message in the corner where I threw my phone—and Camille's multiple sidelong glances—but I'm itching to run and pick it up, even though I know I shouldn't. I know I shouldn't feel this way.

I last six twists of an Allen wrench.

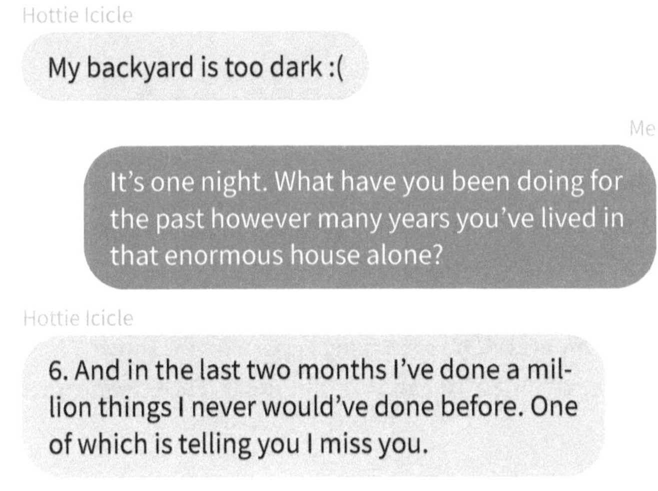

"Having fun?"

I look up into Camille's smirking face, now acutely aware that I'm grinning too wide.

My smile falls as I toss my phone down beside me. "Yeah," I sigh, "but I need to stop."

"Why?" she asks, exasperated. I busy myself by opening a bag of screws. "Maren, you're allowed to have fun. You can do things for yourself sometimes."

"Something happened last night," I admit.

She folds her lips into her smile and raises her eyebrows in mock surprise.

"I mean, something different," I add. "On top of that." I can't look Camille in the eye, so I crawl back to the pile and start sorting identical pieces together. "I pretended it was real. I imagined that Locke actually liked me, that I was his girlfriend. It *felt* real, Camille."

"It's okay if it's real," she counters.

"It's not. I said I wouldn't let my feelings get in the way, and now, here they are. I couldn't even last a month and a half. I'm pathetic."

"It's not pathetic to care."

I scoff. "It is when you set out to do the opposite."

Camille opens her mouth, hesitates, then closes it.

"What?" I question her.

"You obviously haven't cared about looking at the internet lately," she says, "or watching that stupid reality show."

"Is there something on the internet I should be aware of?" I ask, narrowing my eyes. "Did something happen on the show?"

She shrugs. "I mean, yes and no. The usual. There are pictures."

"Of?"

"Things."

"Like?"

She waves her hand airily. "You and Locke in the car. You and Locke talking, walking on the course, smiling and laughing with each other. You and Locke playing golf together. You and Locke kissing. Was he taking pictures of you?"

I blink. My mind flip-flops, wondering who was taking photos of us (not that it really matters), then one harsh laugh comes out of my mouth. "People are nuts. People thought we were dating when I'd literally had one conversation with him. People thought we were dating when we went to dinner together professionally. People thought we were dating when we kissed once and he walked away, when I moved into his guest house, when we became friends with benefits. And guess what? We're *still* not dating. No one is right, and no one knows anything. I literally don't care. People can think whatever they want because they're all wrong. It's not like they have any idea what is actually happening in my life, but sure, let them pretend like they do. I'm tired of worrying about other people."

"My point exactly!" Camille exclaims. "You don't care about the right things. Maren, you've been this carefree human the last few weeks, and I love it. But you should still care about the things that matter. It's okay if you like him."

"I can't," I say, trying to convince myself mostly. "That was the deal. He doesn't want a girlfriend, but then he's suddenly opening up to me like I am one. He's telling me things. Personal things I don't think people know. He's asking me about myself like he wants to get to know me. He knows how to keep his sex life separate. And now I'm left wondering if he's messing with me, playing me like a game."

I'm the mouse—dangling from his paw by my tail as he watches me wiggle and fight for my life helplessly.

Camille stares at me while I try to fit the wrong screw into a hole. "What if *he* likes *you*?"

"Ha," I sputter. "You think I have imposter syndrome about being a photographer? I wouldn't even know what to call myself as Locke's girlfriend. A joke?"

My stomach turns heavy and drops like a rock. I've never considered the fact that Locke is probably telling Conrad all about me. Maybe they're laughing at me behind my back while Locke recalls every position he's had me in.

Heat unfurls across my cheeks, feeling like an inexperienced and childish thirteen-year-old. I can't imagine the things Conrad probably now knows, especially with all the curious attention he's given me.

Camille sighs when I continue, "I don't want to talk about it anymore. Can we just finish this and then watch a rom-com please?" before she nods.

I've been missing this—just me and her. The girl time. I have no friends to talk to anymore, but whatever I said to them would just travel along the grapevine and make its way back to Russ if I did. For some reason though, I still don't want to talk to Camille. I'm on an island alone—in both a good and bad way.

I snatch the instructions out of her hand and flatten it out on the floor in front of me. I stare, holding back the tears wanting to push through. It takes me reading the first two lines and over twenty seconds of pure confusion before I realize I'm looking at the instructions in French.

In the tiniest moment of weakness, I pick up my phone and google Locke Hughes.

The first article has a photo of him kissing my wrist at the golf range yesterday. It only shows the back of my head, but the first thing I notice is Locke's dark eyes—how trained they are on my face, like he can't look away. It's every bit as vehement as I remember.

The headline reads: Locke In Love.

I wonder what the headline would be if the world actually knew the truth.

I TRULY WISH I could do this every day—instead of following men around as they swing clubs and try to hit a tiny ball into a tiny hole.

Emmie is the cutest mini-human to ever exist (I'll reevaluate when Parker, Jr. is born) in her ruffled blush pink dress and white monogrammed bloomers. I'd eat her cheeks in the un-creepiest way possible.

I adjust the bow on her white headband and step back.

Elise looks equally as stunning barefoot in a white maxi dress, and Emmie is the most happy and comfortable babbling baby in her arms.

I want to wrap this feeling around me tight. The sun setting perfectly above the water. The light casting over Elise's and Emmie's smiles. The way Blake coos and then jumps up and down behind me when I want Emmie to look at the camera. I haven't clicked the shutter this many times in months.

These are the little moments of life I want to capture and allow people to cherish—not the moment a golf ball rolls into a hole or when a golfer is in their backswing.

I want people's memories to live forever on their walls, in picture frames on the mantle. I'd be responsible for bringing someone joy.

Honestly, it's like a people pleaser's wet dream, and my career dream wrapped into one.

As Elise spins, I snap a few before I tell them, "Now, walk toward me."

I back up a few feet slowly to let Elise take her time. Every minute I have to stop to make sure I've gotten some good ones, and then I proceed to gush about just how damn good they are.

"Elise! I can't wait to start editing these. You look beautiful. Okay, put Emmie down on the blanket," I instruct her.

With Emmie on her back on the white blanket I laid down in the grass, she kicks her feet into the air and sucks on her toes.

"Someone discovered their toes," I murmur in my baby voice.

Conrad, sitting on the porch behind me, chuckles. I haven't been able to look him in the eye. For the last hour, he's just been staying around the perimeter of this bubble, watching, observing, *judging*.

Since I slept at Camille's last night, Locke and I took separate cars to the tournament today, and when I made it back home, his family was already here.

Instead of sticking around to watch the fuss, Locke took off on his golf cart to practice.

After snapping a million and one pictures of Emmie kicking happily, I motion to the back porch steps. "I'd love to take some of the whole family if that's okay."

"Why do you think I look like this?" Blake says, laughing. She looks sun-kissed and ready in a flowing white shirt and jeans. "I was hoping you'd ask."

Conrad smirks at her as he rises from the black wicker chair. "You're lucky Maren is so nice." When he sits beside Blake, he drapes an arm over her shoulder and kisses her temple before looking back at me. "Actually, we all got lucky Locke likes you so much."

Blake pipes up before I can since my tongue is now lead. "Psh, no, I think we're lucky you like Locke so much. We're obsessed with you *almost* as much as he is."

"Oh," I choke, then cough out, "No, it's not that. Us. We're not an us. You know. I just needed a place to live."

"Like Locke would do that for just anybody," she says, amused.

I laugh uncomfortably. "Don't believe everything you read."

...or see with your own two eyes?

Jesus. Stop talking.

There are pictures of us kissing—what the hell must they think about me? I can only imagine the comments under those pictures. It's not the internet strangers' opinions I care about though. I care about what Locke's family thinks of me. Do they think I'm a gold digger? A groupie? And why do I suddenly care?

Blake guffaws, but Conrad rubs his hand over his mouth like he's rethinking what he said.

Elise is silently kissing the top of Emmie's head, who is babbling incoherently, while she peers at me like I'm the Mona Lisa and she can't quite find my eye line.

I'm not sure where to look myself. They're all smiling at me like I'm God's gift to Locke, so I just shove my face into the camera to cover the embarrassment taking over my cheeks.

They pose for me, but I already know I'll love the ones where they're passing Emmie around, kissing her, laughing when she drools the most.

I wish Locke was here so I could capture his dimples.

No, no I don't, I tell myself.

When we're done, I smile from ear to ear. I'm already itching to get back to my computer and start editing these.

Instead, I corner Conrad before he can make his way inside. "Whatever he said," I start with a deep breath, "or told you..." I will the blush to stay away, which only deepens it faster, more intensely.

Conrad studies me for a beat. "He hasn't told me anything. Locke isn't like that."

My heart slows, but Conrad keeps watching me with a serious upward curve of an eyebrow, like every twitch I make makes him more and more curious about me.

Just as I'm about to retort, he cuts me off.

"My guess is he hasn't figured it out himself yet either. Just so you know."

He disappears through the door before I can ask him what the hell that means, so I turn on my heel, more confused than ever. But all I want to do is lie in my bed with my laptop and make these photos even more gorgeous.

I follow the path through the palm trees slowly, flipping through my camera. When I make the last curve, I look up to see Locke lining up a putt on the hole in front of his guest house.

He's concentrating so much that he didn't hear my footsteps. I stand completely still as he crouches and studies the twelve-foot gap between him and the hole. He's probably played this six-hole course a thousand times, and yet he's still taking three practice swings and crouching again.

When he finally steps up for his actual putt, on instinct, I raise my camera and take a picture of him.

Locke snaps his head in my direction just as his club taps the ball.

I gasp under my breath. He *can* hear my shutter.

But Locke doesn't look mad. A smile radiates across his face, dimples pinching his cheeks, and he doesn't even look to see if his ball rolled into the hole.

Is it possible that he *does* like me?

"Hey," he says, letting his golf club fall to the ground before walking toward me.

My nervous system ticks up, blood speeding through my veins. My stomach loops. My heart squeezes.

Fuck.

That was the hottest fucking thing I've ever seen—him dropping his club like he doesn't have a care in the world besides me.

And double fuck, I *definitely* like him.

THE FALL
Locke

Maren's camera falls to her waist, hanging from the strap around her neck. I wrap my hand around her throat and pull her into a kiss.

Her hands grasp my forearm, almost like she's telling me to squeeze harder.

"God, Locke. That was even hotter," she says into my mouth, standing on her tiptoes to kiss me harder.

I pull back and whisper, "What?"

"Nothing," she says, dazed.

"I missed you last night. Your texts aren't enough," I say, brushing my thumbs along her jaw. Her lips part a millimeter, a glow emanating from her face. My pulse skips. "You look happy. I should've stuck around to watch you take the pictures you love. I'd like to see what you look like when you're actually enjoying yourself as a photographer. Will you come have dinner with us?"

She blinks, eyes glassy like she's just woken up.

"I have... want to," she stutters, "edit these photographs for your aunt."

"Okay." My voice sounds more even and nonchalant than I feel. An uneasiness thrums along my veins. "Come over if you get bored or change your mind."

Maren nods, promises me if she does, she will, and then leaves me standing here alone, wishing I could drag her out of her house and throw her over my shoulder.

The door clicks closed, and I'm left in the setting sun, unsure what to do with myself. So, I guess I'll just leave my golf cart where it is and walk home—try to exercise out the anxiety in my nerves.

This is what it's like to lose control of your emotions. I've let my addiction to her overshadow rational thought. I cannot have her whenever the fuck I feel like it, and she doesn't want me monopolizing her time. She isn't *mine*, no matter how many times I've said it. I'll obsess over her in silence, suffer through the withdrawal.

When I step back into my living room, my phone buzzes in my pocket.

Maren

> I freaked out. I don't know how to handle whatever your family thinks about me.

Me

> What do you mean? They love you.

What I really want to say is:
Come back.
They love you more than they love me.
I'll protect you.
My phone goes back in my pocket where it belongs before I text something stupid.

"Where's Maren?" Conrad asks, walking in from the kitchen, beer in hand, and sitting down on the couch.

I snatch the beer and sit in the chair across from him. "Did you say something to her?"

"Okayyyy," he says, looking at his empty hands and shrugging. "And no, just that we're happy how much you like each other."

My knuckles turn white against the brown bottle. "Are you trying to freak her out?"

Conrad clasps his hands together and lets out a breath. "Am I freaking *you* out?"

"No idea what you're talking about," I say, throwing back the beer and chugging.

He sighs. "You're going to ruin this, Locke, if you don't admit it to yourself."

I glare at him. If he thinks I haven't recognized the situation I've put myself in, then he's not paying attention. I swipe a thumb over the condensation on my bottle, watch a drop zigzag down and cling to the bottom edge before it falls to the ground.

"I'm fully aware of my predicament," I say. "Somehow, I've stayed away from alcohol and drugs. But if it's not those, then it's golf. And when I want to slow down, it becomes a person. I can't escape it, Conrad."

"I've watched you watching her for the last few weeks. This is different. Maren is different."

"Look," I say. "I'm trying to control my feelings and using every ounce of self-control I have. Every day I feel like I've lost it. I'm going out of my fucking mind."

"You're letting her in," he sighs. "You were jealous of another man hitting on her, and now you feel vulnerable. You don't usually let that happen."

With his elbows on his knees, Conrad hangs his head when Elise and Blake traipse through the living room on their way to the kitchen. They both beam at me. Elise winks.

"Do you have a point?" I ask, turning back to him.

Conrad's shoulders rise and fall as he takes a deep breath before he looks back at me. His eyes hold steady, almost like he's daring me to look away. "I'm watching you fall in love with someone before my eyes, and you think it's because you're addicted to her."

I'VE ENDED UP OUTSIDE of Maren's door to prove to myself that Conrad's full of shit.

But after I knock, wait anxiously, panic for a minute that she's not home, before she finally opens her door, I know the real reason why I showed up on her doorstep as soon as I see her smile.

It's one of surprise, but also genuine happiness that I'm here.

"Hey," she says. "How was dinner?"

"Exhausting," I tell her. So exhausting I've been tossing and turning in bed for over an hour.

"It's late. You should get some sleep for the last day of the tournament tomorrow."

And the real reason I came. "I don't want to sleep alone."

Her hesitancy washes over me like she poured a bucket of nails on top of me. The sting starts in my brain and cascades down to my feet.

"I'm sorry if I woke you up," I say abruptly, words stilted.

Her eyebrows quirk. "You didn't. I've been in major editing mode. I didn't even know what time it was until you knocked and scared me." Then she seems to realize at this moment that I'm in my boxers. "Where are your clothes?" she asks, eyes stuck to my torso. A hint of a smile tugs at the corner of her lips when she sees my tattoo again.

I shrug. "I put these on to walk over here, and I walked over here because I want to be next to you when I fall asleep."

It's that simple. Nothing more to it.

Now, have I ever had a thought like that about a woman before? No.

"You look tired," she says, reaching out and taking my hand to pull me into the doorway.

"Ouch," I tease, folding my body around her. Relief stretching across my chest.

Maren melds, tucking herself into me and making it easy for me to maneuver her. I pick her up around her thighs, wrap them around my waist, and carry her up the stairs.

She throws her arms around my neck, scrunches her nose, and whispers, "Hot but tired."

I click my tongue before I bite her earlobe.

"Locke," she giggles.

When I make it up to the loft bedroom, I crawl on my knees to the middle of the bed and scoot Maren's laptop over.

Her screen comes to life and illuminates brightly in the dark room with the picture she took of me putting earlier.

"You're editing my picture." I smile and allow my heart to warm as I place her down under the covers. Maren quickly rolls over, cheeks pink, and shuts the laptop before she sets it on the nightstand.

"I can't believe you can actually hear my shutter. I thought you were lying," she says.

"God," I chuckle. "It used to annoy the shit out of me."

She narrows her eyes at me. "I knew you hated me."

"I never hated you," I say. "I hate having my picture taken. Clear distinction."

"Sure," she jokes, rolling her eyes.

"I don't hate it anymore as long as you're the photographer. I like knowing you're close, watching me." I tangle my feet with hers and close my eyes. "Bore me to sleep and tell me about your cameras. Why're you always carrying two?"

"The exciting world of cameras and lenses," she laughs, locking her body into mine. "Sometimes I have to stand *very* far away according to picky professional athletes, so I need a telephoto lens. You don't really want to hear about it. I was trying so hard to not talk so much when I was showing you how to photograph me golfing. It's hard to shut up when you love something so much."

"But I do," I say seriously, holding her tighter. "I want to know everything about you."

She pauses, and I wait patiently with my eyes still closed. Her voice starts slow and then falls into a comfortable rhythm, excitement ticking through her tone.

"Telephoto lenses capture an object and bring it closer using a long focal length, so that's my camera with the huge lens. Other important factors: shutter speed is how fast a camera takes a picture. Motor speed is how fast a camera lens can focus. Even though golf is slow as shit, you swing your club like one hundred and twenty miles per hour. Golf ball speeds can average over one hundred and fifty. So, depending on the shot I'm taking, I need all those things to get the best photos."

"Yours are the best, you know," I tell her. "I've been looking for them now. In the newspaper. Online. I hunt for your little alliteration beneath every photo, but I think I've gotten good at picking yours out as soon as I see them. Something about your angles."

Maren doesn't reply, and I fight the urge to open my eyes to see if she's staring at me like I'm crazy. I feel crazy. I can see Maren in photographs she's not even in—photos of myself, and Russ, and Landon, and a hundred other golfers. She pours herself into them, takes each one with a little bit of love.

But at least she's still here, wrapped up in my arms. At least she still wants me near her.

At least I won't be crawling out of my skin tonight because she decided enough is enough. Right now, I just want to be existing with her on the verge of sleep.

"Locke?" she whispers eventually.

"Maren," I whisper back.

"Are we still fake friends?"

My eyelids flutter open, but Maren's are closed. Like maybe she's scared of the dark and doesn't want to see it. Whatever *this* is. I trail my thumb across her cheekbone before I lift my head to kiss her lightly on the lips.

"No, but I don't know when this stopped being fake."

THE DECLARATION
Maren

TWO THINGS I'M GOING to do:

1. Not freak out.

2. Remain professional.

Because I'm still left wondering: if I openly like Locke, will this all come crashing down around me? I could make one wrong move, say one wrong thing, and destroy everything.

God, but I'm so happy—for him.

I'm happy *for him* because I didn't do anything.

It's Locke who won the tournament. He puts in the time and the work. He has the drive.

It's me who simply takes pictures of him.

But at the same time, I can't help the selfish little hole in my stomach that screams I have more of a right to be happy than these strangers. Everyone around me is clapping for him and calling his name and whispering about his eagle on the seventeenth hole.

It's also me who feels like I *know* him now, who thought he was a completely different person. Maybe I'm suddenly the lucky one. Maybe he's etched me as a blip into his tiny circle, and I get the rare pleasure of seeing the real him.

It's also Locke who's smiling at me as he stands there awkwardly waiting for the trophy presentation to start.

I've pulled more smiles from this man in the last two months than the last six years I've had this job combined, and I have no idea how, other than wanting something for myself.

The trophy, a cup-looking shape made completely of glass and shimmering in the sun, sits next to him on a black podium.

Locke's face turns back to a slight scowl as soon as the television cameraman steps up to start recording.

After the president makes his speech congratulating Locke, I snap photos of them shaking hands and Locke holding up the cup in front of his chest.

He's not looking directly into the camera. Instead, his eye line is just an inch off, always on my face in some capacity.

When I straighten, he places the trophy back on the podium and strides toward me with long steps. Skirting around my tripod and making me squeal like a silly girl, he picks me up with his arms around my waist.

I don't know whether to laugh or hide my face. "Locke!" I exclaim somewhere in between. "Congratulations!"

"Winning is much more fun with you," he says, planting a kiss on the side of my neck. "Take a picture with me."

"I got them all," I promise, brushing a fingertip over his left dimple. "They're perfect. All the angles."

"No, *with* me." He roves his eyes across my face and drops his voice. "Please."

I nod, before I can second guess the thoughts whirling in my head, and whisper, "Sure."

Locke slides me back down to my feet. "Jeffrey," he calls, "will you take our picture?"

It takes everything within me not to swivel my head to determine who's staring and who's got their phone camera trained on us. Not that any of them know me or care to know me.

He leads me back to the podium by the hand, fingers intertwined with mine, before he throws his arm around my shoulder and brings me in tight.

This feels like a declaration.

For now, I'm not going to overthink. I'm going to allow myself this moment, this day, this week. Whatever. However long it lasts. I've already screwed it up.

I wrap my arms around his waist. Locke buries his face in my hair and kisses my temple.

Jeffrey winks at us before he starts snapping away like we're rare birds. I swear I hear him mutter something about *lovebirds* behind his camera and chuckle to himself.

"Your face was made to be in front of a camera," I tease, looking up and sticking out my tongue. "Smile."

"My smiles are yours," he whispers into my ear.

AFTER THE TROPHY PRESENTATION, it's a jumbled crowd pushing along the path into the clubhouse.

Locke and I are separated when the path splits so he can walk in the back door to get ready for the press conference.

When I set up next to Jeffrey inside the banquet room, he looks at me a little too long.

"Don't say anything."

"I didn't."

"Yeah, but don't."

"I won't," he confirms, holding back a smile with the slightest twitch of his lip. "No more birding jokes."

As soon as I turn toward the table, I know one person who will definitely say something: Russ.

His eyes are fueled by hate watching Locke sit on the other end of the table. Locke looks completely oblivious and unaffected.

I wish I could disappear into the wall. Just flatten my back and become the paint. I want nothing to do with whatever I think Russell is going to do or say.

How can I possibly feel bad? I don't want to make *him* feel bad.

The amount of times I had to listen to him bitch and compare himself to Locke is one hundred times too many.

There has always been something about him that gets under Russ' skin.

He'd come home annoyed that he was paired with him all day, that Locke won, or that he had to film a commercial with him or attend the same function as him.

"What'd he do?" I'd ask Russ empathetically.

"Nothing," he'd huff. "He didn't do anything."

Silly me. I used to think Russ didn't want to talk about it, so I'd back off. Now, I realize he meant it literally.

Locke was doing *nothing*, other than not caring, which just made Russ madder.

"Alright," a reporter starts. "Congratulations to Locke Hughes, the winner of this year's Palm Beach tournament, and runner-up Russell Ashe, who both join us now. Locke, let's start with you. That eagle. What was going through your mind on that swing?"

His eyes flick to mine so quickly that I second guess what I saw. "That Conrad, my caddie, better be right. Which he is ninety-nine percent of the time."

Half the room chuckles.

"Russell," another speaks up, "you battled back from sixth to second. That was some amazing golf."

"Just not amazing enough," Russ sneers. "But who could ever compete with Locke Hughes?"

The next reporter pounces. "This dynamic you've both found yourself in. Are you able to compartmentalize and leave your personal issues off the course?"

"I have nothing to compartmentalize with regards to Russell," Locke says.

After four mundane questions about golf, one reporter steers back to personal territory. "Russell, with the season finale of *Triple Bogey* airing this week, how are you feeling, and will you be renewing for a second season?"

"Bittersweet, I think," he replies. "I'm ready for a break, but this past year has been one of the best and hardest of my life." His eyes find mine in the back of the room. "But I think in a couple of months, it will be even better, and we'll be back gracing your television screen."

We. I almost laugh out loud. There will be no Russ-Maren *we*, even when Locke is sick of me, because I'm sick of the Russ-Maren game.

The same reporter turns to Locke. "And Locke, we've now gotten a glimpse of your life behind the scenes for the first time in your professional career. How—"

"My personal life will continue being my personal life," Locke interrupts him before he throws a sidelong glance at Russ, "well past the next couple of months. Let's keep the questions pertaining to golf."

"Where's the fun in that?" Russ quips.

The other half of the room chuckles.

When the press conference is over, Russ holds his hand over his microphone and leans to his side to get as close to Locke as possible on the other end of the table.

Locke flattens his microphone against the table and wraps a fist around the end.

They exchange inaudible words. Looks. One fist on a table. And then Locke pushes his chair back and strides off.

Screw golf. This feels like a game of chess.

Two kings battling it out with their own strategy. One always on relentless offense, the other playing strong defense. And we're all their little pawns being used and discarded.

◯◯◯

Hours later when I open my front door to the sound of a knock, I blink at the sight of Locke in a tuxedo on my welcome mat.

"Why do you look like that?" I question him before I look over his shoulder and lower my voice. "Are we role playing?"

He smirks. "The charity auction."

"I forgot," I say, squeezing my eyes shut.

"Forgot?!" he teases. "We talked about it earlier on the way home."

"Well, I *may* have picked up my laptop and started editing your family's photos, which then led me to forget that time existed."

Locke tsks playfully and sweeps me off my feet as he steps across the threshold of my door. "Is that why you're ignoring my texts?"

When he sees my phone charging on the kitchen counter, he detours to allow me to pick it up before he proceeds to carry me up the stairs.

Hottie Icicle

Have you ever seen an icicle in a tuxedo?

It's hot.

:)

I look up and laugh. "Who are you?"

"You like what you see. Admit it. I saw your eyes almost bulge out of your head when you opened the door."

I bite my lip in protest and throw my phone on the bed as we pass. Locke places me back on my feet only when we navigate through the bathroom and into the walk-in closet.

He pulls my T-shirt off over my head and tugs my leggings down. He bends down to his knees, so I use his shoulders to keep myself balanced as he slips each pant leg off. Then he rustles around in the top drawer of the closet island to find me a thong.

Determined, sweet, purposeful. He's very many things.

"What did Russ say to you earlier when no one could hear you at the end?" I ask, curiosity overpowering.

"Nothing. He's an asshole," Locke scoffs and bends back down to kiss my knee. "Don't worry about it." He chuckles when I sigh, because he knows that's the last thing I'll probably do. "In the absolute nicest way I can put it, he told me he'll win in the end."

"Locke," I say, amused, "you're a million times better at golf than he is."

His hand runs up my inner thigh before I step into the underwear he pulled out for me. "He wasn't talking about golf."

"Oh," I breathe. My mind stretches into infinite directions wondering how Russ tried to tear down both of us at the same time before I laser in on one thought. "What did you say back?"

Locke pulls the nude satin thong up, but not before licking me once, slowly, like he wants the taste of me on his tongue the rest of the night. "That he will never touch you again."

My legs wobble as my heart beats wildly into my throat. This man is dressing me—pressing, imprinting himself on my heart.

"You're not..." I start, barely a whisper. Maybe I know it's a ridiculous thought as soon as I think it, but that doesn't stop me. "This isn't, like, a test?" Locke furrows his eyebrows, but I've said it now, and I need to keep going. "You're not playing a game with yourself to see if I don't give a shit. You're not trying to see if you can make me care or like you. Like you're timing me, or timing yourself to see how long it takes for me to fall for you. Right?"

He bores his eyes into mine. "You don't actually think that, do you? That I'd do something like that to you?"

"No," I insist, my cheeks heating. "I don't know. I feel insecure, Locke."

Exposed. Vulnerable. Defenseless. I'm very many things too, but strong isn't one that comes to mind first.

He could squish me underneath his heel without a second thought, but for me, it would cause lasting effects. I'm realizing now I've already given him too much of me.

"I would never intentionally hurt you, Maren."

"And unintentionally?" I ask, running my hands through his hair.

"I don't know," he says as he stands. "I've never felt like this. I do know I would inject you straight into my veins if I could."

I tip my face up toward his, resting my hands against the island. "Why do you talk about me like you're addicted to me?"

"Because I am," he growls, hoisting me to sit on top of it. "I'm fucking obsessed with you. Does that scare you?"

"No," I insist. "I like the way you look at me, like you want me all for yourself. I want all-consuming."

"*You* are all-consuming. You consume my thoughts, and I would watch my life go up in flames just to have the smallest piece of you." He nips at my ear before he pulls my head back, forcing me to look up at the ceiling and straight into a can light. Locke sucks my throat so hard he's going to leave a hickey. "You think I want to get jealous when another man talks to you? You think I want to worry about you getting scared of the dark? I didn't set out to get to know you. I wanted to escape from my life for a little while. I wanted peace and quiet. But now, I want you above everything else."

"Locke, I didn't think you cared," I breathe into the air. My eyesight has been glazed by the bright light, and all I see now is a halo of white. "I've been trying not to care. But it's not as easy for me."

His mouth drops to my boobs, and he sinks his teeth into one before he continues to suck my skin so hard there will be dark hickeys across my chest, marking me as his. I try to grind my pussy against him, but he holds my hips firm before he drops his face and bites one.

"You've altered my brain chemistry." Goosebumps prickle everywhere when he inspects his teeth marks, looking satisfied at the deep grooves he's made. "I care," he says hoarsely, his face now between my legs. "I care because I like you."

Another hickey blooms on my inner thigh from the suction he applies. I'll be black and blue when he's done with me, but I'm actually smiling at the thought. The whole world will know who I belong to.

"God, Locke," I moan. "I like you. Us. This."

I'm not sure I've ever liked anything more.

"I take care of what's mine," he says gruffly before he switches thighs. This time sucking even harder.

He backs up, leaving me cold without his touch, and runs his eyes along the dresses on the right wall before he finds the only formal floor-length dress I own: a sexy navy strapless number that's tight around the bust and waist before flowing perfectly down to my feet.

Locke slips it off the hanger and unzips it. I step into it when he holds it out for me.

I stand in front of the mirror and twirl to give him access to the zipper again, but he brushes my hair to the side. At the nape of my neck, he raises the darkest purple from under my skin.

"Don't cover that one up," he whispers, eyes black and locked to mine in the mirror as he zips my dress. "I want to be able to see it whenever I want."

THE AUCTION
Locke

I'M AN ASSHOLE FOR dotting Maren's skin with hickeys. But at least I never claimed to *not* be one.

She didn't have to spend time covering the ones on her inner thighs, so we're not that late.

And besides, I love that I can see the one on the back of her neck when she turns her head a little too quickly to survey the room.

I cradle my hand around her throat, letting my thumb rest on top of it, as she swivels her head to take in the room.

This building was converted into a hotel last year after it sat abandoned for decades, and the restoration makes it look like it straddles the elegant 1920s and modern twenty-first century with its exposed brick walls, floor-to-ceiling arched windows, and huge shimmering chandeliers.

The band on stage in the center is singing a low-key song without words as everyone finds their seats.

"What would you like to drink?" I ask, leading her to our round table near the front marked with a RESERVED sign.

Maren sits down in a gold chair and crosses her legs. "Champagne, please."

I press my lips to hers and kiss her across the top of her shoulder, breathing in the strawberry scent of her skin. When I straighten, Russell, from four tables behind us, stares at me over the whiskey glass he's sipping from.

Enjoy fucking her while you have her. We both know she's nothing special, but I'll take her from you when you eventually ruin it, just because I can.

I'd love nothing more than to shove my golf club that's been up his ex-girlfriend's cunt down his throat. Let him get a taste of how special she is, because that would be the closest he'd ever get to her again.

Instead (obviously), I flick my eyes back to Maren. I can just make out the hickey buried in her cleavage. Then again, she's mine, and no one else will ever know how fucking good she is for me or get a chance to experience her like I do.

"Of course, beautiful," I whisper in her ear. "Now, sit here like a good, perfect girl and show off what I get to fuck tonight."

Her chest jumps as she inhales a sharp breath. It's not about Russell; it's about *everyone.* Anyone who thinks they can do it better than me. They can't. Anyone who thinks she's weak. She isn't.

I brush my smile along her jaw. "You're going to be wet for me all night, Maren. Get used to it because *this* is the game I want to play, and you win every time."

"You're such a tease," she sighs happily to my back when I start to walk away.

The blonde bartender watches me approach from ten yards away. Her hint of a smile tells me she'd go home with me if I made any sort of move on her. And a few months ago, I'd have zero problem indulging her with some fantasy she has about me until I got bored.

Now, it doesn't matter what, but I'd rather do *anything* else as long as it was with Maren: fuck, fight, talk, listen to camera jargon, lie there in silence and stare at the ceiling.

"What can I get for you?" she asks, her tone resting on the edge of *fuck me, please.* The tone of voice that means she knows who I am and it's not me but rather the idea of me she likes.

"Champagne and a water with lime, please."

She nods and adds a sexy "Of course," before she turns her back to make the drinks.

It's not that I don't find this woman attractive. She's tall, has a nice ass, and looks like she knows how to handle herself.

It's that I'm not interested.

Even if she threw herself at me, I don't want my hands on anyone else.

Is this what love is? Finding the person you'd choose every single time, no matter the circumstances? I've certainly never felt that way before about anyone that I wasn't related to.

And now I want to scratch my skin off where the bartender lets her fingers linger on my hand. She doesn't miss the look I level on her that says not to fucking touch me before I yank back Maren's drink.

Back at the table, Maren is patiently waiting for me while she reads the night's itinerary.

I place her champagne flute on the table next to her arm and hover my hand in front of her face. "Kiss me right here," I tell her softly, running my thumb over the spot where the bartender left her unwelcome presence.

Maren, confused but obedient, inches forward and brushes her lips along my fingers, replacing the scratchy tingle with warmth.

"Thank you," I say.

She giggles with one eyebrow raised. "You're welcome?"

As I pull my chair closer and sit beside her, Maren chokes on her first sip of champagne. Her eyes widen, and for a second, I think she's actually choking, my arms readying to grab her and do the Heimlich maneuver, until I realize two people have walked up to our table.

"Tripp," I say, doing a double-take before I stand to shake his hand.

He extends his over the table. "Locke, man. Good to see you."

Maren tries to contain another cough. Fuck, please don't tell me this is another one of Maren's ex-boyfriends, because Tripp Owens is one of the few guys I like.

She swipes at her mouth with the back of her hand, and I notice she's not looking at Tripp, but the woman beside him. Who I pray to god I haven't slept with, because she looks that familiar. I don't want to sit here the whole night with some past fling.

I rack my brain, though there's no way I've talked to her before. Her face only registers me with a soft smile. But I have no idea how I know her.

"Locke Hughes," I offer, "and this is my girlfriend, Maren."

Maren stands but apparently hasn't found her voice yet. This mysteriously familiar, stunning brunette woman has rendered her speechless for the second time since I've known her.

Or was it because I just called her my girlfriend out of nowhere? So out of nowhere that I don't know where it came from myself, or how a word I haven't uttered in over a decade slipped out of my mouth so easily.

Maren stands like a statue looking at me, her throat stuck as she chokes on words now.

"Willow," she replies as she brings Maren into a brief hug before sliding into her seat and Tripp places a white wine in front of her.

Maren comes to life like Willow shocked her heart back to baseline, her huge smile following. "Maren Murray."

"It's so nice to meet you both," Willow says. "So, are we teaming up to win something or outbidding each other in a full-on war?"

I laugh. "I'll pay good money for the football lesson with Tripp." My arm goes around Maren's shoulder, and I kiss the nape of her neck, let my fingertips glide over my little hickey. "Tripp is a former Super Bowl MVP. Do you like football as much as you like golf? I can play that too."

"About the same," Maren quips, leaning into me.

"Give me a golf lesson," Tripp scoffs, "and we'll be even. I broke eighty-five a couple months ago, and now I'm thinking I missed my calling as a professional golfer. Those birdies have me wanting to get back on the course every damn week, but how am I going to do that with my schedule?"

"Let me know when you break eighty," I joke. "Willow, what do you do?"

Maren and Tripp smother a laugh as Willow says, "I'm a musician."

My brain thuds. "Oh," I chuckle, "right."

Willow is... Willow. The same Willow who Blake went to see in concert last year. Who sells out stadiums and plays during the Super Bowl halftime show. Who I have absolutely never slept with (why the hell did I think that?), let alone met, because I'm not in the same stratosphere as her.

"This is one of those times I wish I paid attention to the internet," I add.

Willow laughs and waves a hand toward me. "I don't blame you."

"Willow!"

We collectively look up to see an event photographer decked out all in black, her brown hair piled high on her head in a messy bun, looking back at us hopefully.

"Do you mind if I take a picture of the table?" she asks.

"Of course," Willow says. "I'd be happy to."

"Oh, god," Maren says under her breath at the same time, laughing into my neck. "Is this how you feel about me?"

I kiss her temple and say, "Not anymore," just as the photographer's flash goes off. A warning would have been nice.

And as all four of us stand and smile for the camera, mine a little less wide than everyone else's, my mind is only on Maren's, hoping like hell she's not thinking about what will be all over the internet tomorrow.

THE GIRLFRIEND
Maren

I'M TAKING A PICTURE with Willow, and Locke called me his girl-friend.

I'm not even sure which one I should be freaking out about more.

Locke called me his *girlfriend*. I don't think he's said that word since he was a teenager. And I doubt he even said it much back then.

When I wake up tomorrow morning, the internet will be right for the first time in months. But whatever opinions they formed about me before won't change.

I'll never get any chance to explain myself, and if I did, they wouldn't care anyway. It'd probably have the opposite effect and dig myself into a deeper hole.

The fleeting moments where I think I should put myself first always get overridden.

One night. I'm going to give myself one night.

"Dance with me," I tell Locke when the photographer finishes her mini photo shoot.

Willow and Tripp fall back into their seats, voices hushed, smiles playing around on their lips. Both of them enjoying each other. And they probably deserve some time because they probably have very busy schedules.

Locke narrows an eye as his hand glides down my back and stops to rest on the top curve of my ass. "And what if I don't dance?"

"I don't give a shit."

When I drop my face into mock surprise, a low hum comes from his chest. A smirk crosses his face without his lips moving. His eyes spark then go black again. "That was so sexy," he rumbles, picking me up an inch off my feet.

"Locke," I giggle as he floats me to the dance floor.

"I have an internal crisis every time you do that, because I love it when you push back." His voice lowers, and it travels across my skin like tires on gravel. "But then I just want to push you even harder to your knees and fuck that bratty mouth until you gag around me."

My breath catches in my lungs. Or they just forget how to work. My pussy is in overdrive though, the thong Locke dressed me in dampening.

We stare at each other, mind-reading.

The band is in the middle of one of those songs you can choose to slow dance to or break out in full awkward body quivering.

Locke takes charge as soon as I'm back on my feet, pulling me flush against him. His left hand wraps all the way around my torso and rests on my upper rib cage. His right hand takes mine and nestles it against his chest.

"You feel incredible," he breathes.

God. I'm putty. And he knows it. I'd follow him to the ends of the Earth just to hear him compliment me. And degrade me. It's quite a welcome mindfuck.

Locke treads that fine line between telling me how he actually feels and making me wet while he does it so freaking well. This little game we're playing, I don't stand a chance. But he's right. Either way, I win.

He nudges his nose against my cheek. "Are you winning?"

I curve my body into his and nod. He's quickly hardening against my leg.

"Both of us are."

"Fuck, I wish I could feel how wet you are. I want that sexy little thong you have on as a trophy later." He pulls me against him harder. "Now, you want to dance. We're going to dance."

He smells like fresh air and leather, like his sheets and his couch and his clothes. His whole damn house. My whole damn house.

And then he leads.

"You can dance?"

"Can and do are very different things, Maren," he muses. "For instance, I *can* dance well, I just don't. I can make jokes. I can smile. I can be sweet... in my own way. I can drive people around and let them rent my house. I just don't." Locke kisses my forehead. "Except for you."

His words drop in my heart, settle at the bottom, and start fizzing.

Why me? sits on the tip of my tongue. What'd I do to get so lucky? But some things probably aren't worth asking. Some things you can never explain—they just happen to you. And sometimes the *why me?* is even a good thing—a great thing—but you're still left wondering if you deserve it.

So, I repeat softly, "Except for me," and I like the sound of it.

One scrunch of my nose gets him to smile.

"I love your freckles," he whispers.

"I love your dimples," I whisper back.

We fall into the rhythm, swaying back and forth with the occasional turn. Locke holds me just tight enough to control my body movements, and it's only us and the cadence of our breathing against each other's chests.

One song turns into two, and I never want this night to end, but eventually the band stops playing, they announce the bidding will start in ten minutes, and I need to pee.

When I open the bathroom door, I'm met with a cold white marble foyer.

The stall doors around the corner are those heavy wood that go all the way to the floor so you can't see if it's occupied or not.

Try number one and two are unsuccessful, but three is unlocked. As soon as I shut the door, muffled laughter echoes across the marble walls. I freeze when I hear "...Maren..." or Erin or Karen.

I press my forehead against the door when I hear Locke's name... or lock?

One girly voice says, "How do you think she managed that?"

"I've been eye fucking him for years. Never got so much as a reaction," another voice says with a laugh.

"You eye fuck everyone," a third joins in.

"Russ said she has no backbone. I wonder what Locke is getting out of it," the first voice says, who I now realize is Lydia.

On instinct, I straighten my back and drop my shoulders away from my ears, like I'm trying to prove to myself she's wrong.

The second girl I can't place. "Everyone's obsessed with them."

"Or hates them," Lydia adds.

The definition of the internet.

"No one hates you. Your little stunt didn't even make it on TV," number two laughs. "She was sitting with Willow. I want to be Maren or her best friend."

"You both sound like you just want something from her, and you don't even know her. She's the nicest person I've ever met," the third girl says with conviction. It's Allie, Russell's best friend's wife and high school sweetheart. "And they look really happy. Some things just happen, and it's not our business. Leave them alone."

"You're no fun."

"Or I know what it's like," Allie counters, "and she only has you to thank, Lydia."

"I should've just gone after Locke," Lydia jokes. "Maybe he'll break up with her soon."

"Since when does that stop you?" unknown girl quips back.

"You two are impossible," Allie sighs.

I sigh.

I'll never escape this. And I can't hide in this bathroom stall.

If Locke and Russ are kings, then I'm the queen—and the queen does what she wants, goes where she wants. I have all the control, even when I feel unworthy of anything, even when I'm the most vulnerable at the same time. I've always been in control, but I've allowed others to hold power over me constantly. And I need to stop letting life happen to me.

The handle clicks when I open the door, and as I step into the sink area, Lydia and I make eye contact in the mirror.

Her eyes go so wide she almost stabs herself with her mascara brush.

"Hey, Allie," I smile, stepping up to the free sink.

She smiles back and defeatedly shrugs, understanding passing between us. After I'm done washing my hands, I tear a paper towel from the dispenser and look over at Lydia.

"Allie's right," I say. "Thank you."

Lydia just watches me with stunned eyes as I walk out the door.

Around the corner, Locke almost knocks me over.

"Are you okay?" he asks. "Do you want to talk about how I called you my girlfriend? I shouldn't have just said that out of nowhere. I'm sorry."

I soothe Locke's worried frown with my finger. "I'm great, and I'm not worried about it at all. I feel the same way," I say, standing on my tiptoes to hug his neck. He relaxes against me, his anxiety physically lessening. "I do wish I wasn't in this long dress so I could climb you, though."

"If you want to wrap your legs around me, all you have to do is ask nicely," he growls, his voice coarse with lust.

I match his tone. "What if I don't want to be nice, *boyfriend*?" Locke blinks, adjusting to the word, then smirks. "Is that your kink?" I ask. "Being dominated?"

"No, not really," he answers. "But I think anything can be my kink with you. Tell me what you want."

"Good." I smile. "Because I was thinking... I want to tie you down."

His groan echoes in the empty hallway. "Apparently, I want you to tie me down."

"And I want to blast *Our Secret Cove* on the way home."

Locke's eyebrows crease. "What?"

"Willow's song," I tell him, exasperated.

He laughs. "Anything you want."

High heels clack toward us, and Locke's eyes flicker over my shoulder where Allie, Lydia, and Locke's eye-fucker must have appeared.

Maybe she's eye-fucking him now, but his gaze doesn't stray from my face for over a second.

He kisses me below my ear. "What's that about?"

"Nothing," I say breathily as his tongue swipes over my skin and creates goosebumps down my arms. "Or nothing that I really care about. Besides, I'm happy. You make me happy."

THE ROPES

Locke

Fuck, this woman.

I don't love her... right? But I love her.

She smiles at me deviously, on her knees on the floor, as she knots the rope around my left ankle tight—tighter than I thought she was capable of tying.

Instinctively, I'm fighting and pulling against the restrictiveness of it, but I'm so fucking turned on, and my brain is rolling on Maren ecstasy.

She stands, proud of herself, and lets her eyes rove every inch of my naked body. My cock twitches when Maren bites her lip in thought.

Her green eyes sparkle. "Comfy?"

"Touch me, baby, *please*," I plead, jerking my arms against the black ropes tied to this canopy bed that I'm now incredibly thankful for. "Anywhere."

I'd take my pinky toe right now.

She shakes her head. "Not yet."

I lift my head as she reaches behind her and slowly unzips her dress. My desperate dick is in the way, so I have to keep craning my neck to watch her undress.

The navy fabric puddles to the floor, and I impossibly get harder at the sight of the purple hickeys dotting her inner thighs.

She rubs a light circle over one with her thumb then trails her fingers up. "These are yours... to ruin over and over."

"Maren," I groan when she slips her long legs out of her thong. I'm going to overdose and die on her, tied to a bed and strung out on my own personal drug. "I'll be lucky if I'm the one who ruins you."

Because look at her. Russell Ashe sure as hell didn't.

She holds out her right arm and drops her underwear at her side, then repeats the motion with her bra.

When she's fully naked, I smile. "Now, be a good girl and come sit on my face."

Her lips part slightly to suck in a breath. Her abs and thighs contract. My words fluster her, no matter how much she's trying to hide it, but every millimeter her body moves is like a zap to my nerves. I wouldn't miss it if her eye twitched.

"Why don't you be a patient boy," she coos, climbing onto the bed on her knees. Her index finger lightly traces up my calf. "I'm enjoying that I have Locke Hughes tied to a bed. There's something about this feeling—having the number one golfer in the world at my mercy."

"I've always been at your mercy, Maren. You can pretend all you want that you haven't had all the power this entire time. You're the princess, like I said."

"Queen," she corrects me.

"Qu—fuck," I pant, fighting the restraints when her tongue swipes around the head of my cock just once. This game is everything and more, so I drop my voice and play back. "You're a slutty tease is what you are."

Maren grins and breathes on my aching dick, "I think you just bring out a little something extra in me."

"If I could move my arms," I say, making the bed creak, "the only sounds you'd be making would be choking on my cock."

She raises her eyebrows in a challenge. "You're going to let a little thing like ropes stop you?" Then she climbs off the bed to pick up her thong that I kept wet all night. "Do you want your trophy?"

I nod vigorously, because I already see where she's going with this, and I want the taste of her on my tongue so fucking bad. Now I wish I would have made her come earlier multiple times, soaking it even more. I'll remember next time, because whenever she wants to dominate me, I'm all in.

She's back on the bed, knees between my legs, and stuffing her wet thong into my mouth without a second thought.

Fuck, she's so sweet. And a torturous devil, because this only makes me want the real thing more.

As soon as her lips wrap around my cock, I thrust, and hot adrenaline flushes through my bloodstream. She's taking me so deep down her throat, keeping herself in total control. Saliva drips from her mouth, eyes watering, as I pump in and out. In and out. I'm fucking that mouth like I've been picturing all night, and she's taking it so well that I'm not going to let ropes stop me from doing shit.

I'm mumbling incoherently, groaning around the wet fabric in my mouth, because I'm not going to spit it out myself. It only makes this better. Turns me on even more. Makes me a fucking animal.

Eventually, though, Maren reaches up to rip it out of my mouth so she can hear the words she's being deprived of.

"Such pretty tears," I tell her when one breaks free, "for my good little whore." The edges of her lips turn up in as much of a smirk as she can manage, and she gags around me before she comes up for air.

Her hand replaces her mouth with slow strokes until I'm moaning her name under my breath. She stops, smiles. Continues. Stops. Continues. Until I'm fucking shaking. Then she drags her fingernails down my thighs as her tongue works over my balls.

"Fuck, baby, your ass is going to pay when I get out of these things," I say, imagining it red and splotchy. "Covered in my handprints."

"Promise?" she whispers, finally crawling up my body and kissing me.

"I promise you the world."

She smiles, and my heart jumps.

Then my mouth waters as she gets on her knees, and I can see her skin glistening along her inner thighs. "Now, give me that perfect pussy. Let me taste you for real."

Maren hovers over my face instead, just out of reach, so I take the opportunity to lick her arousal off her thighs. "Fuck, Maren," I plead, ravenous. The fucking wetter the better. "You taste so good." Her pussy pulses when I lick my lips, savoring it. "Give me more."

Her eyes dance. "What makes you think you deserve it?"

"Fuck," I groan, as the blood pumps heavily down my body, and I almost come. Her pussy wants to sit like it's a life or death situation, but her brain—I'm in love... with her brain. "I don't. I don't deserve anything you're willing to give me." I bite the inside of her thigh. "I'm an asshole who would keep *you* tied up in my house and make you come over and over and over for me. But I'll spend every day trying to deserve it—your thoughts, your feelings, your body. I don't know if I ever will, but I know for sure I'm the absolute fucking best at trying."

She grabs my cheeks, her pupils so blown her green eyes are almost as black as mine. Her thoughts run through them, contemplating the seriousness of what I said.

"Good answer," she says softly, then chuckles. "Now, let's shut you up."

I moan happily. "Please."

THE QUEEN
Maren

LOCKE LOOKS GOOD TIED down; starved of me, satisfied with me, like he's deliriously happy and out of his mind.

I lower myself down onto his mouth.

His hum reverberates up through my stomach, causing a new gush to coat his face.

And with every fiber stitched throughout me, I understand how fucking good it feels to dominate someone, possess them—because he's *mine*. It's beautiful to see him wet with *me* and loving it. It just doesn't feel quite as good as when I'm *his*, but this comes in a very close second, and whenever he wants to switch roles, I'll happily oblige.

I arch my back and ride Locke's face. My hands pull at the roots of his hair, holding his head right where I want it.

"This tongue is perfect," I say, when he finds that rhythm and pressure that make me gasp. "You're mine." He moans something back incoherently. I look down at him just as his eyes fall closed, like he's lost in a fantasy with traces of a smile crinkled in the corners. "Look at me when I'm being your dirty slut and watch me come."

His eyes flutter open, and they're so dark, almost bottomless, that I feel like I could tip forward and fall into them. I grab the headboard to steady myself from the lightheadedness.

He groans like I've sent him to heaven, pride bursting from the corners of his otherwise expressionless face. "Fuck," I make out from the semi-words he's muttering against my clit. His arms are straining, desperate for friction that he can't give himself.

"Locke," I moan as my orgasm builds. My hips have a mind of their own, grinding down against his mouth. My thighs shake and clench around his head. I can't look anywhere else except his eyes as I read every emotion that flicks like Morse code across his face.

And he just watches me, intensity burning like coal in his eyes stuck on mine, as I shamelessly come undone for him.

When I've regained some semblance of brain activity and lift my jelly legs, he follows with his head to take one last lick, even though his face is covered. "I could watch you come like that forever. Come back and do it again. I'll edge myself for hours for you. Just use me."

"No," I say, after consideration, shaking my head. "I want to sit somewhere else."

I slide myself down and rub my sensitive clit along his shaft. Locke sucks in a harsh breath at the contact.

"Part of me never wants this to end, but don't touch me unless you plan for me to be inside you," he warns hoarsely. His body tenses, and all the veins in his arms swell under his skin.

Instead of listening, I rock my hips to watch his eyes roll back in bliss.

"Where's all your self-control, Locke?" I whisper playfully.

"Maren," he says, voice low like he's mustering all his strength. He lifts his hips off the bed to match my tempo and grinds back. "It's going to be the pleasure of a lifetime watching you ride my cock."

Only Locke could take one sentence and make it sound beautiful and filthy at the same time.

I lift and take him in my hand, lining him up to where I'm dripping wet.

As I gradually sink down around him, he stretches me, fills me perfectly.

"Shit," we both hiss at the same time.

Immediately, I need more. More friction. More movement. More body contact.

I angle, thrusting my hips into Locke's, and wrap my hands around his neck to try to find anything more that I can.

"Fuck, play with those nipples," Locke murmurs, reading my mind.

Straightening my back, I take my breasts in my hands and throw my head back. I roll my nipples in between my thumbs and index fingers, causing a zing to radiate outward and a moan to escape my lips.

But still, I know what would feel even better.

I lean back over, cradle my hands around the back of Locke's head and bury his face into my cleavage.

He sinks his teeth into my left boob before sucking my nipple into his mouth. He's mastered the balance between soft, sweet nips and heated pain—or he's become so familiar with my body he knows exactly how to drag moans out of me.

Locke switches sides, not allowing me to go silent for longer than a second. I slow my pace, immersed completely with how deep he is, how full I feel.

"You take every inch so well," he says gruffly. "Fucking gorgeous. Use that cock to make yourself feel good." I rise and gradually lower myself back down again all the way, and Locke hums. "Good girl."

His praise twists through me, and a satisfied sigh leaves my lungs. Suddenly, slow doesn't do it for me anymore. I need it hard and fast and wild.

Locke senses my shift and tugs on a rope eagerly. "Give me one hand, baby. Just one." He smiles, all dimples, when I narrow my eyes. "I'll make it worth it."

Without bothering to stop rocking on his dick because it feels too good at this angle when he hits my clit, I untie the rope around his right wrist. I trust him completely, and I know he will make it more than worth it.

As soon as it's free, his hand is all over me. Across my boobs and stomach, cradling my hips, smacking my ass. He sweeps it up my leg and runs his thumb over my clit. Electricity jolts, molten lava pooling in my stomach at his touch. But three circles later, he abandons that plan and grasps my throat to pull my face to his.

"That's it," he tells me when my hips pick up speed at the intimacy. "Show me how much you like riding my dick like the whore we both know you are just for me."

His words brush against my lips as he talks a millimeter from my mouth. His kiss is forceful, and his tongue presses against mine in a frenzy. My entire body prickles when he sucks on my tongue.

He squeezes just enough around my neck, and my head fills with delicious pressure. "Stick out that tongue," he instructs.

When I lay it out flat, he places his middle finger down, wetting the pad of it thoroughly. Then, with his eyes never straying from mine, he runs his tongue along the tip, mixing our saliva, before his hand skates down my back and grabs my ass hard. He presses his fingers into my cheek, feeling me bounce until he spreads it, and with his wet middle finger, circles around my back entrance.

My breath hitches in anticipation against his mouth.

I've never done this, I tell Locke telepathically. He looks back in understanding. *But I want to. I want to give you everything.*

"Do you want to come with my finger in your ass?" he asks, voice deep and surprisingly earnest.

I nod before I remember my words. All of my words are his. "Yes," I whisper.

"Good," he says. "Because I want to take everything from you. I may be the one tied down, but you're mine, and I will own every part of you, Maren."

Locke tips his chin a centimeter to kiss my lips as he presses his finger into me. He swallows my moan.

This new feeling thrums along every pleasure pathway in my body, heightening my euphoria in a way I've never experienced.

"God," I moan, wanting to be his good little whore. I press back, driving his finger deeper.

He smirks. "I'm going to fuck you into this mattress, and you're going to love every second of it."

Words almost hold more power over my brain than the physical, because that takes my body up an incredible notch.

Locke and I breathe heavily, sweaty and wild, as we ride each other. I push down, he pushes up.

Our orgasms build together quickly, each of us nearing total derangement, fervor, passion—a state of being without a known definition.

"Such a good fucking girl," Locke murmurs affectionately. "Come for me, Maren."

His words push me over a ledge I never knew I could reach. This is what it feels like to fuck. To make love. To be a slut. To be used. To be appreciated. To be worshiped.

And when he starts to tremble with me, Locke catches his name moaning out of my mouth with his, and I feel him come inside me.

I'm *his*.

My entire body pulses and pulses in rapid fire at the thought until I can't take it anymore, and I collapse down on top of him.

I sure as hell won't be able to walk tomorrow, and I wasn't even the one who was tied down.

THE HOBBY
Locke

I LEAN AGAINST THE doorway of my bedroom, where Maren's been holed up and glued to her laptop for three days.

Her face is so focused, she doesn't even notice the motion in her peripheral vision.

"Are you going to let me see yet?"

Her head snaps up. "No! They're not ready yet," she says, lowering the screen like I can somehow see through the back of it.

I cross the room in four strides and lie down on my stomach across the bed, mirroring her position.

Maren slides the computer to the side and kicks her feet up into the air playfully to see if I'll copy her—which of course I do, because I'll flirt with her any chance I get.

"All the hurricane shutters are down. The wind is starting to pick up."

She motions to my huge bedroom window. "What about that one?"

"It's the strongest pane of glass in the house, coincidentally called hurricane glass."

"Thank you," she smiles. "You're the best. Is your phone charged?"

I roll my eyes. "You're the only person I'd text anyway."

"Well, mine is." She pats her laptop. "And my computer."

"We have a generator. And I'm going to see them eventually," I tease.

"Of course," she sighs. "*After* I edit them."

"Then show me Camille's maternity shoot." Maren hesitates for a split second, but I don't miss it. "What?" I question her.

"NothingImadeawebsite."

"Nothingyoumadeawebsite?"

She nods as hurriedly as her words, and a dusting of pink spreads across her cheeks. "AndanInstagram."

"Why're you embarrassed?" I ask, grinning.

"It's silly," she says, holding her palms over her cheeks.

"No," I insist, "it's amazing."

She shakes her head. "Sometimes I feel like it's just a hobby, and maybe I should keep it that way. Like maybe if I don't make it feel real, then I won't fail. People won't see me. And it's not like I have any formal training or education, so does that make me a real photographer or just a silly amateur?"

"You take pictures," I state, "so it makes you a photographer."

She squeals "Locke!" when I lift my hips off the bed and pull my phone from my front pocket. I roll over when she pounces, holding it out of her reach. She gives up quickly after I bear hug her down to my chest and type her name into Google.

"Fine," she relents and straddles me, snuggling her forehead into my neck. "Don't make fun of me."

"I would never do that."

Scrolling past the bullshit about us, I find her photographer website on the bottom of the second page.

A photo of Camille in a gray-blue dress surrounded by a garden of bright flowers comes into focus on her homepage.

"Maren." My voice drops to an overly deep and serious tone. "This picture is beautiful. When did you make this website?"

"Yesterday," she says shyly. "I was dreaming—like I could make it real."

"It is real."

"Camille said I needed one," she insists, slight defiance in her voice, like she has to explain herself.

"What?" I question her again. I'll drag every wiry thought out of her brain if I need to and then soothe them all.

She digs her chin into my sternum when she sighs. "Sometimes I wonder if I'll ruin it."

"Ruin what?"

"The joy of taking photographs. Taking something I love to do for myself and making it a job. Putting pressure on myself to 'make it.' It's just another thing I need to do to please people, and it will become less and less about doing it for fun."

"I understand that," I say. "Doing something for fun and doing something as an obligation to other people, getting paid for it, can sometimes change things. But remember why you do it and hold tight to it."

She closes her eyes, smiles like a daydream runs through her head, then nods, almost like she's clinging to my advice.

I navigate back to Google to find her Instagram account. She has two followers, Camille and Elise.

"Elise must have found me on there," Maren laughs when she opens her eyes and sees my screen. "I swear I didn't tell her. She's sneaky."

Each new one that appears as I scroll through her photos of Camille and her baby bump has my jaw jutting into the top of Maren's head. This isn't even my thing, but it's hard to argue that these don't look professional.

"Camille made my job easy," she says.

"Nope, don't do that shit. You're a fucking good photographer."

"I'm still learning. Who's going to want to hire me without experience?"

"Do you want me to follow you?"

She picks her head up and laughs. "You have an Instagram account?"

"Of course." I roll my eyes. "Graham runs it. I don't follow anyone though. I can't remember my password, but I can text him."

"No," she huffs. "Please don't."

"Why not? You'll get noticed. People will follow you. People will book you for sessions. Sessions? Is that what you call it?"

She shakes her head. "Yes, that's what you call it. And no. Seriously, I don't want that. I want to make it on my own. I want people to follow me because they like my pictures, not because I'm your girlfriend. And eventually, when someone figures it out, I'm going to have to turn off my comments."

"Fiiiine," I sigh, pinching her side. She nestles back into me where she belongs. "*Seriously*, look at the light. How do you do that?"

She shrugs. "I don't know. That's my favorite part. Okay, no, I do know. Time of day and weather mostly. *Aperture*. They all have unique challenges, so it's just about learning to work with them all. But like all things, people like different styles of photography."

"What's your style called?"

"Um, natural light, I guess," she says. "I like to enhance the bright and natural colors."

I kiss the top of her head. "It suits you. You're like the light, you know."

She blinks, doesn't say anything. Just purses her lips.

"You are," I insist. "You shine when you walk into a room. Everyone is attracted to your smile. You make people happy, Maren."

"I've always thought of it as a bad thing. Light in pictures is a good thing. Light as a person just means you cater to everyone else."

I frown. "I think it's a brave thing."

"In my experience, people only take and take. They disguise themselves as a friend or a boyfriend, but really, they just want something from me. And I try. I try to give them what they want, but it never works out for me. I don't get the same in return."

"The world needs more people like you," I say. "Otherwise, it would be full of selfish jackasses."

"Yeah, but at what cost, Locke? The cost of myself?"

I squeeze her, and the lights start to flicker. "You know, I never wanted you to change. Actually, I think we're maybe even similar, but we choose to deal with it in different ways. I get burned, and I shut everyone out. You get burned, and you try again. I admire that—I admire you. You just needed help learning how to cut the people who burn you out of your life; stand up for yourself. Cancel out the noise."

"I know," she says. "You were right. The silence is better."

"But only the right type of silence," I say. "For instance, I like when you talk."

"How'd I manage that again?" she jokes.

The lights flicker again before we're plunged into darkness. She jumps just the tiniest amount before she holds me tighter.

"Why are you scared of the dark?" I ask as the lights come back on.

She pauses. "It makes me feel alone. When I was young, my mom used to sit with Camille at bedtime. I got left in my room by myself because I never complained or expressed how scared I was. Camille needed my mom more, cried about how dark it was. The shadows on the wall terrified me too, but I'd try to picture them as happy things, like flowers or ballerinas. It's silly, just my kid brain doing things that's carried into adulthood."

"Lots of silly things are carried into adulthood," I chuckle. "Just like the old therapy joke, it's all your mother's fault."

"I shouldn't blame her, but I do sometimes. I've tried to please her my entire life, but it never seems like it's enough. When did everyone else's praise become more important than praising myself, liking myself, living for myself? And maybe more importantly, why? It will never be perfect—*I'll* never be perfect. When and why did everyone start caring so much about the stupidest shit? I don't feel like I'm enough for anyone sometimes, and then I try too hard, and suddenly, I'm too much. I never figured out how to be in between. At least I figured it out before I turn thirty. Don't know how many years I'm late though... five? Ten?"

"Maren, you're just right. And it's never too late. I think some people never figure it out."

A forceful gust of wind whips through the backyard, and the lights go out again.

"It takes a minute for the generator to kick on," I tell her.

My eyes take a second to adjust before the moonlight reflects off the pool and creates shadows on the wall. I know Maren is watching them too.

The buzz of the generator starts to hum through the walls, and before the electricity comes back to life, I whisper into the dark, "How did you get so tangled up in my life?"

And why do I want to do absolutely nothing to unravel it?

33

THE THOUGHT
Maren

MY ONLY THOUGHT BEFORE drifting off to sleep: Locke Hughes is falling in love with me.

THE HURRICANE
Locke

I CAN FEEL THAT Maren is awake before she speaks.

She flinches almost imperceptibly, her breathing quickens, and her fingers curl against my tattoo.

After a minute or two, she whispers, "What's wrong?"

"Nothing," I lie. "I can't sleep. The wind's too loud."

"What time is it?" she asks.

"Almost three a.m."

She places her palm against my sternum. "Why is your heart racing?"

"That's my normal state around you lately," I say, covering the back of her warm hand with mine.

"Because you think you're addicted to me?" she asks slowly.

"If you could be in my mind," I say, "you'd understand."

"Explain it to me instead."

I pause, my fingers trailing over hers, racking my vocabulary for the right words. "Every time you so much as move an inch, my brain gets a shock, like you complete a circuit within me. My skin can't take it when the warmth of yours wears off, and I want to crawl out of it when another woman touches me even innocently. There's something explosive coursing through my veins when you're near, and you'll probably give me a heart attack eventually. When you talk, my muscles relax. And when you decide you don't want me anymore, I'll be so deprived of dopamine, Maren, you're going to have me wishing I wasn't in my own body." I chuckle. "Too much?"

"You know," she says, kissing the bottom of my ribcage, "I feel the same way, more or less. And I don't think I'm addicted to you. That's what happens to me when I like someone."

Her words hang in the air. Like. Or love? Do I want her to love me?

Every cell in my body crawls, responding to my question.

"My insides knot every time you step near me," she adds. "When you look at me with your deep I-want-to-eat-you expression, my blood pressure drops, and then when you show me your dimples, it races back, flooding my heart. I'd tie you to me if I could, in a non-creepy way. Maybe even in a creepy way. *Definitely* in a sexual way. And I want to take pictures of you every second. I want to consume every little piece of you, Locke. There is no 'when I decide I don't want you anymore,' I promise. I will always want you." She mimics my chuckle. "Too much?"

This woman could never be too much. I'd take and take and take, guard every precious piece, and I'd never get tired of it.

"No," I say, "you're all-consuming. Hey, you want to go outside?"

She laughs. "In the hurricane?"

"Yes," I insist, throwing off the comforter. "It'll be fun."

In my black boxer briefs, I grab Maren by the ankles and throw her over my shoulder. She squeals and kicks the air.

She's in my white T-shirt, and I have no idea if she put underwear on or not, but I guess I'll find out fairly quickly when we step out into the rain.

No, I'll find out now. I slide my hand up her leg to her bare ass and smile. As soon as she wakes up tomorrow morning, she'll be rubbing this greedy pussy on my cock to wake me up—if she still wants me.

Downstairs, the back door takes extra effort to open against the wind, and when I step out on the porch, we're immediately pelted with rain.

"Ouch," Maren laughs. When I move to put her down, she shrieks. "I'm going to blow away!"

"I'd hold you through a tornado," I promise, but she doesn't hear me in the wind.

It howls and whips around the house, but I keep walking straight out, keeping her draped over my shoulder. The palm trees lean heavily to the left, and I'm careful not to step on the branches that litter the ground around the pool.

Finally, I reach the dock, and we're completely soaked. I lower Maren down to her feet, but she keeps her arms around my neck.

"It's chilly," she says. "Did you bring me out here for a wet T-shirt contest?"

"No," I reply. I needed out of the bed. I needed stimulation. I needed chaos. Something to make me not want to pull out my hair by the roots. I don't want to be able to feel anything, because I don't understand what I am feeling.

She stands on her tiptoes to kiss me before she steps back and holds her arms out by her side. With her head thrown back, she smiles at the sky. The wet fabric of her shirt clings to her breasts, just see-through enough, and her nipples peak in the cold.

"How do I look?" she screams over the wind, hair whipping around her face.

"Perfect," I whisper.

Maren looks back at me before she starts to twirl. Her cute little ass peeks out from beneath the hem of my T-shirt as it rises up her legs. "I can't hearrrrr youuuuu!" Her laugh carries across the water on a gust.

I wish I could be every single raindrop caressing her skin, carry her laugh around in a jar to hear it whenever I wanted—but maybe that's not obsession, maybe it's just the way I feel. Maybe it's love.

"I know," I continue. "You look like a force. Like you're happy. You look like a dream, one I never want to wake up from. You look like you're mine. I want to keep you all to myself because I'm selfish, but I want to show you off to the world at the same time because

I'm lucky. You look like someone who deserves everything, someone I don't deserve. And you look like the woman I think I'm falling in love with."

Abruptly, she stops twisting and cocks her head to the side, like somehow she heard me, even though I know she didn't. Maybe she sensed it—my shift or the mood or my intensity.

What? she mouths, unsuccessfully pursing her lips to hide her smile.

"Nothing," I say, shaking my head. Droplets fall from the ends of my bangs, so I run my hand through my hair to push it back. The urge to tell her a secret I never thought I'd say out loud gnaws at my brain, but it's not a question of if anymore but when. Because I can't not tell her, even if it means she pulls away. All of my secrets are her secrets now.

I drag her into me flush against my body, wrapping my arms around her lower back. I tip my face down to hers and speak against the shell of her ear. "I want—need—to tell you something."

She peers up at me, eyebrows knitting together from her smile. "I like secrets."

"It was me," I let out. "I interfered with your reality show." Confusion replaces her smile. My body is on fire despite the rain, but the only way to put it out is to keep going. "I got them to agree to never show what happened."

Her jaw drops, and she blinks through the raindrops weighing down her eyelashes. "How?"

"Maybe threatened, maybe bribed. I'm a persuasive motherfucker when I want to be, but that's beside the point."

"Why?" she asks.

The same question I've asked myself a million times in the last few months.

I would never have done it if I hadn't been walking down the hallway that day and heard Russell's grating laugh coming out of the private lounge in the country club. They must have been the only ones in there, because it was so early in the morning, but I'd been up before dawn to practice.

"You want them to air that?" I'd heard his caddie say. I paused and lingered in the hallway outside the door.

"Why not?" Russ replied, still amused. "All publicity is good publicity."

His caddie laughed while pointing out the obvious. "That's fucked up."

I could almost feel Russ' indifference shatter out of the room, like his shrug caused a fissure across Florida. "Maren will get over it."

I'd known. We'd *all* known what he'd done. This is a small world—golf world. I stay out of people's shit, but this particular thing, I just couldn't. I couldn't live with myself, knowing I could stand up for her.

It took me all of three seconds before I made a rash decision and turned around. No one would ever know it was me, I'd make sure of it, but I also knew that over my dead body was that fucking saga going to air.

As soon as I made it outside, I had Graham on the phone to demand he give me the producer's personal phone number within the hour. Sometimes it's very useful to pay someone so much.

"I don't know," I tell Maren. "Because I saw me in you. I know what it feels like to be manipulated and used, and trust me, I feel insane now. I haven't been stalking you or obsessed with you, and this wasn't some elaborate plan to mess with you. I watched you for years bouncing around like light. I knew what Russell was doing, but I had no clue if you knew, and I wasn't about to get involved. And then he just stole it all from you. I wasn't about to let him make it worse."

She pauses, taking that in. Her face is coated with rain, but she doesn't bother to wipe it away. "And you cared?"

"Yes, Maren, I *cared,* but you never would've known if you hadn't asked me for help and came bounding into my life. I felt like I'd done my part, and I wouldn't even agree to help you until I realized I could get something out of it because I'm an asshole more often than I care."

Her wide, stunned eyes blink again rapidly. "Did you get Craig to stop filming me?"

I shrug. "All that took was a look. I suspect because he thought we were dating, which I had *zero* intention of doing. I would have died with this secret, and now—now, I'd die for you. I don't even know how I've gotten from point A to point B."

Maren bursts into tears, and I have no idea if they're happy or sad. Maybe I've reached my limit, shown my hand, that I'm too fucking much. I forgot what I'm good for—a boyfriend isn't one of them.

"If this is too much for you..." I start, not wanting to finish. However, whenever, this ends, I'll be in the same place: a hollow version of the man I used to be, using everything and anything to fill the void Maren will leave.

Then a laugh comes bubbling up, brightening her face. She jumps into my arms and wraps her legs around me. The rain and her tears mix together on her wind-blown cheeks.

"You'd die for me?" she breathes.

"Yes," I say with a laugh. "Of course, I would. We just established that I'm insane."

Her kiss is electric. "Locke, getting to know you has been one of the best—and most fun—times of my life."

Maren has destroyed my life as I know it.

Now—*just say it, Locke.*

But I don't. Because how do I say that?

THE EPIPHANY
Maren

I wake to calm.

The sun streams in through the crack in the curtain, hitting my face just right. From what I can see, the sky looks extra blue.

Last night runs through my head. He *helped* me. Selflessly. When no one else would. And it only makes me love him more—the man who hates people is the most caring of them all.

I roll over to see Locke staring at me, big dark brown eyes surrounded by sunken dark circles.

"Good morning," I whisper. "What time is it?"

"Almost eleven."

"Did you sleep at all?"

"No," he sighs, reaching out and tugging me into his chest. The scent of rain still lingers on his skin.

I place the palm of my hand on his cheekbone and play with the blond hair behind his ear. "Why not?"

"Multiple reasons," he answers before he takes a deep breath. "One of which is I heard from my mom after you went to sleep."

"Is everything okay?" I ask, stiffening.

There's a wave of heat radiating off Locke's body that I just now notice. His skin is slick with sweat, but somehow freezing at the same time.

"She left me a voicemail." His face pales, his eyes squeeze closed, like he doesn't want to play it back in his head. "She was hallucinating."

I press myself against him as if I'm trying to meld us together to absorb some of his pain. "Are you sure?" I ask, unsure myself if this is even the right thing to say.

"Considering I haven't died in a plane crash, yes."

Definitely not the right thing to ask. We wince in sync. I have no experience with this, but I figure the best thing I can do is be there for him.

"I didn't want to be gone when you woke up," he adds, slipping out of the bed, "but I'm going to go talk to her."

Sitting up straight, I grab his hand in reassurance. "I'll come with you," I offer, but Locke takes his hand back, almost in embarrassment.

"No, just stay here." He turns away from me so quickly, without looking me in the eye, it stings my heart.

He pushes through the French doors to the bathroom, but I get up and quickly stick to his heels. I lean against the vanity as he splashes cold water on his face then avoids me in the mirror and busies himself in a drawer looking for nothing.

"Look at me," I urge softly.

Locke pivots with his back to me and heads for the closet instead.

So, I follow.

"Look at me."

He doesn't—just pulls a crumpled black T-shirt off the floor and puts it on.

"Look at me!" I demand, gripping his elbow and fighting his strength to get him to turn.

He blinks back the tears I only now notice when his eyes catch mine.

"Hey," I say, my tone laced with concern.

He tries to shrug me off. "Let me get dressed."

"Let me come with you," I plead.

"Why?" he scoffs, turning to fully face me. His face is now rigid with no sign that he was ever about to cry. "So you can see what a shitshow this is? How despite everything I do for her she turns back to drugs? You want to watch me break?"

"No," I say. "I want to come because I want to be there for you."

With his shoulders hanging, Locke slumps down to the ground against his drawers before he buries his head in his hands.

His breathing becomes erratic after a few seconds. "I'm scared," he forces out. "That you will think differently of me. That you'll see me in her. I'm scared you won't want this anymore. Because nothing good comes from letting people in, letting them see the fucking mess of my life behind the curtain. I won't be this idea to you anymore. The shininess wears off, and suddenly, I'm real. Real becomes too much. And I'm fucking terrified that I'm going to turn into her when you leave me. Maybe I'm already her. Taking from you like a selfish asshole, sustaining myself, living for the next hit you give me. You're all I think about."

I sink down into his lap, and with my legs straddling his thighs, I lift his face to mine. "I'm not here for you to call me a good girl, Locke, or live in your house, or use you for anything. I know who you are, and I'm here because I care about you. Not Locke the golfer. Not Locke the sexy, brooding mystery. I like *you*. Because you're more than you give yourself credit for. You're not selfish. You love deeply. Deeper than most people are maybe even capable of. Nothing I see is going to change my mind about you, nothing's going to make me feel differently about you. I want to come because you need me, even if you won't admit it to yourself, just as much as I need you."

I try to hold back my own tears, but I'm not as strong as Locke. Two break free and one slides down each of my cheeks.

His eyes flash pain mixed with clarity before he presses his lips to mine. I taste my own tears, and Locke holds me so tight against his torso that my breaths become shallow.

When he pulls back, I've never seen someone look at me the way he is now—an epiphany so intense swirling behind them, and it terrifies me in the best way possible. It's almost like I know what's coming, but there's no possible way for me to prepare myself. Even if I had a century, his next words would still be like a wrecking ball to my heart.

I'm ruined. And Locke Hughes holds all the pieces.

"I love you, Maren."

My chest constricts. He relaxes like he's been holding it in for days, weeks. Locke's irises are more golden than I've ever realized, the tiniest lines bursting from his pupils that you'd miss if you were any farther away than an inch. Everything about him is more than I thought was possible.

And at this point, there's no hesitation when I reply, "I know. I love you too."

THE INTERVENTION
Locke

THE RIDE TO MY mother's house is silent.

My hand never leaves Maren's thigh, like if I let go of her for even a nanosecond, she'll have second thoughts and jump out of the moving car. I tighten my fingers around her hard enough to leave an imprint.

This woman sitting beside me loves me, but I still think it will take time to adjust to that thought. The vulnerability she's handing to me because she trusts me not to hurt her, abuse her, manipulate her, take advantage of it. And I've never wanted to prove to someone more that I'll guard her like my life depends on it. Because in theory, it does.

It's the most beautiful cloudless day, and you'd never know there had just been a hurricane if I wasn't weaving around huge branches lying in the street every other block.

This is the calm before the storm. After the storm. In between the storm.

I've never felt more exposed, but I wouldn't dare to be this exposed with anyone else. Maren is about to enter the darkest part of my life, but how can I love her correctly if I don't show her all of it? I *want* to show her all of it, no matter how crushing the weight, because I want to be fully seen and still loved. The rarest love of all that deep down everyone wants—but also might be next to impossible to attain.

But if I show her all of this, and she still wants me...

My mom's house sits on a quiet cul-de-sac in a gated community. You'd never know from the outside, with its Spanish tile roof, peach stucco, and impeccable lawn, what living on the inside is like.

I wonder sometimes how often she's even here. How many nights she spends elsewhere to escape. Because even with everything I give her, she isn't happy.

When I pull into the driveway, Maren peers out her window, deep in thought. Possibly thinking the same things that I am.

"It *looks* idyllic, I know," I say.

She rubs her thumb in a circle on top of each of my knuckles, trying to relieve the tension knotted through my forearm.

"When I'm here," I continue, "the only memories I think about are staging interventions with Elise, checking to see if she's alive, dropping her back off from the hospital after an OD, her hosting dinner in a moment of clarity only for her to become more and more incoherent as she shoots up in her bedroom." Maren massages my neck when I lay my forehead on the steering wheel. It takes everything in me to breathe steadily through my pulsing temples. "I don't care that I'm thirty years old. I'm still her child, and you shouldn't ever witness your mother like that."

Her voicemail plays back in my head, her words like sobs, wishing she had more time with me, wishing she could have shown me she could be a better mother, that she loves me, that she's sorry. She couldn't understand why she'd survived the nonexistent plane crash.

Maren kisses my hand before I open the car door and start up the stone path to the front door.

I ring the doorbell as soon as I'm close enough, before I lose any of my last un-frayed nerves.

No sounds come from the other side of the door.

I try again and wait. And wait. I don't have enough strength to open the door and face what might be inside, so instead, I press my forehead against the wooden door.

After a minute, Maren's hand lightly grips my shoulder. I didn't even hear her get out of the car.

"What if she's..." My words are barely audible, and I can't manage to finish the sentence. My worst fear. And what if I speak it into existence? If I never say it, it can never happen.

She unfolds my fist and takes the key from my sweaty palm. "Let me go in first."

"Maren, I can't let you do that," I say, sounding stronger than I feel.

But she shushes me and unlocks the door. "I can be strong enough for the both of us right now."

It swings open to the empty foyer, and past that, the quiet living room that looks straight out of a Florida real estate catalog.

Maren knocks and calls out, "Mrs. Hughes?"

When no one replies, she squeezes my shoulder. "Stay here. I'll check if she's home."

What she's really thinking is 'alive.' It's what we're both thinking.

I shake the thought out of my head and step into the foyer after Maren. She smiles reassuringly at me with closed lips as I stuff my hand in my pocket to thumb the tee I have there.

"Mrs. Hughes?" she calls again, louder and farther inside this time.

Maren disappears down the hallway. I hear a soft knock followed by a door opening and closing. I'm mapping out my mom's bedrooms in my mind as Maren repeats it three more times.

She shakes her head at me when she reappears before whipping her head toward the sound of the sliding glass door out of my eyesight.

"Who are you?"

Relief rushes down my spine at the sound of my mom's voice.

Maren's shoulders jump before I can almost see the relief cascade down her body too as her muscles uncord.

"I'm your son's girlfriend," she answers. "Maren."

There's a pause before Mom replies, "Right. The one he loves," like she's been reading articles about us.

"I love him too," Maren says, "and he wants to talk to you."

My mom's eyes snap to me when I take three steps out into the living room and instantly fill with tears. She has to catch the handle of the door and lean her weight against it from the shock. She looks tired, the same dark circles around her eyes I saw around mine in the mirror earlier. Her blonde hair wild, like she just woke up but never went to sleep at the time.

"Hey, Mom," I say.

"Locke," she whispers through her tears.

"Can we talk?"

She nods slowly.

Maren and I sit on the couch.

I set the timer on my watch for thirty-three minutes, giving myself that three minute buffer. I don't know how this is going to go, but I'm determined, and this will only bring out my best (or worst, depending on you look at it) self.

But when I look up, I already know I'll win this argument based on how defeated she looks. Not that I would have lost, because I wasn't walking out of here without her anyway, even if it took hours.

My mom sits, listens.

I get lost in the conversation, the tears, but it won't matter how long I have to talk. It won't matter if she doesn't think she can do it. I'll talk and talk and talk. I'll never shut up as long I can get her to agree to walk out of here with me and check in to rehab.

And eventually, I'm leading her to my car.

I watch her in my rear view mirror as I pull out of the driveway. She looks tired, so exhausted that she might fall asleep mid-thought.

She's tried twice already to get sober, and even though she relapsed, she's going to attempt to try again. And that's what matters to me.

My mom is willing to get better. She wants to keep trying, fighting.

And every time, I'll be here for her.

Maybe the third time in rehab will be the charm for her. But this doesn't magically end. I don't think there is an ending to addiction.

The timer on my watch goes off, ringing through the car, and Maren snaps her head in my direction. She reaches across the console and wraps her fingers around my wrist, hitting the button to silence it with her thumb.

She narrows her feisty eyes. *I love you*, she mouths.

I mouth it back and lace my hand in hers.

But then again, maybe I shouldn't be giving anyone advice—I'm an asshole.

MAREN AND I WALK back out into the Florida sun. Palm trees line the path to the parking lot, so I watch the shadows move in the breeze as we walk. I take one last look behind me. The rehabilitation center, with its grand glass opening and high white walls, almost looks like a resort.

I've never talked so much in my life during each of my now three trips here.

But it's worth it—to have her and her doctors and therapists lay out a specialized and personal treatment plan, to discuss our feelings so I can be involved in the process and support her in the best possible way. She knows that I'm here for her, and I will do everything in my power for her to get the best possible treatment.

I stop short and gather Maren into a tight hug. "Thank you," I whisper into her neck. "I know you felt like you didn't do anything, but you did. So much. Thank you for being here because I couldn't have done this without you."

She won't ever realize how much her presence calms me and lights me up at the same time. I'll never be able to put into words what she does to me. Because it's inexplicable.

"You're welcome." She traces her fingertips up and down my back before she pulls away to look me in the face. "I'm not going anywhere, okay? We're going to do this together every step of the way, and I'll support you while you support her."

I nod as she presses her palms against my cheeks. Her thumbs sweep under my eyes. I'm sure they're dark as hell. Between not knowing how to say those three simple words and my mom's phone call, I haven't slept in two days.

I let out a breath. "I need sleep."

"Let's go home," she says as she presses her lips to mine and takes my hand in hers. Her green eyes brighten against the sun when she turns her head up to look at me and smile, scrunching her freckles up. "No tournament for you this week. No work for me this week."

I smile back, exhausted. "Less."

"Less sounds fun," she agrees.

THE BEGINNING
Maren

LOCKE SHUFFLES OUT THE back sliding door.

His gaze shifts from me to the rising sun, just a fuzzy slice of orange over the water. The sky is otherwise a deep dark blue.

I'm bundled up under my favorite blanket on the porch swing bed with my legs tucked up to my chest.

Locke, in his black boxer briefs, climbs in next to me, rearranges the blanket around both of us, and forces my legs down so he can nuzzle his head in my lap. He stretches out his long body, pressing against the rail with his feet.

"Why are you up?" I whisper, braiding my fingers through his disheveled hair. "I thought you'd sleep longer than"—I tap my phone on the armrest—"ten hours."

He squeezes an arm around my legs and smiles lazily. "You weren't in bed. I can sense when you're not sleeping next to me."

"I'm sorry."

"It's okay." He purses his lips. "I thought for a second you went back to *your* house."

"I don't live with you, silly," I tease.

He hums in protest. "We'll see about that." Then Locke reaches up and brushes the tip of his finger along the underside of my jaw. "I wonder how long you can hold out."

"We'll see, won't we," I play back, nipping at his finger.

"What're you thinking about?"

"Everything," I chuckle. "Did you sleep okay?"

He nods his face back into my lap. "Yeah," he says. "I feel good. You know, it's always kind of weird, this feeling after she checks in."

I take a sip from my coffee mug, continuing to scratch his scalp with my nails, to give Locke time to elaborate. Less gets you more with him—I think it always will.

"Watching her fill out the paperwork and be eager to stay. Unpacking her things because she knows she'll be there for a while. Actively listening like she's invested in what they have to say. When we walked out, my brain immediately quieted. I know exactly where she is. That she's safe. I don't think I even realize how much anxiety I have about her until I get that relief, experience the shift. But you being in my life has made such a difference, Maren. I've never been able to open up to someone like this. I've never really wanted to before. My life forked, and I wouldn't go back and take the other road for anything. Because I can't *not* talk to you anymore."

I plant a kiss into his forehead. "You can tell me anything. Everything. And I'll never change my mind about you. I *know* you now, Locke, and that blows my mind every single day." I laugh. "I can't believe I asked a stranger to help me not give a shit, and I ended up failing miserably at that, because I care about you the most."

"I failed miserably too," he says playfully, pinching my hip. "It was my job to teach you not to give a shit, and talk less, *and* not have my photograph taken. And now look at me—us. I think we both rubbed off on each other and found the perfect balance."

"Who's the better half?" I pinch him back harder.

"You," he laughs. "And you don't even have to pinch me. It's always you."

It's always me, I repeat in my head. *Always me and him. All-consumed.*

"You know," I say, "when we were driving to that very first dinner in San Diego, and all throughout dinner for that matter, all I could think about was what it would be like to be liked or even loved by you."

He picks his head up. "Is it everything you imagined?" he jokes.

"It's better," I insist. "Different too."

Locke smirks. His eyebrow ticks up. "Different how?"

"Maybe I mean I'm different," I muse out loud, chewing on my lip. "I did text my mom a little while ago and tell her I'm not cutting my hair because I like it long and I'm a twenty-nine-year-old woman."

"You're such a badass," Locke teases.

"Right," I grin. "But you are just like I thought—I feel so incredibly special when you look at me, when you smile, when you hold my hand or tell me you love me. I experience the intensity. But I used to think I didn't deserve it, and that's bullshit."

"Definitely bullshit," he agrees, snuggling deeper into my lap. "I'm in love with you. I love you. I love saying that now."

"I love *you*."

I take a deep breath. Then listen to a few birds chirp. Drink my coffee. The silence welcomes both of us for a while before Locke yawns.

"What now?" I ask.

"Shut out the shit you shouldn't care about. Care the hell out of the things you should." Locke shrugs. "Live."

"Live," I repeat. "Happy."

"Happy," he says sleepily, closing his eyes. "Because you deserve it. You deserve everything, Maren. This is the beginning."

None of the other things matter because we're happy for now. I'm happy with myself, and there's no guarantees, so all I can do is keep going; living.

And yeah, sometimes I'm just not going to give a shit.

THE MASTERS
ONE YEAR LATER
Maren

I$_T$'s so quiet on the eighteenth hole, you could hear a pin drop in the grass.

Locke finished nearly twenty minutes ago, five under par, before he retreated to the clubhouse to watch the rest play out on television.

Russell has been battling to five under, one hole behind Locke all day. And right now, he's positioned to win if he makes this putt for birdie.

It will be an incredible shot if he does; about ten yards out, just a straight line. One swing of a club away from his lifelong dream.

I've got my monopod ready, another camera strapped against my left shoulder in case.

Russ crouches to examine his ball and the path it has to travel. He rises before stepping back to have another word with his caddie.

I still don't understand how many different ways there are to discuss *hit the tiny ball in the tiny hole.* But of course, they confer with each other for another three minutes—checking their book, examining the club, clearing nonexistent obstacles in front of the hole.

He nods, chuckles, then his face forms into a look of mean concentration.

I went through this tournament twice with him, but he'd never been in a close enough position to win either of those. I can only imagine how nervous he is, how close he feels to being able to grasp something so significant with his fingertips.

And I'm going to capture the moment when he putts. If it goes in, he wins. If it doesn't, and instead he makes par, then he and Locke will go into a sudden-death playoff.

Russ finally steps up, and I hold my breath along with everyone else as his club connects with the ball.

It hurtles along, and I snap a thousand pictures, capturing his putt like stop-motion as it curves along the edge of the hole and drops—Russ' amazing winning putt is perfection.

"SMILE!" I EXCLAIM. "YOU just won the Masters!"

Despite everything, I'm still excited for him.

Russell lifts his lips and shows me his teeth, but nothing reaches his eyes.

Everything he's ever wanted—the silver Clubhouse trophy he holds up next to his face and the gold buttons of his green jacket glimmering in the sun—right in his hands.

And he doesn't even look happy.

But it's not my job to worry about his feelings. It's my job to take his picture.

And it will be my job to take his picture tomorrow—but hopefully not for forever. I have a spring family portrait session this week and a newborn shoot the next. While it's only a couple hundred dollars, and I won't be quitting my day job any time soon, maybe one day I will. I have a real website with galleries that aren't just my family and regular bookings. It's steady enough right now, especially since Elise tells everyone she knows (and everyone she doesn't know, like the barista at the coffee shop yesterday). And I have a lot of social media followers, but I have to limit the comments because they mostly talk about how hot Locke is and debate why he's not in any of my pictures.

The most important thing is though—I'm happy, which only seems to piss Russell off more. Locke was right. This is the best revenge, and I don't even want revenge anymore.

I turn my head over my shoulder and smile. "Lydia! Come get in the photo."

She practically squeals in excitement, while managing to ignore me somehow. Every time I see either her or Russ, it amazes me how they faded to black in my mind. Nothing about them bothers me.

Russ looks bothered though. His mouth pinches like he wants to say something, some explanation that maybe I deserve but don't care enough to hear. I've heard enough of his voice to last me a lifetime.

He stares at my hand, then his blue eyes glint in the sunlight when he scowls back at me, over and over. Maybe the ring on my finger is catching the light at just the right angle and blinding him. Maybe that's what really pisses him off more. That he has no control over me or my thoughts—because he doesn't even cross them. Unless he's standing right in front of me.

Lydia hangs on him, beaming in the same bright sun, in her cute floral sundress. She keeps smiling, so I keep taking pictures. She looks like she could do this forever.

I'm happy for Russ. I wish he could feel the same.

When I'm done with their pictures, I finally turn to Locke.

He's standing on the edge of the crowd with his mom, Elise, Conrad, Blake, Emmie, Camille, Parker, and my nephew, Parker Jr., as they have a conversation around him.

All of his attention is on me.

I raise my camera to my eye and snap one picture.

Locke playfully frowns as I inspect every inch of him though my viewfinder—his blond hair that I get to run my fingers through, his broad shoulders I lay my head on, his abs that I've memorized every curve of. But my favorite is his layers underneath, the ones he reserves for me.

Come here, pretty girl, he mouths, before flicking his eyes down with a knowing smirk to my now pulsing pussy and continuing down my legs.

I snap my camera back on its tripod, but when I turn, a woman with a media badge is speaking into Locke's ear and he's being whisked away to the post-tournament press conference.

Instead, I make my way over to our families and start with my sleeping nephew, kissing him on his forehead.

"He conked out on the eleventh hole," Camille says softly. "But he was clapping and cheering for you."

We just had his 'One Happy Dude' one-year-old birthday party, which is incredibly fitting because he's the happiest baby I've ever met (only because I'm the world's best aunt) at Camille's house last month, where I captured every second of his cake smashing.

Both his and Emmie's photos hang in my and Locke's hallway (I lasted six months before I 'officially' moved in, by the way, because that seemed more appropriate, and Locke bet himself he could make it happen in four). They're already the best of friends because Locke and I have group babysitting night.

Then I go around the circle. Camille gets an awkward hug because she has to hold little Parker. Big Parker picks me up off my feet in a hug the same way Phillip does next.

Each one praising me like I'm the one who just played a week of golf and almost won the biggest tournament in the world.

Elise, who's holding Emmie, kisses my cheek. "Congratulations," she says, beaming, and squeezes my arm. "Second is still amazing." I've gotten used to people acting like I have something to do with Locke's accomplishments, so I just let it roll off my back.

Blake hugs me tight after I smush Emmie's cheeks.

Conrad, dressed in his white caddie uniform, throws an arm over both of our shoulders and teases me and Blake for wearing almost matching golf dresses. Then he picks us up by our waists and shakes us.

"Conrad!" Blake cackles.

"You're a nuisance," I joke.

"We *almost* won," he laughs, putting us back on our feet.

Locke's mom, Joanna, holds me the tightest, the longest. A little over a year sober, she takes it a day at a time—working, repairing family relationships, going to therapy.

This has become my little family. My friends. We all live life, together, one day at a time—there for each other.

MY HEART CLENCHES, AND I smile at how remarkably similar this photography closet looks to the one at home. I *feel* at home. I rest the reflective umbrellas into the corner and lay the tripods on the second shelf.

All in one motion of events, the light flicks off, the door clicks shut, and my gasp gets sucked out into the pitch black.

Now temporarily blind, I turn slowly and nudge back into the wall.

"Locke," I whine softly under my breath.

"Maren," Locke whispers so close to my face it surprises me.

He presses my body against the wall with his.

"Saving me for last," I tsk.

His fingertips trace the curve of my cheek before he brushes his lips over mine in a slow tease. "So I can have you the longest."

"You already have me forever," I say, untucking his polo just so I can slide my hands up his warm plane of a torso.

The engagement ring he proposed with last month snags on the fabric.

In true Locke fashion, he'd whipped me around on our staircase and dropped to one knee out of nowhere. Because he'd been obsessing about it in his pocket for all of two hours since he'd picked it up from the jeweler and couldn't wait for his original plan to play out. I think that's how we'll get married too. Maybe one day I'll wake up and say that we should get married today, and he'll agree to a destination wedding with just the two of us, because neither one of us really wants to wait. Neither of us wants to be patient enough.

Maybe I'll suggest it tomorrow when we wake up and then go to sleep a wife.

He chuckles. "What're we going to do with all that *time*?"

With the tip of my nose, I find his dimples in the dark and smile against them before I press my lips to his and let my tongue taste his bottom lip to satisfy my craving. "You played amazing. I'm so proud of you," I say, nuzzling into his neck. "Are you upset?"

"That I came in second?" His laugh rumbles softly in his chest. "This is better than when I won last year and when I won years ago."

"What? How?"

"Winning and having no one," he says, "doesn't come close to losing and having you, Maren. Everything is better with you in my life. And this year you're wearing this ring, and everyone knows you're mine forever. Reporters won't stop bugging the shit out of me. And then next year, you'll be by my side again. And the year after that. And then eventually whenever the year comes when I'm not playing golf anymore, you'll still be here. And that's better than a trophy. *You* don't come in second."

"Locke Hughes has a way with words," I say, dropping my hand over the zipper of his pants.

"That's definitely not my bicep," he murmurs when I rub him.

I hum back then smile, even though he can't see me.

"Are you going to rupture my eardrums again, Maren?" he says, voice deep.

"Maybe when I scream your name," I breathe.

"Be a good girl," he says with a smile in his voice, and I wish I could see his dimples. His body contracts, flattens me harder against the wall, and his voice turns to gravel. "Let everyone know who you belong to."

I melt. Over and over from his touch. From his words.

"I'm yours. Forever, Locke."

I've given everything I have to him, and I'll let him whisper in my ear for the rest of my life. Perfect praise doesn't exist, but Locke gets pretty damn close.

Acknowledgments

This book is a love letter. This book is a hate letter.

And I almost think that is how it will be received. Either you loved it or you hated it—no in between. But isn't that most books?

While I hope you are in the percentage that loved it, even if you aren't, thank you for reading it. The entire time I was writing this book, I could never shake the feeling that something about it is different, but I still can't put my finger on why.

This book is personal in so many different ways, and there is a part of me in all of the characters.

I shouldn't say never, but I'll *probably* never write another book like this again.

Phew. I don't really have the words—except that I can't believe I published this. I shouldn't really give a shit though, right?

Thank you to the best author friends a girl could ask for: Rachel LaBerge and Mariah Montoya. If you haven't, you should go read their books.

Thank you to my alpha and beta readers. This crazy book is better because of you.

Thank you to my family. You put up with how much this sometimes consumes my life. Finally, here's a much-needed break.

And lastly, thank you to my readers. Each and every one of you who reads, rates, and/or reviews my books holds a special place in my heart. You make a difference in my life, whether you know it or not, and whether you give me five stars or one, I appreciate you.

About the Author

Grace Pearce writes stories that strive to leave you with a smile. She lives in southern Louisiana, but her husband may one day get his wish to move to a state with less humidity. She is the author of *Leigh Makes Three*, *The Ex List*, and *Perfect Praise*.

Connect with her on Instagram @GracePearceWrites
www.GracePearceBooks.com

Titles by Grace Pearce

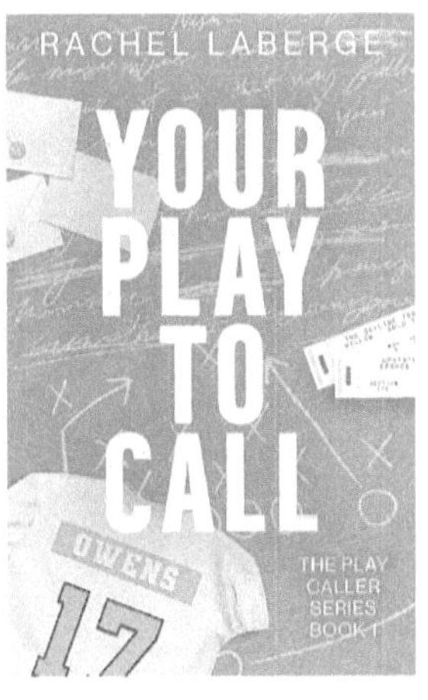

Your Play to Call
by Rachel LaBerge
Football x Popstar

Sunshine x Sunshine

Golden Retriever MMC

Texts on Page